THE WORLD TURNED UPSIDE DOWN

The Girl From Ipanema

AJAX MINOR

PARK PLACE
PUBLICATIONS

Park Place Publications
Pacific Grove, California
parkplacepublications.com

Cover design Gene Harris
Interior design Patricia Hamilton

"This book is just as good if not better than the first which is usually hard to accomplish! Again this book was a fast paced read that went by fairly easy for me. I didn't find myself rereading parts over and over because I felt lost. I really enjoy this series and can't wait for the next book!"

—**Dallas,** Amazon Reviewer

"Aficionados of sci-fi, geopolitics, and adventure wrapped up in fantasy will surely find something with which to engage the mind in the second of Ajax Minor's Ur Legend trilogy, The Girl from Ipanema. A number of familiar characters return from his first venture, Sun Valley Moon Mountains, which will please those looking for some continuity. The tenor of this second volume, however, has changed from the pure fantasy of the first to a darker, more sinister world view. Thankfully, the quirky humor remains."

—**Margo W.R. Steiner,** Amazon Reviewer

FOREWORD

———

Dear Reader,

For those of you who have read *Sun Valley Moon Mountains* (*SVMM*), Book 1 One of the Ur Legend trilogy, and have no need to refresh your memory of the storyline, you may sail on to the first section of *The Girl from Ipanema:* Pyongyang. With one qualification. Please read the last paragraph of this foreword for a brief disclaimer. For those who for some odd reason have decided to forego *SVMM* and plunge into *The Girl from Ipanema*, what follows is a synopsis of Book One.

Jaq and Kate, after ten fruitless years of trying, finally gave birth to a daughter, Ur. Tragically, she suffers a catastrophic accident. The couple flees New York City for Ketchum, Idaho, and some peace. There, Ur dies seven months later.

The book begins about a year after Ur's death. Around Christmastime, the couple begins to experience a series of paranormal events. Jaq arrives at work before dawn one day and finds himself, in an instant, in a verdant field occupied by a solitary house. Within, he relives the traumatic moment of Ur's birth and is then pursued and cornered by a monstrous spider, only to find himself once again in Sun Valley. Kate hears the sounds of Ur's raspy breathing coming from the baby monitor she has kept for over a year. For respite, they indulge in their shared passion, a day fishing on the Lost River east of Ketchum. There Jaq glimpses strange figures on the ridge line of the massive Big Lost Mountains looming a mile above the valley floor. Finally, they catch and release a Fantastical Fish, splashed with shining hues of purple and rose and silver, in a rain of tears and blood.

Kate is convinced that Ur, while dead, is in danger and asks Jaq to speak with their friend, Nicholas Marduk Beele, the local Jesuit parish priest. He affirms Ur's existence but assures them that she is in no immediate danger and will alert them if the facts change. The facts change. On Christmas Eve, Nick sends a note to meet him on the banks of the Lost River. They discover that he is much more than a simple priest and he offers to guide them to rescue Ur from Tiamat, an ancient being known as the Creatrix, who holds worlds together with her mind. And who is also his mother.

Passing through a crack in space-time, the three arrive on Luna, a satellite of Mir and analogous to Earth's moon. At Old Spall, a community of humanoids, they accept the help of one, Kak Zhal, to lead them to Hades, Tiamat's lair. On the first night Jaq strays and Kak Zhal is sent to find him. Nick and Kate continue on with the aid of Rock Cats, creatures sprung from stone, and cross the Styx over the objections of Bildad Proud, the ferryman. Meanwhile Jaq and Kak Zhal traverse Hades through a dense fog and meet Jaq's heroes from *The Iliad*: Hector, who gives him his sword, and Odysseus, who offers advice. Kate and Nick meet Achilles, who gives Kate her spear.

At last they reach Tiamat's lair, where they find an immense arachnid, and their daughter Ur. Jaq proposes single combat to decide who keeps Ur and Tiamat accepts. After a fierce battle, Jaq triumphs, wounding Tiamat with Achilles' spear, and Tiamat's form returns to that of an old woman. She implores Ur to stay so that the child might teach her about Love, and Ur tells her she will think about it.

The five leave but must fight one more battle on an icy lake with dangerous rock creatures, Sand Banshees and Dust Bats, and finally with Bildad Proud himself, who wants to rule the underworld with Ur. They triumph, for the moment, and head off to New Spall to return to Jaq, Kate and Ur's original world-line. New Spall turns out to be the house in a field in Jaq's first strange experience. There Ur tells her parents that she is staying to teach Tiamat the meaning of love. Though heartbroken, they accept her choice, as all parents eventually must, and return home through the space-time portal.

A year later Kate awakens Jaq to tell him they must go to the Lost River. There they find Ur, carrying a small bundle. It is Tiamat. Jaq, when he wounded

Tiamat, stole her immortality and she decided to live her life as a human. Again, Ur leaves to take Tiamat's place and hold worlds together with her own mind, and Jaq and Kate head home to Ketchum in silence with 'Mattie'.

– Ajax Minor
April 2017

THE GIRL FROM IPANEMA

PART ONE – PYONGYANG

CHAPTER I

———

A small splash of red, unsuspected, unsolicited, intruded. Discreet yet distinct. Then it spread. Like a nasty stain, absorbed by the medium it had infected. Again and again it spilled itself into focus, pulsing like some sad, torn artery. *Jumong!*

Mattie's eyes snapped open and, for a moment, she scrabbled about the bed frantically. *Jumong!* The dream had had something to do with Jumong.

Sitting up, she pushed herself back against the wall. Red neon flashed across her face with monotonous regularity. "Silly dream," she muttered.

Mattie shot a glance at the clock. Ticking like a bomb, it sat squat on the nightstand. Soft, weak dawn light had smudged the glowing green hands. Mattie snatched the thing off the table. 6:50 a.m. "Shit."

Bolting out of bed, she threw on a pair of panties that sat in a lump on the floor and then yanked on the dresser drawer. The handle fell off. Mattie exhaled audibly. "I really don't have time for this." Digging her fingers behind the drawer and peeling off a chunk of veneer, she finally managed to get the thing open.

 "And this is the best hotel in Pyongyang. Jesus." Shaking her head, she turned to sprint for the bathroom, then stopped and walked instead over to the open window.

Peering over the ledge, she saw Jumong's limo parked on the street. As always, he had been punctual as hell. He'd be knocking at her door in five minutes. Or Fuong Ba would. Jumong considered it impolite to go to a lady's room alone. At least, that's what he'd told her. Jumong was very, very old fashioned. By Western standards. *But this is North Korea, isn't it? And you are an anthropologist, aren't you?*

And why *had* she become an anthropologist, anyway? Other disciplines were too easy, for one thing. She could prove math theorems standing on her head. And her memory was eidetic. Total recall. But people weren't subject to the same type of analysis. Their behavior was more subtle, and fluid. Oddly, she had always had the feeling that she was not observing cultures, but another species.

Waves of red neon light from the hotel marquee across the street shimmered in sequence after tedious sequence off Mattie's slick brown skin. She noticed that she had been sweating.

She ran a finger across the large scar on her torso, right next to her rib cage. Her parents, Kate and Jaq, had always told her that she had been fed through a tube when she was an infant because of a congenital GI problem. But the scar had always struck her as too big and too ragged for a surgeon's cut. The doctor had been either a rookie or on drugs, she figured.

Suddenly, the slick sweat that covered her torso set, like lacquer. Horny and hard, and bottomless black, the skin around her scar and on her belly failed to move when she breathed. She placed the tip of a finger on the scar, and an image flashed through her mind, like a bat flitting across the sky at dusk. Someone, someone she *knew*, was bashing her in the face with the hilt of a sword.

Breathe! Mattie sucked in a shallow breath that quieted the waves of panic that washed across her chest. The image vanished and the lacquer melted. A tiny drop of perspiration traced a crooked path from the scar, down her abdomen, settling at last in the well of her navel. Mattie blinked, then shook her head lightly.

Rubbing the damp finger against her thumb, Mattie was struck out of the corner of her eye by another burst of red. Lifting her head, she ran a hand through her dense, black hair, removing the offending strands, damp and wiry, from in front of her eyes. Pyongyang stretched before her and beneath her. One mind-numbing mass of gray. Much like its people. Except for Jumong.

Like Jumong, the blazing red fireball of the sun was lifting itself over the edge of the eastern horizon, over the horizon and above the drab conformity of the city. Intruding itself unavoidably upon the scene, punching its way into and through another gray mass of thick, bunched clouds that sat, self-possessed but suspicious, almost fearful, above Pyongyang.

As the sun climbed higher, Mattie could actually see the morning dampness begin to burn off at the city's edges. The slightest intimation of heat tickled her cheeks. A light wind stirred and rushed through the open window, drying her sweat-stained skin. Chilling, though not unpleasant, the breeze made her shiver.

Mattie wrapped her arms about herself, lifting her full, firm breasts higher still. Jet black nipples sat rigid atop her forearms. She lifted a finger and touched one lightly on its tip, wondering what the day with Jumong would bring.

A knock at the door, soft, slow and sudden, made Mattie jump.

"Oh, fuck," she whispered.

Mattie threw on a blouse and opened the door a crack. Staring down at her, across the brass chain of the safety lock, was the face of Fuong Ba. But he quickly averted his gaze, seeing most likely that she was not fully dressed.

'I, um, overslept,' she signed, beneath the bodyguard's bowed head. "I'll just be a few minutes, though."

Fuong Ba nodded, but when Mattie tried to close the door he stayed it with his huge hand, shaking his head. He glanced at the chain. And Mattie thought, just thought, she caught his eyes darting in the direction of her chest. Pulling the fabric of her unbuttoned blouse tighter still in her clenched fist she signed, 'I'll be all right. Really.'

Fuong Ba lowered his hand to his side and stepped back from the door.

Standing in front of the bathroom mirror, a contact lens balanced lightly on the tip of her finger, Mattie studied her own face. Large black eyes, absent whites, absent irises, stared back at her. "Should I tell him, show him?" Mattie asked her own reflection. Shrugging, she popped in the lenses, covering the entire surface of the eye, except for a small hole where the pupils should have been. *What would I say, when I don't even understand it myself?* But the image in the mirror offered no answer.

Quickly, Mattie threw on a sweater, jeans and hiking boots, then closed the door to her room quietly behind her, testing the lock with a deft turn, out of habit. Fuong Ba nodded. A man in simple fatigues sat rigidly in a straight back chair set against the wall.

"Has he been here all night?" Mattie asked, in Korean, looking her escort directly in the face.

Fuong Ba nodded again.

"Jesus," she swore softly, nodding in the direction of the stairwell.

Fuong Ba snapped his fingers and the short, slightly built guard popped up. Mattie could see a bulge beneath his jacket. "Well, go on," Mattie said to Fuong Ba. This time, however, he refused to back down. He stood motionless, unblinking, his eyes boring into Mattie's own.

"Oh, dammit, all right," she said at last, sprinting past the guard. He tried to place a hand on her arm, gently and courteously, but she shook it off and began to run, faster and faster down the stairs, with her escorts in swift tow, until at last she burst into the lobby.

Jumong was outside, slouched against his limo, smoking a cigarette. When he saw her, his face lit up with a broad smile. He flicked the butt into the gutter and ran into the hotel.

"I'm sorry I'm late," she said without a smile. Simply the sight of Jumong had cast a fine, cool spray on her agitation. The sight of him always made her a bit giddy. He was tall, six feet, athletically built, with thick black hair, high cheekbones and brown, bedroom eyes. But she wasn't ready, not quite, to let him know how happy she really felt. She picked at a finger; a habit probably acquired from her mother, Kate.

"Is something wrong?" Jumong asked, in perfect English.

"Wrong? *Really*, is all of this security necessary?"

Jumong glanced around. At least a half dozen men, armed with pistols, concealed automatics and highly visible shotguns, stood tensed about the stark, gray lobby. Only a picture of Jumong's father, displayed prominently above the entrance, served to break the monotony.

"Well ..." Jumong scratched his nose. "These are difficult times for my country. The forces of reaction are at work everywhere." His large brown eyes twinkled. "And, after all, I am ... what would you call me?"

"Crown Prince?" Mattie said.

Jumong's eyes darted about nervously and he placed a finger over his lips, which had curved upward, almost imperceptibly, at the corners. "Please, please, Mattie. You must be more careful. I told you that the forces of reaction are a serious threat."

"Jumong, really." Mattie chuckled, sensing the tension release from her gut. "Seriously, I understand the security for you, but …"

"But you don't approve of police states."

Mattie ignored Jumong. "I mean the security for me. After all, who's going to harm *me*?" For just an instant, Mattie sensed a figure, once again, straddling her, arms raised, screaming, "Fucking Bitch!" She flinched.

But Jumong hadn't noticed. He laughed in a high, clear baritone, and the sound filled the room like a bright, brass bell. "Why, darling," Jumong said, letting the endearment hang for a second or two, long enough for Mattie's deep chestnut cheeks to flush reddish brown, "I'm not afraid anyone is going to harm you. I'm afraid they might steal you."

Mattie's eyes locked onto Jumong's. "Wherever did you learn to be so charming?" she said.

"Why, after all, charm is nothing more than the prized child of politeness. And for we Orientals, as you *used* to call us, manners are an integral part of the process of, what would you call it in your field, acculturation?"

"Yes, we would." Mattie smiled. "But I've made us late."

Jumong shrugged. "But you've made me happy."

"You said it's a long drive up into the hills."

"On our poor roads, yes. Long, but beautiful," Jumong said, placing his own long fingers, delicate for a man of his stature, on top of her hand.

He led Mattie out of the hotel, followed by her security, and held the door while she climbed inside his car. Fuong Ba settled himself into the front seat alongside the driver and pulled down the front visor, revealing a large mirror. Fuong Ba's eyes caught Mattie's as Jumong told the driver to go.

As they sped off, a spot of black streaking through the great gray city, Mattie glared at Fuong Ba in the mirror and signed, 'Do you mind?'

To her surprise, Fuong Ba replied, 'Yes.'

On the outskirts, beyond the thermal of Pyongyang's buildings, the limo dove into a mass of dense ground fog. In the mirror, Mattie was able to see Fuong Ba's face tense as they lost sight of the escort in front of and behind them.

Jumong placed a hand lightly on Fuong Ba's shoulder. "Relax," he said slowly and in a gentle voice. "The enemy is as blind as we are this morning. Besides, a tactical nuke couldn't pierce the armor of this car." Jumong chuckled. But Fuong Ba shook his head, then dug his fingers into the dashboard and leaned forward, peering intently through the windshield.

Perhaps Jumong was right and the enemy, the forces of reaction or whoever they might be, was as blind as they were. Perhaps no enemy existed at all. Mattie, at that moment, didn't much care. What was it he had called her back at the hotel?

"Darling," she said softly and in English.

"I beg your pardon?" Jumong said.

"Darling. Wasn't that what you called me?

"Why, yes, I guess it was," Jumong said, his eyes, brilliant as dark bronze coins, dancing.

"A little presumptuous, don't you think?" Mattie said.

"A little premature, maybe." Jumong cleared his throat. "I feel as nervous as a schoolboy on his first date." Jumong reached into his jacket pocket and tapped a cigarette from its pack. "Do you mind?"

'Hmmm?" Mattie narrowed her eyes, trying to appear as stern as possible. "Of course I mind," she said, clipping the consonant. "In this tiny cab? I just washed my hair. Anyway, it'll kill you."

"But Mattie," Jumong said in a pleading tone, "you need to show a little more understanding. You're an anthropologist and I'm Asian and you know how we love our cigarettes."

"Frankie gave them up. So can you."

"Who is Frankie?"

"Frances Howard. A friend of my parents. She disappeared before they brought me home." The image of a small, slightly built woman with short, dark hair flashed through Mattie's mind. Someone was standing next to her. A man. A tall man … Mattie could feel her abdomen tighten.

"Disappeared?"

"Well, she left Ketchum rather abruptly."

Jumong regarded Mattie thoughtfully. "Anyway, whatever did she give up her cigarettes for?" Jumong said.

Mattie pressed her full, dark lips into a smile and placed her hand on Jumong's. "For love," she said softly.

"Well, then," Jumong said as he rolled down a window, "you've got me." And with that he tossed the pack of cigarettes out of the car. Cool, damp air rushed in. Mattie shivered, but she wasn't entirely certain that the fog was the sole cause.

"So, will you indulge me in my one remaining vice?" Jumong poured a small cup of green tea from a pot and offered it to her. A hint of jasmine filled the air. "It'll take the chill off."

Mattie took the tiny, white porcelain cup in her hands and felt the warmth of the tea spread through her fingers and up her arms. They sat for some time in silence, sipping slowly as the limo piled into great pillows of fog, only to emerge, once and again, into a thin, gray mist that caressed the dark, delicate shoots of rice that filled the fields lining the roadway. While the hot liquid warmed Mattie's belly, the chill did not entirely go away.

A sudden, unpleasant thud jostled everyone in Jumong's car. "I'm sorry," he said. The limo vibrated lightly on the uneven road surface. "Resources. We've simply run out of money for concrete. And besides, hardly anyone lives up here. Except for the Old Man."

"Who's the Old Man?" Mattie asked.

Jumong smiled and shrugged. "Who? Or what? A legend, probably."

"But not a myth?" Mattie said.

"Now you're being the anthropologist."

"Legends have a basis in fact, myths don't."

"A legend, then. Maybe we'll meet him. That's where we're going on our hike today."

"And where is *that*?"

"Deep into the forest." Jumong leaned forward and spoke in a low, leaden tone. "To look for him."

Mattie leaned over and held her face close to Jumong's. "Deep. I'd like that," she growled in a whisper, placing her hand on his thigh.

Jumong sat up, his eyes flaring and his mouth dropping open in mock surprise. "Now who's being ... premature?"

Mattie smiled back but swallowed very hard, surprised at how much she wanted Jumong at that moment.

CHAPTER II

As the car climbed and cornered through a thick white cloud, Mattie threw her head back and let out a laugh, sharp and steely. Like a knife, it must have cut through the last of the morning moisture, as the car exploded into bright sunshine. Mattie gasped. As far as she could see, the landscape was awash in brilliant fall color. Thick, low, leafy deciduous trees, tinged with red and yellow and orange, were punctuated by outcrops of gray and pink granite, all set against a soft, damp, blue autumn sky. Sunlight bathed the hills in warm, white-yellow light.

"Oh, Jumong!" Mattie exclaimed. "Let's get out right here. Let's! And we can walk and walk *forever*."

"No. We're headed higher, toward Myohyangsan mountain. The conifers are magnificent. And you'll have to see the rhododendrons in the spring. You don't have rhododendron in Idaho, do you?"

"Of course not. But I have seen them." Mattie closed her eyes and she thought, just thought, she retrieved a memory of the first rhododendron that ever bloomed. But of course, that couldn't possibly be.

Mattie sat back and stretched. Her eyes caught Fuong Ba's. He had lowered his hand from the dashboard. Fuong Ba did not blink. But she did not blink much either. And the chill she had been feeling was gone.

Soon, thick clusters of scrub, pulsing the warm tones of Autumn, gave way to the green of fir, pine and spruce, and sky's bright blue. Her energy and excitement grew as the car climbed higher. At a spot where a particularly wide, particularly swift stream shot underneath the roadbed, Jumong's caravan slowed, then glided, in almost perfect unison, to a stop.

Mattie bolted from the car. "Oh, it feels good to stretch," she said. She turned her back to the car door, pressed her palms flat against the glass and arched, thrusting her breasts skyward and letting her head drop limply from her shoulders. A light wind dueled with her black hair, pushing a few stray strands about with soft gusts.

"Mattie, please, the men," Jumong said, in English. While his lips were smiling, his eyes were not.

"Really," Mattie said, exhaling audibly. "This is not the nineteenth century."

"No. And this is not California."

Mattie straightened up and ran her fingers through her hair, laughing. "Oh, boy," she said. But her smile vanished when she caught a glimpse of Fuong Ba, his face still, his expression as implacable as the tall spires of stone that stood sentinel all about the landscape, locked in the embrace of the thick evergreens. Not a muscle moved across his pinched, narrow forehead, guarded by a crop of short, black bristles; nor down his smooth, yellow-brown cheeks, nor his broad, bulging jaws. Nothing moved. Nothing at all, except for his eyes, which darted like a swarm of insects, surrounding her frame in a cloud seemingly reflecting raw appetite. Still, almost in complete contradiction, Mattie thought the intent that lay behind the eyes was thoroughly clinical.

Mattie averted her gaze and thrust her hands into the pockets of her jeans.

"What's wrong?" Jumong asked. "I've never known you to be the sensitive type."

"May I ask a question?" Jumong nodded, smiling. "How can Fuong Ba perform as a bodyguard if he is a deaf mute? Wouldn't his back be a blind spot?"

Fuong Ba had turned around and was scanning the forest. "Try it."

Mattie set her jaw. "Okay." She darted for Fuong Ba, meaning to grab his arms from behind. But, when she was only a meter away, he turned and caught her by the arm.

He scowled. "Just curious," she said. Mattie thought she saw the faintest hint of a smile, like the brief brightening of the sky after a storm. Fuong Ba nodded, let go of her arm, turned his back and resumed his surveillance.

"He can feel the slightest compression in the atmosphere around him. A compensation, I guess. You were brave to try," Jumong said.

"I like risk."

Jumong raised a dark eyebrow. "You are either brave, then, or foolish. I'm not yet sure which. However, I haven't known you for very long, have I?"

"No. But that's what my little trip is all about, isn't it? Getting to know one another."

"Indeed," he said.

Jumong's words fluttered across Mattie's consciousness like the wings of a small bird, dimly recognized, in a very dark barn. She found that she was not alone in that place apart that held her most distant memories. It was beginning to fill up. Perhaps it would unfold as well, she thought.

"Yes," Mattie said, flashing a smile, her bright, white teeth carving a dazzling slice across her nut-brown skin, her eyes dancing. "So let's get on with it." Mattie looked back down the road at a string of a dozen military vehicles, all beige, all with a splash of red on the doors, and frowned. Jumong regarded her with concern. "I'm sorry, I just feel as if we're on maneuvers," Mattie said.

"I am." Jumong's eyes narrowed.

"Oh, stop it," Mattie said, chuckling, and laying her hand on Jumong's arm.

"I'm the head of the army!" Jumong cried, feigning indignation. "What else would you expect me to do? Besides," he continued, lowering his voice in a conspiratorial tone, "the enemies of the people are everywhere." Mattie laughed. "But I promise you," Jumong said, laying two fingers over his heart, "while we will not *be* alone, we will be left alone." Jumong nodded in the direction of a small path that bordered the rushing stream and took Mattie's hand. Before they disappeared around the first bend in the trail, Mattie shot a quick glance back at the convoy. Fuong Ba's eyes no longer followed her. He appeared to be in deep conversation, signing to one of the officers. The captain shot a glance up the trail. His expression, sour and brutal, caused Mattie to swallow hard from fear. But the fear was not for herself, for the officer's eyes followed Jumong.

The sun soon burned off the last of the morning mist. The forest palette of greens, both deep and delicate, punctuated by knots of yellow and orange, was set against a cerulean sky. Now and then a chubby cumulus cloud, like some smoky Buddha, would float across their field of vision. Here and there a renegade maple would apply a dab of rouge as if the woods were blushing at the attention they were receiving.

The trail followed the river closely, its pitch and the river's rising as the stream narrowed toward its source. Occasionally tumbling over rocks and sending up a fine spray, the water would burst into a fountain of color, glistening where a shaft of sunlight had penetrated the forest canopy.

After a while, Mattie's and Jumong's skin began to glisten. Jumong stopped and wiped his brow with a sleeve. The two sat down on an old piece of deadfall, covered with thick, soft piles of emerald moss.

Jumong offered Mattie his canteen and she drank greedily. Mattie flicked a line of perspiration off her upper lip. "I hope I didn't overdress."

"No, no," Jumong said. "You'll be glad for the flannel on the hike back. It'll be all downhill." Jumong leaned back and looked Mattie over from head to toe. "No, in fact, you're dressed perfectly. I love the look."

"The look!" Mattie laughed. "Jesus, jeans, boots and an old plaid shirt and sweater?"

"When I studied in the States I bought everything from Bean," Jumong said. Mattie raised an eyebrow. "Really. Look at me. Boots, rag socks, cordu—"

"And that old Mao shirt, or whatever it is." Mattie grabbed the canteen from Jumong and took another swig of water. "Mao's an anachronism. Discredited, really."

"Really?"

"Sure," Mattie said, sitting up very straight and pressing her palms into the wet moss. "Even China's embraced capitalism. Only your country and a few other loonies cling to the old system."

Jumong threw his head back and let out a great laugh, the sound clear and loud and honest. "Now you know very well that my father has begun to institute market reforms."

"At a glacial pace."

Jumong frowned. "So is that what you think I am? A loony?"

"No, no. Of course not." Mattie wriggled uncomfortably as if her bottom had been attacked by a swarm of termites. "That's just it. You were educated in the States. You understand Western ideas. You think Western. It's who you are."

"Is it? Perhaps. Although I don't know yet who I will become. That is a function of circumstance and, if we're lucky, choice. *What* we are is more fundamental. It is part of the raw material for the process of becoming." Mattie's shoulders slumped and she frowned. "Did I say something wrong?" Jumong asked.

"No, it's just that you sound like my father," Mattie said.

"Is that bad?"

"No."

"You don't sound convincing," Jumong said.

"I'm not convinced."

"Do you love your father?"

"No."

"Does your father love you?"

"I don't know." Jumong placed his hands, lightly, on his knees and regarded Mattie with an inviting silence. "He was always kind and offered me every intellectual indulgence. He taught me all he knew, from fishing to Philosophy. He valued the mind above all else, you know. But, I mean, every time it seemed as if he made a move to become, um, closer, he'd back away. He would hug me and I could feel the tension in his body. There was a distance." Mattie exhaled loudly and stood up.

"Now who's backing away?" Jumong said in a calm voice. He extended his hand and Mattie accepted it. Gently, he guided her back down onto the log. "You were trying to escape our conversation."

Mattie averted her gaze, then in a swift movement, raised her head and locked her eyes onto Jumong's. "They adopted me," she said laconically.

"You never mentioned that," Jumong whispered softly. "Another choice, then."

"Choice?"

"That your father—Jaq, is it?" Mattie nodded. "A choice that your father made. You are part of who he is but not what. You are not a part of his genetic—stuff."

"But we were talking politically, weren't we?" Mattie said, rallying.

"We could be talking economics. Or social theory. Communism.

Dictatorship. Capitalism, Democracy. The individual. The mass. What matters is how we treat one another."

"The Golden Rule?"

"An acceptable moral template. Communism and Christ have much in common, you know. To each according to his need, the shirt off your back—" The image of the tall, dark man intruded once again on Mattie's thoughts, but she couldn't hold it. Jumong was speaking. "…much in common. And not. Christ would have embraced Kant and his categorical imperative. The individual as the focus of moral decisions."

"Would he?" Mattie said. "Are you sure?"

Jumong laughed. "Of course. It's written in the gospels. In black and white—"

"But *he* didn't write the gospels."

"No, I suppose he didn't." Jumong frowned. "But we have to make inferences. And utilitarianism would have been hard for him, I think. The greater good for the greater number. You see," Jumong leaned forward, his face lit by the fire of an argument he'd had a hundred times, "the human being is both a social and a solitary animal." Jumong tugged on the sleeve of his Mao shirt, "This shirt reminds me that socialism touched the East with a message of growth and productive energy that not only helped to bootstrap us into the twentieth century, but a message of community that speaks to our culture. We feel comfortable with the concept of responsibility. You with rights. Isn't that so?"

"Me?" Mattie said.

"Well, not you specifically. You, the West." Jumong rubbed his lips with his thumb. "But what about you, Mattie? Aren't you a democrat?"

Mattie tilted her chin and narrowed her eyes. "There is a third way," she said in a flat voice.

"Ahh," Jumong whispered. "I see. You are, at heart, a despot."

"Take your Marx and Lenin, your Jefferson and Locke, and give me Hobbes and his Leviathan. Or, when I'm feeling particularly magnanimous, Plato's philosopher king."

Jumong hopped off the log and settled on one knee. He bowed his head. "Your majesty. I am at your service."

Mattie slapped Jumong's arm with the back of her hand. "Oh, stop it. You're a damned dictator yourself. Or will be soon." Mattie spread her arms. "So dictate."

"Very well," he said, taking Mattie by the hand and lifting her off of the old spruce log. "We've a legend to verify. And we're, um … How have you told me your mother would phrase it, burning daylight?" Mattie smiled broadly and shook her head. As they set off, Jumong squeezed Mattie's hand gently and she squeezed back. But neither said another word for a very long time.

At last the trail split from the river. Mattie and Jumong had to climb an outcrop of rock that rose ten to twenty meters off the forest floor to intercept it. While Jumong picked his way carefully from ledge to ledge, Mattie shot straight up the face. Working in uncanny synchrony, her fingers and boots exploited the tiniest of hand and footholds, and her arms and legs exploded her body to the next elevation. Although Mattie had grown up in the Rockies and considered herself an accomplished climber, she had never experienced such a sense of virtuosity. Yet it felt familiar.

With one last burst, she leapt up and onto a small, grassy glade that guarded the outcrop. "What was that all about?" Mattie muttered to herself. Wiping her forehead with her sleeve, she froze as she caught a glimpse of her hand. Soft sunlight, muted now by a thin layer of high cirrus clouds, shone off a surface that appeared hard and black. Just like this morning, she thought. But this time her throat did not tighten, her breathing did not stop. She simply lowered her arm and stared as the hand regained its former, supple texture.

"Hey, Spiderwoman!" she heard Jumong shout. "How about a lift?"

She turned around and caught sight of Jumong a few feet below, panting hard but smiling. Bending, she extended her hand and then, with one fluid, powerful movement like a human hydraulic, Mattie hoisted him up and onto the grass.

"What—" Jumong gulped a large draught of air, "was that?"

Mattie shrugged. She knew perfectly well what Jumong was referring to. "I've climbed all my life."

Jumong cocked his head. "I'll say." He turned Mattie around slowly. "Well, what do you think?"

Some twenty yards ahead the trail began again, snaking its way in a jagged parabola atop a narrow ridgeline that framed a deep valley. In the distance and directly ahead, on the north-facing headwall that guarded the valley, large boulders were capped with a light dusting of snow from the previous night. On their side of the trail, thick stands of fir and spruce spilled down the western-facing flank to the floor below. The river they had followed all morning cut a dull, silver slice up to a series of falls and small cataracts that tumbled down the rocky eastern facing side.

"It's lovely," Mattie said in a whisper.

Jumong spun her around. "Not as lovely as you."

"Oh, Jumong, that's corny."

Jumong shrugged. "I didn't grow up speaking your language. I'm not as clever with it as I'd like to be." Jumong's lips drooped at the corners.

"Poor baby," Mattie said, stroking his cheek. Then she smiled wickedly. "Not clever with the language, but very cunning nonetheless. You're a born manipulator." Mattie growled, gripping Jumong's ears lightly, pulling his face close to hers, and kissing him hard.

"Mattie, the men!" Jumong said in mock horror. At least a dozen elite troops had followed the two, slipping along silently, concealing themselves always and completely with the rugged raw material of the forest, maintaining a respectful, yet carefully close distance.

"But you said yourself, Jumong, that they would see but they would not watch."

"Yes, I suppose I did. They are good, aren't they?"

CHAPTER III

Mattie peered intently into the thick wood surrounding the small glade where they had stopped. Suddenly, the material world dissolved. Everywhere everything melted into a diaphanous scrim. Bright bits of energy blinked in a quantum dance as the constituents of being communicated with one another in shimmering sequence. Mattie saw through the world. "Good," she said, "but not that good." Jumong gave her a puzzled look as Mattie began to point to a rock here, a tree there, a bush, a boulder.

Jumong frowned. "Out and at attention," he shouted in Korean. The small guard emerged from cover. Jumong's eyes widened and then he gave a hand signal. The men disappeared once again from view. "Remarkable," he said, simply.

"I was a Girl Scout," Mattie said.

Jumong grunted. "I suppose I ought to give you a field commission right on the spot."

"Not until we've successfully completed our mission, sir," Mattie said.

"Our mission?"

"The Old Man's hut. We haven't reached it yet," Mattie said.

Jumong grinned. "No, we haven't." He pointed to the valley below. "Do you see that small rectangle of stones?" Mattie shook her head. "Oh, come now. You seem to see everything else. There, just below the last cataract above the valley floor."

"Yes, I see it now. That's it?" Mattie said, a note of disappointment in her voice.

"Well, yes. Legend has it," Jumong said, lowering his voice, "that the hut appears when the Old Man is at home." A small cloud covered the now sallow sun. Mattie shivered. "I did see it once before. My brother, Kang, and I—you'll meet him …"

"I'd like that."

For a moment, Jumong stood silently. "No, you won't." A puzzled look crossed Mattie's face. She realized that Jumong had never spoken about his brother. "Anyway, it was getting dusky, it was early summer, the air was moist and not a breath of air stirred. We were playing at being commander. Suddenly, there it was …"

"It?"

"The hut. And something moved."

"And?"

"And we ran like hell," Jumong said, laughing. "Or Kang did. He's something of a coward, you know."

"And a bully, I suppose," Mattie said. "His reputation …"

"Is justified. But we were kids and I didn't want him to know that I knew, so I ran too. I always wondered, though, if I really saw anything." Jumong stared down at the small square of rocks. "Are you game for a hike down?"

Mattie nodded. They crossed the soft grass and she stopped once they hit the trail again, taking a slow, deep breath. Sharp scents of pine and the thick, sweet odor of juniper, all cradled gently in the soft, mildly astringent decay of autumn, filled her nostrils. She shut her eyes.

"Now you know why they call these mountains Myohyang. 'Mysterious and fragrant'," Jumong said.

Mattie sniffed. "Where were you and Kang when you saw the Old Man's hut?" she asked rather abruptly.

"Hmmm?" Jumong said, apparently caught off-guard by Mattie's change of tone.

"I said—"

"Yes, I heard. There …" Jumong pointed to a spot up the trail, perhaps three or four hundred yards ahead.

"I smell smoke coming from that direction," Mattie said. "Didn't you say he was supposed to be a charcoal burner?"

"Yes, but I don't—"

"You weren't a Girl Scout. Come on." And Mattie charged ahead.

The trail sloped gently upward along the ridge line. At a point where it began to level off, Mattie stopped. Jumong was right behind her. The increase in elevation now offered a vantage point to view the higher peaks of the Myohyang, already topped with snow. Puffed like pregnant pastries, she thought. Mattie reached out her hand and her mind ran it across the flanks of the distant range. Feeling them stir beneath her touch, she remembered their birth. How could she not? Puffed like pregnant … Mattie, all at once, was aware of her reason for being there.

"Mattie …" Jumong was calling. She turned and looked Jumong over from head to toe, her eyes taking his measure.

"I'm sorry. Your mountains aren't only fragrant. I became lost for a moment. But I've found myself." Mattie turned to the east and away from the valley. Ten or twenty yards of loose scree disappeared into a thick stand of pine. Beyond and at the bottom lay a clearing. "This way," she said, and stepping lightly over the small stones that guarded the woods, she began to descend. She looked back at Jumong who stood quite still for a moment. Motioning to his men, who had had no choice but to abandon cover and line up single file on the narrow trail, Jumong followed.

Needles from a hundred summers crunched pleasantly beneath Mattie's boots as they picked their way down the slope. Fortunately, the pines were well spaced, not dense and dirty like the lodgepole stands back home in the Rockies, and the going was easy. The high cirrus had scattered and clear, yellow afternoon light dripped down like syrup through the trees and warmed their backs.

Go Jumong, this man she had traveled thousands of miles to see, seemingly on a whim, had been named after the legendary (or was it mythical?) first King of Goguryeo. His mother, Yuhwa, had been impregnated by the sun. Mattie felt the thick heat of the afternoon sun bore through her back and into her belly.

She began to run. Suddenly, the acrid odor of pitch was erased by the smell of burning wood. She ran faster. She could hear the footfalls of Jumong and his men behind her, patting like large drops of rain on silk. Bursting out of the pine stand, Mattie stopped abruptly at the edge of the clearing they had seen from the ridgeline. Deep grass, buffeted by a light breeze that had come up all of a sudden, tickled her knees. Jumong pulled up beside her, his men forming a tight semicircle behind and around them.

"But there was nothing here," Jumong whispered.

"Of course there was," Mattie said, "we simply couldn't see it from our point of view." Before them stood a modest structure of split spruce. Two windows, framing a simple plank door and covered with lacquered paper in place of glass, had been thrown open to the air and light. Wisps of gray smoke snaked from a chimney fashioned from large river rocks.

The door catch clicked, echoed by the rattle of a dozen weapons raised to the ready. "Joe!" Mattie shouted. Hearing rifles cock, she turned quickly, shouting "No, wait!" But her words were wasted.

Jumong and his guard stood motionless, bathed in a light that seemed now all the more golden, richer, thicker, as if it could be spread with a spatula. Like insects in amber, they all existed in one singular moment in time.

A very large hand gripped Mattie's forearm. Dark eyes danced in a flat, broad face that seemed to have been fashioned from bronze. Deep lines of laughter streaked from those eyes, supported by high cheekbones and separated by a nose that seemed an anchor to all of the pieces of personality that surrounded it. Jet black hair, pulled into a tight ponytail, was streaked liberally with iron gray.

It was Indian Joe, all right. Her father's best friend back in Ketchum. Proprietor of a Native American artifacts store. Part-time philosopher, full-time gambler. That's why Jaq had liked him so much. Not for the gambling, but for the philosophy. Mattie had never liked philosophers much. In fact, she had never liked them at all. An image flashed in her mind. A cave. She and her father were talking. It was an unpleasant conversation.

Mattie blinked. No, she had never liked philosophers. Except for the Indian. He let you teach yourself. Mattie didn't like being lectured. Maybe Jumong was right. Maybe she was a despot, after all.

"*Jumong!*" Mattie motioned frantically toward Jumong and his men. "Joe, what's happened to them?"

"Nothing. They're all right. They're right there in their own space-time." Joe loosened his grip on Mattie's arm.

"Then where in hell are *we*?" Mattie reached out and tried to touch Jumong, but her fingers passed through his cheek as if he were a hologram. Her hand began to shake violently.

Joe placed it between his enormous palms. "We're *elsewhere*," he said gently.

"Elsewhere," she whispered. Of course. As a child, she'd heard Jaq and Joe drop the word when they talked, while she played with bone whistles and Blackfoot war drums in his store. But she'd been elsewhere herself, though she couldn't quite remember the details.

"Come on," the Indian said. "We don't have much time."

"Time?" Mattie said, glaring at the ghosts around her. "It seems to me as if we have all the time in the world."

"Sure we do, metaphysically speaking. But they're almost ready to start the third quarter and I've got a grand on the Broncos."

Mattie's jaw dropped. Joe started back toward the cabin at a trot. "Oh, and bring your boyfriend."

"He's not my boyfriend," Mattie snapped.

Joe stopped and scratched his cheek. "No, I guess he isn't. He's a hell of a lot more. Which is why you're here. Give him a hand—"

"But —"

"Bring him over. You know how. You've done it before. Today is a day for memories, isn't it, Mattie?" Joe said, then disappeared into the hut.

Mattie took a deep breath and gently pulled Jumong from the amber. Sucking in a deep breath himself, he blinked a few times and then regarded Mattie for a long moment. Jumong glanced at his men. "I suppose we shouldn't keep our host waiting."

"You … you're not startled or surprised or … or frightened or anything, are you?"

Jumong's face flushed deep bronze. "Frightened? I've always believed in the Old Man. Why should any of this surprise me?"

"Well, it surprised the hell out of me," Mattie said, "and I know him. Scared me to death, in fact, when you and your men …" Mattie stared at Jumong's troops. "You are brave."

"It's in my genes," Jumong said. "That's why you came to me, isn't it? I think I understand that now. And I think you know it as well."

Mattie's jaw tightened. "Your genes? Yes, I suppose that's one reason. But only one." Their eyes locked for an instant, and Mattie sighed. "Come on, let me introduce you to the Old Man."

Stepping through the doorway ahead of Jumong, Mattie glanced around the single room of the cabin. A simple wooden table, surrounded by four straight-back chairs, sat in front of a large window opposite the doorway. One corner served as kitchen area, filled by a bar fridge and small sink. A few dishes were set neatly in a drying rack on the sink counter. The opposite corner contained Joe's bunk, the mattress covered by a maroon blanket decorated with simple Native designs and tucked in tightly at the corners. Above the bed she spotted, to her delight, his dream catcher, its web reflecting the incident rays of the sun that penetrated the cabin, spinning gold into hot, bright white silver. The mandala was quite different, though, from typical Southwestern designs. Joe once had said a spider had fashioned it. Mattie's abdomen tickled.

Joe was sitting, as he always had on Sunday afternoons in the fall, in an enormous easy chair that he called his throne. In front of a large flat screen TV monitor, his attention was absorbed by the thoroughly dichotomous repetition and unpredictability of athletic contests.

Joe had not looked up when Mattie and Jumong entered the room. He was scribbling away furiously on one of his scratch sheets as the five-minute ticker scrolled across the bottom of the screen. At last, the Indian scattered the sheets on the floor, the only concession in his home to entropy. "Either of you like a beer?"

Silently, they settled themselves on the sofa. "No, I guess not," Joe said, answering his own question. The announcers were segueing into the next snap.

"You like football, Jumong?"

"Yes. I got into the college game at Stanford. And I rooted for Oakland." Jumong shrugged. "I guess I like the underdog."

"Stanford the underdog?" Joe said shaking his head. "Anyway, the Broncs are losing today, but I've got a soft spot in my heart for them."

"Which means you've got three points," Jumong said. "Not bad with a minute forty left and the Seahawks with the ball on their own twenty."

The Indian smiled. "Smart young man you've got there," he said.

"I always liked the 'Hawks," Mattie said. "But, then, I always bet with my heart."

The Indian's eyes drooped. "Not always, Mattie. Not always."

"Wilson takes the snap," the announcer was saying. "Uh oh, looks like a busted play."

The Indian shook his head and grunted. "Wilson should've retired years ago." "He's heading for the sidelines and the Bronco's safety runs into his own man! Wilson's off. Forty, across mid-field, thirty-five, twenty, touchdown Seahawks!"

Mattie was jumping up and down, pumping her fists. The Indian sat slumped in his chair, one enormous hand draped over his forehead. Jumong regarded them quietly.

Joe pounded his fist on his thigh. Mattie walked over and sat down on his lap. "Maybe they'll return the kickoff for a score," she said sweetly.

"Nah. Their special teams stink." Joe punched the mute on his laptop.

"Oh, Joe," Mattie said. And she planted a kiss on his forehead. "Is it that bad today?"

"No," Joe said. "I'm only out the vig, so far."

"Well," Mattie said, "there's always the Sunday night game."

The Indian's face brightened. "You're right." He kissed Mattie on the cheek. "Just like old times. You always made me feel better when I had a bad day at the track." Joe lifted Mattie gently off his lap and rose from the chair. "Mind if I smoke?" he said, picking up a pack of Kools.

"Did it ever matter?" Mattie said.

Joe took a deep drag on his cigarette and coughed a few times, being careful to cover his mouth. He turned his easy chair a few degrees so he could face Jumong and Mattie, who now sat together on the sofa.

"Want a twag?" Joe asked, offering the pack of Kools to Jumong.

"No, thank you. I gave them up."

"Yeah?" Joe stuffed the cigarettes back into his shirt pocket. "When?"

"This morning."

The Indian pressed the cigarette between his lips in what passed for a smile. He took a deep drag. "Well, you'll be over the worst of it if you can sit there and watch me suck this baby down."

"No sweat," Jumong said. Joe raised an eyebrow. "Discipline. My father, and the Party, drilled it into me. Since I was a boy."

"Since before that," Joe said softly. "But we're not here to talk about you, Jumong. That's not why I brought you both here."

Jumong's face flushed. "Brought us here?"

Joe coughed again. "Well, not exactly. Let's call the whole thing a planned coincidence."

"An oxymoron," Mattie said.

"The universe is a strange place, Mattie. But you know that already," Joe said.

"You need to talk to Mattie, don't you?" Jumong began to get up.

"Sit down. Please. I do need to speak with Mattie, but I also needed to meet you. None of this, of what's happening, bothers you, does it, Jumong."

"Should it?" Jumong said.

"It must all seem a bit unusual. Especially for a thorough-going materialist," Joe said.

"Sure. But while I believe everything has a natural explanation, that doesn't mean we're capable of explaining everything," Jumong said.

"So, Mattie," Joe said, "he's brave and he's disciplined and he's smart. You've chosen well. But it sounds as if he's a bit of a philosopher as well, and you never did like philosophers much, did you?"

"Except for you, Joe."

"Did you, Mattie? Did you like me?" Joe said.

"Very much," Mattie said.

"And your boyfriend here?"

"I love him."

Joe took a very deep drag on his Kool, then blew out the smoke in a thin, tight wisp. "Aaah," he said. "So your sister did teach you a thing or two after all."

Mattie chuckled nervously. "My sister?"

"I didn't know you had a sister," Jumong said.

"I don't. But, uh, I did. Step-sister." Nervously, she fingered a button on her shirt. "She died before I was born. I never knew her."

"Didn't you?" Joe said.

"Excuse me," she said with a smile. The Indian nodded.

CHAPTER IV

Mattie rose and walked stiffly across the carpet to the kitchen table. Placing her hands on the back of a chair, she stared out the window, straining to catch a glimpse … All day memories had intruded on her consciousness. Memories? Unremembered actually, yet familiar. They had come without her willing them.

Sunlight splashed softly on the spruce and pines, sank, then settled on the forest floor. A small bird with a crown of fuzzy copper feathers lit on the sill. Cocking its head, the bird's jet-black eye, matching Mattie's own, locked her gaze. It tapped the window lightly with its beak and flew away. Though she tried to follow its flight, the bird quickly became lost in the tangle of the forest. Leaning forward, Mattie thought, just maybe, she saw its copper top bobbing about amongst the pines.

Out of the corner of her eye, she caught a glint. Glowing dully yet seductively, like quicksilver, the Indian's dream catcher pulsed in the corner of the room. Among the interstices of the web and deep within her own mind, she saw a small girl with auburn hair, cobalt eyes, and a very, very serious expression. "Ur," she whispered, then drew in a sharp breath as tiny fingers dug into the old scar on her side.

"She taught me to love. I remember now. It wasn't easy for her, was it, Joe?"

"It wasn't easy for you," he answered.

"But I do love you both." Mattie held out her hands to the two men.

"Mattie, all this talk today of love and genes … I have to tell you, it's giving me ideas that aren't terribly respectable," Jumong said. Mattie laughed. "I am more old-fashioned than you might think."

"So is she, young man," the Indian said. With a grunt, he pushed himself out of his chair and walked over to the small, pot-bellied stove that heated the cabin, and flicked his butt inside.

"That's right," Mattie said, her words surfing over the top of a throaty laugh. "Things will have to be done properly. Our child—"

"Child?" Jumong said.

"Joe can tell the future, Jumong! He'll be like his father, won't he, Joe? Brave and disciplined and smart and a great leader."

"Brave and smart and disciplined, yes," Joe said.

"And a great leader," Mattie repeated.

A silence suddenly gripped the room, suspending them like Jumong's men, but not in time. Rather, at the edge of an abyss whose rim they did not care to cross. "But Jumong will be a great leader. He's going to take his country, maybe the whole damned world, someplace it's never been."

"He will," Joe said, nodding gravely. "But as a teacher."

Jumong shrugged and smiled. "Can you really see the future, then?" he asked the Indian.

Shaking his head, his eyes dancing, the Indian answered, "No. But I can see possibilities."

"Is there truly a difference?" Jumong asked.

For a moment, it almost looked as if the Indian might have smiled. "Your young man *is* a philosopher, Mattie. Don't say I didn't warn you."

"A philosopher and a teacher," Jumong said thoughtfully. "I could do worse in life. And what about Mattie, Joe? What have I found in her?"

Brushing Mattie's cheek gently with the back of his hand, the Indian spoke softly. "A great queen."

Mattie smiled and kissed the Indian's hand. "And a despot?"

"That too."

Suddenly, the postgame show was interrupted. An anchor was speaking: "The asteroid will transit the moon tonight and be highly visible in the night sky. The militaries of the great powers will launch their weapons to deflect the threat. Remarkably, calm is prevailing across the globe. Scientists have convinced everyone, it seems, that Necros poses no danger." Scenes of calm in all the capitals were projected on the screen. "Now back to our sports report."

The Indian began coughing violently. Deep gurgling sounds rose from his chest. Mattie thought he might throw his lungs up. Gripping his arm, she began to strike him on the back, but he pulled away gently and waved her off.

At last, the Indian bent over a wastebasket and, with one mighty wretch, spat. "It's time to go," he said.

"Joe," Mattie began, "you know you really should—"

"It's time," Joe said again, gesturing toward the door.

Standing at the edge of the Indian's divot in space-time, facing his own mute corps, their eyes still searching for some unknown menace, Jumong turned to the Indian, his own eyes bright. "But please, before we go, tell me—"

"When you return," Joe said, patting Jumong on his shoulder.

"When," Mattie said, her voice rising. "Not if?"

Centuries of sorrow seeped from the Indian's eyes. "When."

His face grew more animated. "Jumong. DPRK first caught sight of Necros."

Jumong laughed. "One advantage of the disadvantage of lack of generating capacity. Our night sky is pretty dark."

Joe nodded. "I know you haven't been invited to the party but you might want to double check the numbers on the payload required to divert the threat."

"Do you think there is a problem?" Jumong asked.

The Indian shrugged. "Hey, I'm no physicist. Still…"

Mattie glanced at Jumong, his own face taut, his eyes fixed on a point beyond the Indian. "Joe?" Bright green grasses rippled in the sunlight where the cabin had stood, bowing before a cool breeze. Mattie heard the rattle of weapons. Jumong's men, their eyes tense and focused, searched the clearing.

"I'm certain I saw something, someone, sir," a young corporal said, addressing Jumong.

"Perhaps you did," Jumong said, smiling. "But by now it's elsewhere." The soldier regarded him with a quizzical expression. "And it's getting late. Lieutenant?" With that, the troop scrambled back up the slope and through the pines.

Perched again atop the ridgeline that sheltered the river valley of the great Myohyang, Mattie and Jumong paused to catch a breath. Though the sun still sat well above the western peaks, its ecliptic was low enough that it would soon begin to descend abruptly toward the horizon. "We should move so we're back in town before dark," Jumong said.

"Right. It'd be nice to clean up before dinner." Mattie looked up into Jumong's face, and then lowered her eyes. "Unless, of course, you have plans," she said flatly.

Jumong lifted Mattie's chin. "How unlike you, Mattie. How indirect. It's charming."

Mattie grinned. "Well, every once in awhile I have to practice at being female."

Jumong's eyes roamed over Mattie's figure. "You don't need the practice."

"Thank you," Mattie said demurely. "But I am hungry. Let's go—"

Gently restraining Mattie's charge, Jumong spun her around to face east, the direction they had just abandoned. Jumong pointed at the empty clearing, already beginning to disappear into the shadows. "Did you hear what he said about us?"

Pursing her lips into a pout, Mattie nodded. "Sure. But what about you? You're supposed to *lead* this country one day, Jumong. You have new ideas."

"And so, I'll teach them. To whoever will listen."

"But it's not who you were brought up, meant to …" Mattie smiled weakly. "I'm worried, that's all."

Jumong pointed toward the plains further to the east. "There. Look." Slowly, the lunar disk, thick and creamy, as if it were being freshly poured from a celestial churn, and limned crisply by a sapphire sky, began to climb above the horizon. "Will it be a guide to a lost hiker? Will it light a page of poetry for a dreamer? Will it incite lovers to riot and excess?" Jumong laughed. "Now that's corny, hmm?"

A pang gripped Mattie's side. Throbbing, her scar proclaimed its existence. "Home," Mattie said, through clenched teeth.

"I'm sorry?"

"Let's go home. I'm just a little worried. I need to sit next to you quietly and hear you tell me that everything will be okay. Okay?"

"Okay," Jumong said. "But let's just watch the moon clear the horizon." Mattie leaned her head against Jumong's shoulder.

As the moon burst into full view, Mattie straightened up. Neither said a word. Pulsing in the moon's lower quarter, red and angry like a boil, ripe with infection, sat Necros, stewing quietly.

The rogue asteroid, Necros, had appeared only a few days before from behind the moon. There had been riots in some of the Muslim countries, people panicked over the possibility of an Armageddon brought on by the godless, secular West, but by and large, the world waited stoically for the great weapon, Science, that had dispatched nearly every other problem, to rescue the planet. Necros would be struck by multiple missiles from this and that direction at such and such velocity and detonate with a force that would alter the planetoid's trajectory ever so slightly so that it would be sent spinning directly into the center of the sun to be deep fried.

"It seems," Jumong said, "the moon will become a mere target. But for tonight only."

"Let's hope it's the only target," Mattie said. Staining her mind's eye, Mattie's dawn dream belched bright blood. Jumong's legs could not be seen for the carnage, but his face was pale and pasty. Her side ached. Jaq had often told her of his own pain over Ur, a "hole in his soul," he'd called it. There had been a time, Mattie sensed, when she could have changed outcomes. Would have changed them. But no longer. Her mother, Kate, had told her that we all must play the hand we're dealt, make the best of a bad situation. And a good one. Kate was a true Stoic. It was how she had dealt with the death of Ur. *Deal with it!* Mattie braced herself. Somehow, she knew that she could no longer affect the future, but she damned well knew that she could deal with it.

Jumong's jaw bulged. "Are you angry?" Mattie asked.

"I was just thinking about what Joe said. I hope the West, in its wisdom, has done its calculations properly."

"Is your pride wounded because they didn't ask you to participate?"

Jumong's face softened. "A little, I suppose." He smiled. "But pride comes before the fall, doesn't it. So we must take care."

Another image flashed through Mattie's mind. A gaunt, ugly, tormented countenance. *Proud! Bildad Proud!* And there was the smell of roasted flesh. *What does it mean?*

A soldier was running toward them, jostling through the thin ranks of Jumong's guard on the narrow trail. He stopped short a few feet from where they stood and saluted. "Sir," he said, "you must return, quickly. Your father is very ill."

"This isn't good," Jumong said to Mattie, the skin around his eyes pinched tightly. "The people won't take this as a good omen. Not tonight." Jumong glanced at the moon, bright white now except for a single crimson stain. The red fires of the setting sun seemed to have ignited Necros, which loomed larger and appeared to shine more brightly.

"An omen?" Mattie said, gesturing toward the asteroid.

"Despite fifty years of rationalism, despite a diet of dialectical materialism, people cannot discard five thousand centuries of superstition and inchoate fear. It's in our genes" Jumong smiled, though not gently. "I have to be there, if …" But he left the sentence unfinished as his eyes filled with tears. "We have to hurry," he said hoarsely.

CHAPTER V

———

By the time they hit the main road, the sun had already set. Dark was descending like a shroud, covering the Myohyang in mist. All of the trucks and jeeps in the small convoy had been turned around. As Jumong approached the spot where the river dove beneath the highway, an officer, short and trim, saluted. Suddenly, four fighter jets roared overhead, a bright red star visible on their tail sections in the moonlight.

"Our jets…" Jumong said, his question obvious though unfinished.

"General Kang ordered them to scramble. It's very bad, sir, with your father." The officer bowed his head slightly, then snapped his fingers and shouted an order. Instantly, a dozen engines roared and two dozen lights snapped on, piercing the gloom with their sallow light. "Please, will you ride in my car?"

"And my brother, Kang?"

"Is with the Great Leader already."

Jumong nodded. "Oh, and get Pak Wei on the phone on the double. Tell him I need him to crunch some numbers." The soldier saluted.

Jumong gripped Mattie by the shoulders. "I'll call you, when I can."

"I'm coming," Mattie said simply.

Jumong shook his head. "You can't. My father wouldn't understand." He gestured toward his men with a nod. "*They* wouldn't understand. The country wouldn't understand. Not yet."

"Get going," Mattie said softly.

Moving more swiftly than Mattie could have imagined for a man of his bulk, Fuong Ba scrambled to climb up into the car beside Jumong, but Jumong stayed him with a hand. "I want you to take Mattie back to the hotel," he said. "And stay with her. These are not safe times."

"No!" Mattie saw Fuong Ba sign emphatically. "Nor is it safe for me to leave your side tonight. Let Chung Soon go with her."

Mattie had not noticed until then, but standing close by, out of the glare of the headlights and mingling with the deepening shadows, was an officer of medium height, but powerfully built. With a head of closely cropped hair like Fuong Ba, he had a nasty scar that ran from the middle of his forehead, across the orbital bone of the eye and down his left cheek, intersecting the corner of his lips and making them turn up at one end in a snarl. It was the man she had seen talking with Fuong Ba as she and Jumong had set out on their hike.

Suddenly, a small, thick, damp cloud rolled down the watercourse and rumbled across the road. Like clammy fingers, a few trailing wisps insinuated themselves beneath Mattie's shirt collar, already damp with sweat from their brisk return. She eyed Chung and shivered. His own gaze was flat, but she could feel that it operated as a window for a keen intelligence.

"Jumong," Mattie said over-loudly, signing simultaneously, "couldn't they both come with me? Please. I'd, um, feel safer." Mattie felt quite certain that she would feel safer. But from whom?

Fuong Ba shook his head violently, but Jumong placed a hand lightly on his shoulder. "I have almost fifty of my elite guard with me. I can't send that kind of force back into Pyongyang with her." Fuong Ba began to object once again. "I can't," Jumong repeated. "Take care of her. Both of you. It's an order, old friend." Fuong Ba bowed and stepped back from the car. "And you," Jumong said to Mattie with a smile, "don't you dare give them as much trouble as you give me. I have other things to worry about." His eyes began to fill with tears, but he turned away quickly and gave a sharp order to the driver.

With a loud roar, its wheels spitting gravel, the Jeep sped off down the road. Four trucks raced into the van and five more followed Jumong.

Mattie waited until all twenty taillights had disappeared around the first bend. Her eyes locked on Fuong Ba. She glanced at Chung, who had not moved a single muscle in all of those minutes.

"Please," an older soldier said to Mattie, "will you come with me?" With a slight bow, the officer opened the rear door of the limo she and Jumong had taken from Pyongyang that morning. Mattie glanced at Fuong Ba, whose features remained impassive, as if etched in granite. The chill that had stolen over her collar seemed to seep into her bones.

"Yes, let's get going," Chung Soon said. He was smiling now, but still, Mattie was unable to see the intention that lay behind his eyes. *How can I deal with two of them?* She would think of something. She had before. The shadow of what she had been passed across the lens of her mind's eye, but this time less darkly.

"Yes, let's do," Mattie said, and crawled into the back seat. Fuong Ba followed. As Mattie settled into her seat, she saw that two soldiers were already in the limo. One sat, grimly next to the door and another was perched, back straight, on the edge of the bench that faced to the rear.

Just as Chung Soon was about to crawl into the limo, a hand stayed him. "No, no," the older officer who had been holding the door said. "It'll be far too crowded with all of us in the back."

"Then you hop in front," Chung said, smiling. His eyes caught Mattie's and, for the first time, she saw them soften. *Maybe …*

"Hey, Chung Soon!" a voice called. Two men stood at his side. "Come with us."

"Yes," another voice said. "We can follow. It's a better security protocol. Besides—" The man leaned and whispered into Chung Soon's ear. Chung Soon scratched his chin and looked directly at Fuong Ba, who glanced around briefly, then nodded.

"Right, then," Chung Soon said, rubbing his hands, "it's all settled. See you at the hotel."

As an aide slammed the rear door of the limo, Mattie could hear Chung Soon laughing. Listening carefully, she thought of John Faddle, a stockbroker and one of her parents' best friends when she was growing up in Ketchum. Consummate salesman turned consummate politician, Faddle had purposefully taught Mattie the many manifestations of bullshit. Chung Soon's laugh was a bullshit laugh. But who, she wondered, was the joke on?

The older officer who had first addressed Mattie ordered the soldier sitting opposite her to exchange places with him. The soldier's jaw muscles bulged as he regarded Fuong Ba with a fixed gaze, but the officer settled back into the soft cushions and allowed a broad, self-satisfied smile to fill his flat, flaccid face. "Surrounded," Mattie said in English.

"I beg your pardon?" the officer said.

"I said, I am surrounded by so many men."

"Does it make you uncomfortable?" the officer asked. While Mattie considered her reply the man sucked slowly on one of his teeth.

"Why, no," Mattie said, at last. "In fact, I'm flattered."

The officer grinned and nodded, all the while continuing to make loud sucking sounds. "You really must stop that," Mattie said.

"Excuse … Oh, I'm sorry. Does the sound annoy you?"

"Oh, no," Mattie said, "it's just that I'm awfully hungry."

"You're—" The man wrinkled his nose and shook his head, then shouted to the driver to go. "Your American humor is very, uh, very…:

"Decadent," Mattie said. "Yes, I know."

While the grin had vanished from the officer's face, Mattie smiled sweetly, but her stomach twisted and felt as if it were pressing against her scar, rubbing it raw. Turning to Fuong Ba, she saw that he sat quietly, his huge hands resting on his thighs, his eyes locked onto the soldier sitting opposite, who might as well have been a mannequin were it not for a tiny tick that flashed at the corner of one eye. Though no one said a word, the silence in the car rose to a deafening pitch that seemed to drown out the roar of the engine as they sped away.

* * *

The broad rump of darkness had, at last, spilled over the edges of the Myohyang massif. Chung Soon strode easily alongside the two soldiers and into the glare of their truck's headlamps. As they approached the vehicle, the two men drifted, almost imperceptibly, away from Chung Soon and as they did, his shoulders and forearms tensed slightly.

Chung Soon walked directly into the glare of a headlamp. "So," he said, "what about that shot of Kentucky bourbon you promised?" The men's boots stopped crunching the small stones that lined the road. Only the sound of the truck engine, purring patiently, and the rush of the river could be heard.

One of the men, the larger of the two, laughed. "Yes, the shot we promised you." Chung Soon leaned against one of the jeep's headlamps, his right arm draped casually over the fender. The men had stopped perhaps four or five feet from Chung Soon.

Grinning, the smaller man drew his sidearm. "You know," he said, "you always were an arrogant son of a bitch."

Chung Soon rubbed his scar. "So this is personal?"

"We volunteered," the big man said. "To that extent, yes, it's personal. But no—"

Pulling a pack of cigarettes from his pants pocket, he grabbed a twag and jammed it into the corner of his mouth. The small man took a lighter from his shirt pocket with his free hand, never for an instant taking his eyes or his weapon off Chung Soon, and lit the cigarette.

The large man took a deep drag. "No, you see, tonight the great Go Jumong is going to have an accident." Chung Soon frowned. "Oh, no, nothing like that. Kang wouldn't kill his brother, but Jumong's convalescence will take a very long time. And with the Great Leader himself gone, the country will need strong, effective, uh, guidance. Besides, who could tell Kang and Jumong apart anyway? Don't you agree?"

Chung Soon folded his arms. The big man shrugged. "Whether you agree or not is of no importance. But you know enough, and where you're going, the knowledge won't do you much good anyway." The smaller man cocked his revolver.

"Just one question," Chung Soon said. The big man flicked an ash onto the ground. "The Great Leader is ill, then? That is not a deception?"

"*Was* ill."

"So Kang killed him and is waiting for Jumong at the compound."

"Actually, no," the big man said. "Kang is at People's Defense Command." Chung Soon wrinkled his forehead. The big man pointed his cigarette at the big red blotch that now covered the greater part of the moon's surface. "Remember. Tonight the nations of the world are cooperating to take out a common menace."

"But we weren't invited to participate," Chung Soon said, straightening himself.

"So? What's the English phrase? We're going to crash the party," the big man said.

"I see," Chung Soon said slowly as he took a step forward.

"Hold on," the big man said, pulling his own revolver. "No closer. You're good, Chung Soon, but not five feet good."

"Then you haven't paid attention," Chung Soon said.

The big man frowned. "Anyway, I'm tired of talking," he said.

"So am I," Chung Soon said. And with that he leapt to his left and at the smaller man. As he did, the glare of the headlamp hit both men in the face. It gave him just enough time.

With a flying kick he knocked the gun out of the smaller man's hand. Landing behind him, Chung Soon hit the soldier in the head and from behind with a roundhouse kick. A loud noise, like the snap of dry wood, was heard and the force of Chung Soon's blow drove the smaller man forward, knocking the big man off balance momentarily and forcing the gun to fly from his hand.

Chung Soon bounced lightly on the balls of his feet. For an instant, the big man eyed the revolver, lying near the body of his smaller companion who was sprawled on the ground, head and shoulders at an awkward angle,

"You're good, Park," Chung Soon said, a smile playing at the corner of his lips. "But not five feet good."

With a snarl, the big man raised his hands and lunged at Chung Soon. But Chung Soon stopped his punch with a deft block, seizing the big man's hand between his own raised forearms. A belch of air was heard as Chung Soon delivered his foot to the big man's midsection.

Chung Soon paused, just long enough for the big man to look up. Their eyes met for an instant. Then, with a cry that rent the blackness surrounding them, Chung Soon drove the index and middle fingers of right hand into the big man's eyes, the first two joints curling behind the bottom of the sockets. Chung Soon focused, then grunted and snapped his elbow back behind his ear. With a crunch, the lower half of the big man's face fell away and dropped to the ground along with his body, all in a pool of vomit.

Chung Soon dipped the toe of his boot delicately between the still quivering lips of the big man. "You always did talk too much," he said, then hopped into the jeep, shut off the lights, and headed at full speed back down the road toward Pyongyang.

Ten kilometers passed, fifteen, and still there was no sign of the limo. Leaning over the steering wheel, Chung Soon squinted, but no telltale red lights were to be seen. All was blackness on the road.

Careening around a curve, Chung Soon tapped the brakes. Perhaps a hundred meters down the road and off to the side, a flicker of movement disturbed the bright whitewash of the moon. With one hand Chung Soon reached up and behind and pulled an automatic off its rack, then ducked beneath the dashboard and leveled the gun at the dark figure that had flattened itself against a berm.

At ten yards, Chung Soon snapped on the lights. Jamming on the brakes, he shouted, "Fuong Ba!" A shot rang out and a bullet smashed through the glass of the front windscreen, narrowly missing his head. Chung Soon ducked down even lower, thrust his free hand out the window and signed his own name furiously. Peeking over the dashboard, he saw Fuong Ba lower his weapon. He bounded out of the cab of the jeep and sprinted toward his friend.

With a grunt, Fuong Ba pushed himself off of the body that had served as cover. Chung Soon placed his boot beneath the shoulder of the fallen soldier and rolled him over. The young soldier who had sat next to Fuong Ba in the car stared up at the blue-black sky with sightless eyes. "So," he said, "there are traitors everywhere."

Fuong Ba nodded, then looked at Chung Soon's right hand, his fingers covered by a dark stain. "Yes," Fuong Ba signed, "traitors everywhere."

"But how did they—" Chung Soon began, speaking slowly and looking Fuong Ba full in the face.

Fuong Ba waved his hand in disgust. "Guns at close quarters always limit options. Even I—" Fuong Ba's hands fluttered to his side. 'But I took this little prick with me.' Fuong Ba kicked at the corpse, then clenched his fists. Relaxing them, he signed, "I want that son of a bitch Colonel Pak Ree. I can still see him sucking on that tooth as they pushed us out the door."

"Still, I don't see—" Chung Soon began.

Fuong Ba opened his coat. Blood stained his shirt and a piece of rag had been stuffed between his ribs. "They must have thought they'd killed me."

"Is it bad?" Chung Soon asked.

Fuong Ba shook his head. "Flesh wound, but it knocked the wind out of me. I'll make it. Anyway, they're taking Mattie to Kang, I know that much. But the knowledge doesn't do us much good, since I'm not really sure where Kang is."

"But I am," Chung Soon cried. Slapping his thigh, he let out a whoop of laughter. "Park—"

"Could never keep his mouth shut," Fuong Ba finished.

"So," Chung Soon said, "Mattie is being taken to Kang at People's Defense."

"Why is she being taken to *him*, and what is Kang doing at People's Defense?"

"As for Mattie …" Chung Soon shrugged. "But it seems as if Kang wants to take a shot at that thing," Chung said, pointing to Necros. Fuong Ba nodded. "Anyway, our orders were to safeguard Mattie. But Jumong …"

"We split up, then. My first responsibility is her safety, no matter what I think," Fuong Ba said.

"And what do you think, friend? Of Mattie."

"She doesn't trust me, but she is good, very good, for Jumong."

Chung Soon smiled and nodded. Then his face fell, his scar curling down his face in the moonlight like a black viper. "They're doing something to Jumong. I don't know what, but it's bad. We have to hurry."

Fuong Ba growled, then signed, "… something bad to Jumong?" He picked up the dead private's pistol off the ground and bent the barrel with his bare hands.

"Fuong Ba!" Chung Soon said. "Don't waste artillery."

Fuong Ba threw the gun on the ground and held up his hands, fingers splayed. "This is all the artillery I need," he signed.

People's Defense was situated only five klicks from the Great Leader's compound. Vehicles raced up and down the road that paralleled the barbed-wire perimeter. Chung Soon's jeep was lost in the confusion. A hundred meters from the main entrance, Chung Soon pulled over to the side of the road. "The place is, how would the Yanks put it, jumping," he said. "Are you sure …?"

"I know every meter of the place. I helped design security, remember?

No one will see me. Or if they do, they'll wish they hadn't." Fuong Ba grinned. "I'll be in missile control in thirty minutes. Once I get Mattie, I'll pull a hijack and meet you … ?"

"I'm going to the infirmary at the compound. A hunch."

"Good luck," Fuong Ba said silently, moving his lips very deliberately.

Chung Soon nodded and Fuong Ba slipped out of the truck and into the night.

CHAPTER VI

With fingers that writhed like a clutch of small snakes, the captain continued to dig his long, effeminate nails into the flesh of Mattie's forearm, all the while pulling her, out of step with his own blistering pace, down the narrow corridor. Rude fluorescents flickered overhead, their brittle light reflecting flatly off the faces of Mattie's guard. Gray walls, gray floors, dull gray metal doors surrounded them like the barrel of a gun.

Turning to the right at the end of the long hallway, Mattie found herself standing in front of a pair of black double doors marked with small red characters that said simply "Command." Sucking, sucking all the while on his tooth, the captain pulled a card out of his pocket and pressed it against a scanner on the wall. Slowly and precisely, he tapped out a long code.

With their own peculiar sucking sound, the doors parted and the captain rudely shoved Mattie forward and she stumbled into the room. Regaining her balance, she turned sharply and glared at the captain. With a wide smile, teeth set perfectly on edge, he took a long, slow pull on his loathsome canine.

Somewhere, deep within, Mattie heard the sound of her past rushing upward to greet her consciousness. Making their way through a labyrinth of new memories, the old continued to push themselves out. Mattie knew, quite suddenly, that she had arrived at the time and place of discovery where she could continue the process of her own becoming.

Cupping her right hand successively beneath each eye, Mattie snapped out her contacts. Shoving them into her pants pocket and staring back once again at the captain and her guard, she saw his smile drain back into his mouth and his men step back a pace. Coldly, she regarded them with eyes set in their sockets like polished onyx.

"Bring her to me!" Harshly, a voice echoed off of the walls. *Jumong!* A shock coursed along the surface of Mattie's skin and she ran to the top of a flight of stairs.

The room was a shallow amphitheater. Ten or twelve rows of seats sloped down gently to a large floor, filled with long banks of desks that ran in parallel, covered with ancient computer monitors, many with green DOS characters glowing. Beyond the workstations and on the walls sat an overly large, almost campy world map, complete with varicolored lights denoting, most probably, strategic locations.

Three men stood huddled over reams of paper that had been strewn over one of the desks. All wore military uniforms. The man with his back to Mattie shouted again, "I said, bring her down here!" Although the voice was Jumong's, the inflection was not. Mattie hesitated, then with pheromones flooding her nostrils and feeling a surge of blood pulsing through her abdomen and thighs, she raced toward the sound, the boots of the guards pounding behind her.

Stopping abruptly at the bottom of the stairs, Mattie drew a deep breath. She was sweating profusely and she felt as if her pants might split at the crotch from the pressure. Wiping her forehead, she said his name once again, this time softly. "Jumong."

The man wheeled about slowly, then leaned back against the desk. Like an icon, Jumong's face seemed to float in the soft green light of the room. Mattie's full lips were parted by a brilliant smile, but the smile evanesced slowly as she watched Jumong's brows knit themselves together tightly.

"Wherever did you get those eyes?" he asked.

Lowering her head, Mattie whispered, "I, um, I'm … sorry. I should have told you. My parents had the prostheses made for me." Mattie lifted her chin and she locked her eyes on Jumong's. "But they told me I didn't have to wear them. They told me they loved me the way I am. Do-do you love me that way, Jumong? Can you?"

"A freak! This will be more fun than I had expected." The man grinned, revealing a row of yellowed teeth filed to exquisite points. Mattie stumbled backward, bumping into the captain, who sank his fingers into her flesh.

Mattie winced from the pain. Clearly, the captain had regained his courage.

With a vicious yank, Mattie freed her arm from the captain's grip. "So you're—"

"It was rude of me. But Jumong always said that rudeness was one of my salient flaws. Along with cruelty and avarice." The man laughed and the captain and his guard echoed woodenly. "I am Kang." He smiled and ran his tongue slowly across his teeth. "The evil twin," he said in English.

"Of course. I've heard of you," Mattie said flatly.

"I am flattered," Kang said, "that my reputation has preceded me. I didn't realize—"

"Don't flatter yourself. There have been only isolated reports in the States." Kang frowned. "And Jumong mentioned you just this afternoon." Kang raised an eyebrow. "In passing," Mattie finished.

His features folding into a frown, Kang raised a hand and tapped lightly on the point of one of his upper incisors. "You're a bitch," he said at last. "I don't really see why Jumong fancies you. You seem more suited to my temperament."

"If that's your opinion," Mattie said, "at least you're honest with yourself."

Kang straightened. "You must be honest with yourself when you're not the favored one." Mattie's features softened. Nothing is either entirely good or entirely evil, her son Nicholas used to say. *My son!* The clamor within began to rise again, but softly, like a cloud of fine dust pluming from a sarcophagus recklessly opened. Rather than a feeling of fright, Mattie was driven by a macabre curiosity to view the face of the being lying still inside. "But there were certain advantages," Kang was saying. "My father was a good judge of people. He did not become the Great Leader because he was bad at his job. And so, I accepted his judgment and refined my own talents." Kang grinned.

"What do you mean your father 'was'? I know he's been ill. Has he—?"

"Died? Yes."

"Then why are you here? Are you certain he's dead?"

"Ah, yes," Kang said softly. "He always taught me to be most certain of things like that."

Mattie took a step forward, but the captain restrained her once again.

Kang shook his head. "Let her go," he said simply, switching to Korean.

Rushing at Kang, Mattie grabbed his shirt in her two fists. "Where is Jumong? What have you done with him?"

Gently, Kang pried Mattie's fingers from him. "I'd almost forgotten about Jumong. Ke Dong?"

The captain stepped forward and bowed. "The young lady here is right. We shouldn't neglect our brother at this sad time. Take your men and leave."

"But, sir, the launch is only twenty minutes away and—"

"And everything has been planned so that the program will execute smoothly. No, flawlessly. Isn't that how you put it?" The man opened his mouth but not a sound came out. "Isn't it?" Kang shouted.

"Yes, sir."

"Good. It's settled. All of you, leave us! Ke Dong. Station your men outside the door and you go to the infirmary alone. Now!"

With a sharp salute, Ke Dong turned on his heel and raced up the stairs of the amphitheater, his men and Kang's two technicians in tow, the heels of their boots battering the steps in double time.

"Ke!" As his men filed out, the captain stopped short and stood at the top of the steps. "Make sure our brother is properly attended to. The country's safety is at stake at a time like this." Ke Dong smiled a tiny, crooked smile and made a sucking noise that insinuated itself into the sudden stillness that had settled over the room. As if in counterpoint, when the captain exited, the heavy metal doors sealing off the command center shut with a soft whoosh.

"So Jumong is with your father's body at the infirmary?" Mattie said, trying very hard to sound calm, objective. Trying very hard to extract as much information as possible.

"No, no," Kang said. "The old man is already in deep freeze. He'll go on display, perhaps tomorrow. Or the next day at the latest. It wouldn't do if he looked less than fresh, would it?"

Jumong! Mattie screamed inside her own skull. Tiny claws, sharp as scalpels, tore at the old scar in her side, as she felt fear and anger flood from her brain and out to the very extremities of her body. But anger, she told herself, *Jaq* had told her, can be dangerous if it isn't controlled. It interferes with judgment, and she realized that she must be very careful around this fellow Kang.

Casually, she strolled down the length of one of the rows of desks and hopped up onto a control station.

"Be careful!" Kang shouted.

Mattie arched an eyebrow above one of her bottomless black eyes, smiled demurely and wiggled her butt into a more comfortable position. "What's this red button?" she asked, with affected insouciance, as her finger hovered over the control.

"I said, be careful," Kang repeated, as he grabbed her wrist.

"Ouch," Mattie said flatly, yanking her hand free of Kang's grip. She smiled unconvincingly. "Boy, Kang," she said in English, "this is some set-up."

"Why, thank you," Kang said, splaying his long, thin fingers across his chest.

"Where'd you get it? Hollywood? It's so *retro*! All you're missing is Doctor Strangelove." Mattie ran her gaze over Kang. "Then, again, maybe not."

Kang's features tightened and his lips twisted into a thin sneer. With unnatural speed, he smacked Mattie very hard across the face.

In an instant of time so brief that it was difficult to say whether or not the intellectual record of the event qualified as a memory, the surface of Mattie's skin flickered, black and shiny and hard. Kang winced, his face reflecting both revulsion and a complete lack of understanding. Mattie felt her anger rush at her scar, pressing against it as if it might break her ribs to escape. In a moment, the pressure within subsided. But she carried from the experience a memory. A vast plain, parched by a blistering sun, and a man. *Jaq! That's who was straddling me in my dream.*

Mattie's side throbbed. She touched her shirt at the spot where it covered her scar. Mattie reminded herself again that she must not allow herself the luxury of anger, as she had that day when she'd faced her father. But other than that single thought, the pieces of her past lay strewn about, still waiting to be put together. At least she'd dumped them onto the floor.

Kang blinked, as if in denial of what he thought he had seen. "Pride. The

West needs to beware its pride," he said slowly, as if recovering. "This room may look 'old fashioned,' but I assure you the equipment is quite effective. We purchased it from the French, after all."

"For what purpose?"

"I suppose there's no harm in telling you," Kang said. "After all, you won't be leaving Korea."

Though swallowing hard, Mattie failed to move a single facial muscle.

"The nations of the West, once again in their supreme arrogance, have decided that we will not be allowed to participate in their little party this evening."

"So the Indian was right," Mattie whispered.

"What?" Kang barked.

"Uh, nothing." *Focus, Mattie, focus.*

Kang turned and pressed a button on the desk behind him, and the display on the wall changed to a view of Necros, red and ugly, framed by Earth's own bright, white moon. "But we're going to crash it. A team of our 'observers' at a Russian silo in Siberia have managed to, um, *borrow* one of their rockets. And its payload should be just enough to change Necros' vector and keep it in the affectionate embrace of Earth's gravity."

"So where's it going to land?" Mattie asked, picking at a finger.

Kang leaned back against a desk and folded his arms. "Well …" He rubbed his chin. "Our equipment, as you pointed out, is somewhat primitive and we are dealing with uncertain initial conditions …" Throwing his arms up and affecting a slightly bewildered expression, Kang said simply, "The West miscalculated badly. Without our payload, Necros would hit a major population center in the U.S. It never would have been diverted out of Earth's orbit."

"So the Indian was right," Mattie whispered to herself.

"What?"

"Nothing. So where will it strike" Mattie asked.

"If we're lucky, the Pacific Ocean. If not, our best guess is Idaho."

"Idaho!" Mattie jumped off the desk.

"Yes. What were you expecting? London? We're not butchers, after all. Hardly anyone lives in Idaho. But we'll make our point."

As Mattie pressed her face close to Kang's, he seemed to recoil slightly as her jet black eyes locked onto his. "The hell, hardly anyone. A million people! Including my parents."

"Very touching, but very Western. Here I am trying to make a point and, in the course of it, saving probably twenty million lives. But you, all you care about is the individual. It's an overriding paradigm.

"Besides," Kang whispered, pulling Mattie against his body, "I doubt they're your parents at all, unless they each have one massive set of recessive genes." *Genes.* The word itself made Mattie dizzy. Her nostrils flared. She took a deep breath. She breathed deeply again. She couldn't stop. Kang's smell, Jumong's smell, seeped into every cell of her body. Kang was speaking but Mattie could not hear the words. "Lily white. Why should you care anyway about your goddamned precious Idaho or your precious America? *Nigger.* Isn't that what they still call you back there?"

Snapping back into focus around the loathsome word *nigger*, Mattie's mind realized that it was in a battle with her body, her instinct, for control of her very self and that it was losing badly. "Hmm?" she said absently. Then suddenly, "Jumong! Dammit, Kang, what have you done to him? Where is he?"

"Where? Why, right here, of course," Kang said, touching himself lightly with the tips of his finger. "We're identical, you know. Genetically identical."

CHAPTER VII

More than just an odor now, Kang's smell, his essence, belched from his body. Every pore in Mattie's skin, every follicle on her head, soaked it up. "Yeah, I know," she said, her voice thick and dusky. Slowly, she backed away, hoping that distance, even a small one, would release her from the grip of the fine net of pheromones that were entangling her. Mattie took a couple of shallow breaths. Kang stared at her breasts, rising, swelling, then falling. "Look, Kang, this is all lunacy. All of it. This silly missile control room, your scheme. I mean, this is the real world; you're going to kill real people. This isn't some fucking James Bond movie. Come on, Kang. Let's shut it all off. Okay? Come on."

Grabbing Kang's hand, Mattie swallowed hard, as if she knew what would happen. Mingling with hers, the sweat on his palms seeped through the surface of her skin and coursed up her arm. She could feel herself begin to tremble, but she didn't let go and led Kang back to the red button. Then she slid her hand from his. Just in time, she thought. Just in time before she drove Kang to the ground and tore his clothes from his body with her bare hands, before she sucked at his flesh and took what she needed.

Large beads of perspiration rolled off of Mattie's forehead and coursed over her cheeks. "Okay," she said, as calmly as she could manage, "let's do it, Kang."

Kang arched an eyebrow, smiled and tapped a finger on one of his canines, thrusting like a dart from his gums. "Oh well, maybe you're right. It's very simple." He flicked a toggle switch next to the red button and the old CRT that stood on the console flashed "Command." With carefully measured affectation, Kang held his hands poised above the keyboard. "Then again," he said, "maybe you're wrong," and he stood upright and clasped his hands behind his back. "Yes, it would be so simple to abort it, or change it, but I think not."

Mattie wiped her forehead with her sleeve. "How simple, Kang?"

"Well, if you enter Bravo Charlie X-ray 573567 Alpha 25 King 7 Queen 49246, then respond to a series of prompts, you can change the course of the missile. I don't mind telling you this because excellent memories are almost always photographic or, if eidetic, they're visual. And if by some chance you could remember the code, you'd have to have a good grasp of mechanics to reprogram the trajectory and send it to a precise target. Even you wouldn't want to risk sacrificing, say, Chicago, for Idaho, would you? And all of this assumes you've overwhelmed me and rendered me helpless." Kang grinned and flicked his tongue across his teeth. "As for the destruct sequence," he said, pressing his face close to Mattie's, "I don't think I'll give that to you." Kang lowered his head and stared at Mattie's breasts. Her light flannel blouse had soaked through and her nipples, erect and hard, felt as if they were about to rip through her shirt. "But there is something else I am going to give you." Pressing his groin against Mattie's thigh, Kang ripped her shirt open. Buttons launched into the dim green atmosphere and rattled in asymmetrical sequence off the desks and floor, their soft clicks tearing tiny holes in the silence.

Mattie shut her eyes so tightly she felt as if she might crush them in their sockets. Kang's hands moved slowly in large, then small, circles across her breasts, his essence mixing slowly, but ineluctably, with hers. This is what she had come for. To mate. *No!* To make love to, to love, Jumong. To love, but to mate also, with Jumong. But this man *is* Jumong. Memories scurried from every cell, converging on the wound in her side, scratching, trying to dig their way out. Somewhere in the babble was the answer, but she couldn't hear it. Until she was able, she had to control the desperate need.

Kang was making soft, growling noises. *Control the need.* Out of the corner of one eye Mattie spotted the red button. *Quickly, before Kang notices.* But her bones felt as if they had been filled with molten lead, hot and heavy. Her arm floated towards its target, but Kang did not see it. As he pressed his groin harder against Mattie's leg, she could feel his tongue flicking lightly across the tips of her nipples.

But Kang had seen, known. As her finger reached a point directly above the red button, his hand shot out and seized her wrist. Panting, he raised his head and looked her full in the face, regarding her with what appeared to be keen interest. Kang cocked his head.

Gritting her teeth, struggling to gain the slightest advantage from his divided attention, Mattie tried with a grunt to reach the button. But Kang held her fast, then smiled and shook his head. "What is it you find so compelling about that red button? You don't even know its function. So, you're a bitch, and not very bright at that. Go ahead, then." Kang released his grip. "Hit the damned thing and find out. Does it abort the launch? Does it override the ability to abort the launch? Does it blow the both of us to kingdom come?" Mattie's hand remained motionless above the control. Kang tsked. "We've established you're stupid, but I thought that at least you'd be curious." Kang slammed Mattie's hand down onto the console, striking the red control. Involuntarily, Mattie's throat released a tiny squeal from the petty pain. "So," Kang said softly, the sibilant whistling through teeth, "what hath we wrought? Salvation or destruction?"

"Kang," Mattie said, the word punctuating her gasps as she pushed herself up onto her elbow, "This is fucking nuts. Stop it. All of it. What you plan to do with your goddamned bomb and what you're doing to me. Let me go. Let me go to Jumong. Please, Kang." Tears filled Mattie's eyes, two small pools of hot tar. Sweat collected in the tiny hollow at the base of her neck.

"If it will make you feel a little bit better, and a little bit better about me, I'll let you in on a secret. We will change the coordinates of the payload's trajectory after the omnipotent ones of the West allow us to join their party. I told you, they miscalculated. They need us." Kang pressed his face close, his breath warm and ether-thick, insinuating itself into her volition. "I'm a blackmailer, not a butcher."

"Good," Mattie said, her chest heaving. "That's very good." While she appreciated his words, she could not feel the appreciation, just the need. Swelling, she felt her labia pressing against her pants, threatening to split their seams. Blue-black nipples knotted, each quivering on its pinched base. The flesh wrapped about Mattie's bones began to quiver. "No," Mattie gasped, "I, I need Jumong."

Kang must have inferred Mattie's intent, if not her meaning. "Need?" he said simply.

"Let me go. Please, Kang. I have to—"

"But I'm afraid that's impossible. You see, your little red button has locked us in. No one can enter and we can't leave. Unless," Kang said, once again with a nasty hiss, "I want to. And I don't want to."

"Jumong," Mattie cried weakly, "I need Jumong. Now." As she spoke, her arms began to shake violently and then, no longer able to support her weight, gave way and her torso slumped back onto the desk.

With a quick, violent move, Kang tore open his own shirt. Hairless, yellow-brown like parchment, his chest glistened, even in the dim light. "I *am* Jumong." Confirming his words, his scent shot from his body.

"Yes," Mattie said, breathing deeply again and again, "you are Jumong," her body screaming what her mind denied.

Kang's eyes flashed, panther bright, and he ran his tongue one last time over the tips of his teeth.

'You are Jumong,' Mattie's body screamed again and aloud. With a quick savage movement, her hands shot out and she began to tear at his pants.

Just as violently, Kang unsnapped Mattie's corduroys and pulled them down below her knees. Shaking one leg, she pulled the foot free, letting the pants dangle from the other ankle. Spreading her legs, a thin, hot river of her own fluids gushed over her thighs and buttocks. With a leer, Kang unbuttoned his trousers and fell on top of her.

Mattie spread her knees and within an instant felt him, tongue-hot, drive deeply within. Pressing his face against hers, Kang chewed at her lips and cheeks, his own teeth making small slices in the flesh. But Mattie could focus on little else but the need until she felt him pulse and groan, then bellow like a mindless beast, collapsing on top of her.

Instantly, Mattie heard the chains fall, which need had used to bind her reason. *What have I done?* She swallowed hard. She rolled Kang off of her and hopped to the floor.

"No, wait," Kang said weakly, pushing himself up on his elbow. Men,

Mattie reminded herself, were far less demanding when their own needs have been fulfilled. Where had she heard that? *Garp.* Perhaps she could take advantage of the fact, and of Kang, to find Jumong.

Jumong. What have I done? Closing her eyes, Mattie pinched the top of her nose between her thumb and forefinger. Genes. They didn't much give a damn about consequences, only results. Genes. She could feel Kang's semen running down her leg. As if she had smelled something terribly offensive, Mattie wrinkled her nose and pursed her lips, then grabbed a loose piece of paper off the desk behind her. Carelessly, she wiped her thigh, crumpled the evidence and threw it in the trash. Quickly, and consciously avoiding Kang's gaze, Mattie pulled her pants back on and buttoned up.

Kang was sprawled out on the console, panting softly. "Okay, Kang, get your shit together. You look a mess and we're going to be very busy."

A smile snaked across Kang's face as he slid off onto the floor. "So, tell me what it is we're up to, commander."

"Shut up and zip up!" Deep within, Mattie could feel her resolve stiffen. Jaq had often spoken of a "steel curtain" that he used to cut his emotion off from his intellect. She felt something like that happening. The son-of-a-bitch had raped her. She had plenty of emotions demanding to be dealt with at that precise moment, but their demands would have to wait. First things first, Kate had always said.

The steel curtain dropped into place with a soft click. But there was more, as if the hard bony surface that had flickered across the surface of her flesh had begun to seep, molecule by molecule, into the very cells of her body. Hardening, she felt both fear and exhilaration.

"First, we're going to put our toys away, like a good boy. Then, when we've made the world safe, you're going to take me to Jumong. And then we're going to find me a good doctor and take care of this thing inside of me."

Kang raised an eyebrow. "Thing?"

"I'm pregnant, and I'll be goddamned if it's going to be yours and not Jumong's." How Mattie knew this she could not tell; but in her belly she felt a stirring. Something without intention but with purpose.

Lightly, Kang tapped the tip of a tooth. "First, we are going to abort nothing." Behind Kang, crimson Necros pulsed dully at its core while it flickered with malevolent portent at its edges. "I may be an evil genius, but the emphasis, I assure you, is on genius. The omnipotent ones of the West have miscalculated. *I told you that.* They need our megatonnage or *that* thing," Kang gestured behind without looking, "will blow a nasty hole in someone's backyard. We don't know whose, but we do know it won't be ours. So you see, our efforts are thoughtfully altruistic. As for your condition …" Kang drew close and placed the back of his hand beneath Mattie's chin, "Though how you could possibly know—"

"Mother's intuition."

"If you're correct, and if you want Jumong's child, I suggest you take no measures, other than to be most scrupulous about your own health and the nutrition of your child during your maternity."

"I'm sorry, I don't—"

"I've told you," Kang flicked his hand off Mattie's chin, causing her head to snap back. "Jumong and I are identical. So, you get what you want, Jumong's genetic son, and I get what I want. My heir. Because I've chosen the time to make my contribution, or will choose it, that will make the child unique, mine. So, we both get what we want."

"Kang," Mattie said, "you're crazy. Why would I ever again, with you—"

"Because you want—No, I don't know how I suspect, but somehow you need Jumong's child." Mattie clenched her fists but stood mutely before Kang.

Silence stretched between them until at last it snapped. "And it's Jumong's child I'll have," Mattie said. "His contribution, our son, will be unique."

"Son? My, we are prescient, aren't we? Well, sorry to ruin your plans, but that will be impossible." Mattie cocked her head and the skin pinched around the corners of her eyes. "You see, Jumong's had a little operation this evening. I believe it's called a vasectomy." Kang smiled, but it was a vicious smile.

CHAPTER VIII

Charging Kang, Mattie raised her arm and threw a fist at his face, but Kang deflected the blow and seized her wrist. "You cocksucker!" Mattie screamed.

"Hardly," he answered with a smirk.

Curling her left hand into a claw, Mattie forced her mind to deny the person that stood before her. It looked like Jumong and it had smelled like Jumong. But its tongue tickled the pointed tips of its teeth, sickly yellow in the dim, thick light of the amphitheater… its tongue, red-bloated, full of poison and death. Just like Necros, which was filling the screen on the far wall. "Motherfucker," Mattie hissed.

Kang grunted. "I did consider that once but—"

Opening her mouth to scream, feeling the bolts that secured her steel curtain, Jaq's gift, strain, then begin to buckle and groan, Mattie forced her anger to withdraw. *Anger destroys reason.* "Why?" she whispered.

Kang folded his arms and nodded approvingly. "You're learning. My father, the Great Leader, consummate son-of-a-bitch, is dead. The people will accept only Jumong in his place. I'm under no delusions. But Jumong is a dreamer."

"He's a teacher."

"He's a fool. I'll rule in fact and our son, or daughter, will rule in deed."

"But Jumong will never—"Mattie began.

"Jumong will accept everything because Jumong will do what is best for Korea and because Jumong can't alter what has been done," Kang said. "And you'll accept it, too. And come to like it—" Kang stepped forward and cupped Mattie's cheek in his hand. Reaching his hand inside Mattie's shirt, Kang moved closer. His breath, garlic sharp, laid its damp hand on her face. No longer did his pheromones hold the keys to her molecular locks.

Snap! One bolt broke free and the steel curtain buckled. Tiny teeth chewed at the old wound in her side. Snap! At first revulsion, then anger, began to seep through the breach. Razor sharp claws, fine and feral, scraped the scar.

"No!" Mattie screamed, and screamed and screamed for seconds and seconds and seconds. Raking across Kang's cheek, Mattie's fingers drove her own nails deeply into his flesh.

Jumping back reflexively, Kang, his eyes wide with surprise, touched his cheek cautiously and dabbed the wounds. Placing his hand in front of his face, he regarded his own blood, rubbed it between his fingers and delicately dabbed a drop, deep gentian now, on the tip of his tongue.

Then Kang struck Mattie across the face. "Bitch," he hissed. "You will do—" he hit her again across the other cheek, snapping her head, "what I say." Mucous, hot and runny, spewed out of Mattie's nostrils and trickled, salty sweet, over her lips and into her mouth. "When I tell you." Kang hit her again, opening a cut on her lip. Bright blood, with its astringent ancient flavor, washed over her gums.

All at once, Kang was hitting her, again and again. Hot saliva, mixed with bitter bile, flowed freely. "Bitch," he was screaming. "Nigger!" Stinging pain seared her scalp. With a dull thud, Kang's fist landed in the middle of Mattie's face and broke her nose with a sickening snap.

The levee broke, blasting through the old scar. Memories escaped, burst the confines of their long confinement and rushed toward the light, blinded at first, then blinking at the white-hot, tungsten glare of an old sun.

Lying on her back, someone was pounding her on the forehead with a hilt of a weapon. Jaq! She remembered now. Jaq was not her father.

Jaq had lost his own daughter, Ur, Mattie's sister. No. Ur had not been Mattie's sister. And Mattie herself—Tiamat had been her name—had been responsible for Ur's death.

Because he had controlled his own anger and provoked hers, Jaq had won the battle, driven his weapon deep into her side when she lay supine, bereft of reason. Anger is the enemy of reason. *Think, Mattie.*

Quicker than the eye could follow, quicker than thought, Mattie seized Kang's fists. Gently, but powerfully, she pushed them away from her, but did not let go. Kang's eyes, hot razors a moment before, opened wide, small delicate saucers now, china brittle, ready to crack, then crumble in their sockets.

Mattie's own eyes reflected off the backs of her hands, plastic black, chitin hard, flawless. Only the green overheads that cast their incident light betrayed those eyes, while dancing in soft sparkles off the slick, ebony surface of her skin.

Slowly, Mattie squeezed Kang's hands until she heard a sharp snap, bone bursting from bone. Although he tried to speak, tried to cry out, his tongue lay stuck against the roof of his mouth, stuffed in the back of his throat.

Mattie glanced around the room. Its elements danced their own bright dance, atoms joined to atoms that blinked into and out of existence. And she remembered that she had started it all. She looked back at Kang, still mute, yellow-white now, and saw that he shared the same basic genes with the small dust mite that crawled along his eyelash with its own purpose and sense of time. She had created all of that, too. It had been her idea.

But she was not God. She heard her own father speaking to her. Though she could not see his face, she could see the back of his head, slick black hair shining bear-grease bright, tied together and falling like a dark comet over his shoulders. What was he saying? It didn't matter.

Though she had created the universe she now inhabited, she had not anticipated love. Its existence had frustrated her. Its meaning had eluded her until Ur had taught her and Jumong had fulfilled its promise.

"I'm going to see Jumong, now," she said, in a voice that was dry and dust-ancient. She recognized it. It had been her own.

"Jumong," Kang croaked. "Yes, I'll take you."

Deliberately, Mattie walked Kang backward, his forearms firmly in her grasp, until he settled against the wall, his body framed by the projection of blood-red Necros.

"No, I think I'll go alone," she hissed. Two sickening snaps split the silence between them. Kang groaned; his knees buckled.

"Mattie, please, I'm trying to save the world, not destroy it. I lied to you. To frighten you. Imagine," Kang swallowed hard, "me trying to frighten *you*. But the West did miscalculate. Our payload will give them the power they need to deflect that thing away from Earth." Kang tried to wave his hand at the projection on the wall, but it dangled limply from his wrist. He lowered his head for a moment, retching softly. "Your precious Idaho is safe. I'm not all evil."

"Of course you're not entirely evil. Nothing is entirely good or bad. Simply, it's our responsibility to express one and hold the other in check. But the emphasis we choose determines our moral worth, hmm?" She thought of the Indian. "You just fell on the wrong side of the fifty-yard line."

Mattie smiled, although she wasn't sure that the expression passed for a smile at all anymore. Kang gasped. "You violated me and you've violated your brother, whom I love."

"But our child. You said yourself there's a child. It's my contribution. It—" Mattie twisted Kang's elbows and his forearms flopped like a marionette. Saliva, hot and runny, began to pour out of the corner of Kang's mouth, spilling onto Mattie's hand. Kang coughed, then retched, green-black bile splattering onto his chin. He squeezed his eyes shut.

"Yes, it is," Mattie said, once again with a peculiar hiss. She was remembering now. "Your contribution. And there's one more you'll make."

Chest heaving, breath coming in short gasps, Kang opened his eyes, filled now with tears of pain, searching Mattie's face for some small shard of pity. Then his gaze strayed, becoming unfocused, vacant, as if he knew he would never find the redemption he sought.

"You cautioned me, Kang, to be mindful of the welfare of the child. To nourish it."

Kang moaned deeply. Two bright black fangs, hard, bony, protruded from what had been Mattie's jaws. Sharp points drooped at the ends. Once, twice, she clicked them. Behind her, Mattie heard Kang's Praetorian Guard banging uselessly on the metal doors. With a smooth, swift motion, she drove her fangs deep into Kang's neck and up his carotids.

Slowly she sipped, making a peculiar sucking sound. She thought of the bastard Ke Dong and began to suck harder. Kang had stopped screaming. He had stopped moving, breathing. Kang had stopped altogether.

Tiamat released her prey. Carelessly, she tossed the remains aside. They hit the floor with a hollow rattle, like a large basket dropped from a small height.

Outside the amphitheater, the pounding grew louder. Metal crashed against metal. Shouts were heard. Mattie closed her eyes and breathed deeply. When she opened them, she saw that her flesh was brown and supple again. Flexing her fingers, she told herself that she must not do this thing again. Become, will herself to be, what she had been. Nor did she need to. She had Jumong and Jumong's love. She had become, had chosen to become, human and she must let the thing play out. It had been her decision, after all.

Breathing deeply once again, her lungs filling with air, Mattie's nostrils flared as they were stung by the smell of ozone. She could hear arc welders crackle as they bit into the steel doors. It would all be so simple. She could wipe out Kang's guard with a thought. From somewhere deep and apart, the Indian was speaking to her. Already, she had interfered too much. He had exiled her once for that. She must not interfere again. Except …

Stepping over Kang's husk, one thought possessed Mattie now. *First things first.* She hoped Kang had been right about the missile and that she would not need to interfere.

BCX 573567 Alpha 25 King 7 Queen 49246. Blinking bright green, the prompts were displayed on the screen in slow succession, like frogs leaping from a pond. Mattie drummed her fingers, then ran them through her hair. She growled and slammed the desk. "Jesus," she swore softly, "we're a few years away from Q-computers and this fucking thing's in DOS." At last all of the prompts appeared. Mattie raised her finger, then paused.

Seizing the mouse, she clicked, opened the hard drive and connected to the Internet. "You've got mail," the computer chortled. Mattie felt the urge to laugh and it felt good. "How quaint! I hope Kang paid his bill," Mattie said aloud.

A quick search told her everything she needed to know about Necros and the West's plans for it. "I'll be damned, Kang, you were right," Mattie whispered, turning to Kang for a moment. Crumpled and yellow, like the paper she'd used to wipe her thigh, he lay on the floor. Discarded. "Too bad, Kang. You weren't all bad. You were just bad enough."

Mattie returned to the prompts and checked the specs of the Russian payload and the missile's trajectory. She frowned. Kang had underestimated as well. Necros would never escape Earth's gravity; the combined megatonnage was simply inadequate.

Of course, no one could be blamed for the error. There were simply too many initial conditions, too many possibilities. Mattie let herself smile. Omniscience would be a terrible bore. As the Indian had quipped, that's why God slept so much.

Outside, softly at first, a drill bit whistled on its axis, then biting into steel, began to scream. *It won't be long now.* What should she do? Mattie looked at the image of Necros, then back at the computer screen. She shrugged and felt a flush of relief drain the tension from her shoulders. There was nothing to do. Necros would be deflected by Kang's program. Not enough to be shot into space and swallowed whole by the sun, but just enough, by thoroughly blind chance, to take a bite out of Earth, barely missing any populated areas. There would be consequences.

Winter is coming, she heard a voice whisper inside her head. But this wouldn't be another fantasy, but a brutal reality. There were always consequences. But chance had saved her. She would not have to interfere.

The drilling had stopped and they would begin setting charges. What should she do? Though she had begun Everything, she was not omnipotent. She had powers, but they were—what had her son Nicholas Beele called them?— mere parlor tricks. She wouldn't kill the soldiers but she couldn't let them kill her, either.

Perhaps she ought to morph into a tiny, harmless red spider, scamper down the desk and across the floor, climb the wall—it wouldn't do to get squashed by a jackboot—then exit by one of those vents in the ceiling.

The vents! Someone, some*thing*, breathed on the other side of the grate nearest the doors. "Dammit," Mattie spat. Whoever was in the duct system had removed the grate. Mattie caught the flash of a small mirror, glinting in reconnaissance. She held her breath. What was she? Human? Creatrix? Regardless, she knew that her love for Jumong was her center. How could she have failed to comprehend love for so long, so many eons, until a small, dour child with copper-colored hair and bright cobalt eyes, and no smile at all, had taught her its meaning?

Within the duct the intruder shifted, his clothing rustling softly against aluminum. Would she save herself and lose the world, and Jumong, by meddling again? Would she die and lose Jumong? Mattie swallowed hard and clenched her fist.

A head popped through the opening in the ceiling. Mouth agape, Mattie controlled an impulse to shout aloud; springing up the stairs, taking steps two at a time, she felt her heart pounding in her ears. Twice within minutes, she had been saved from circumstance and, perhaps, from her own self.

Fuong Ba extended a hand and pulled Mattie up and into the duct. As their eyes met, his flew open as they dove into the dark, bottomless pools that floated in Mattie's face. But Fuong Ba did not hesitate, not for an instant, until, checking the room quickly before he closed the grate, he paused. Mattie sat scrunched on her haunches. "Kang?" he signed. Mattie nodded. Fuong Ba studied her face for a split second. He put the grate back in place and signed, simply, "Quick. Come," and they crawled on all fours for all they were worth. As Fuong Ba pulled Mattie out through the exhaust vent on an exterior wall, behind a thick planting of shrubs, an explosion was heard, and felt, as a shock wave propagated through the compound. Silence. Then cries erupted. Obviously, they had found what was left of Kang.

"The infirmary," Mattie signed hastily. "Jumong's in the infirmary."

Smiling, Fuong Ba signed back. 'Chung Soon was right."

"Chung Soon? I—" Mattie began.

"He usually is," Fuong Ba finished, and the pair disappeared into the blackness.

CHAPTER IX

Fuong Ba dragged the two young guards who had been posted in front of Room 217 across the floor and stuffed them in a storage closet. Fuong Ba held each of the soldiers by the nape of the neck with a delicate touch, like a lioness carrying her cubs. Chung Soon had not killed them. After all, they had simply been following orders. How sweet their faces are, Mattie thought. Thin and supple, the cheeks hairless, unspoiled. Like two adolescent angels. Or Buddhas. Mattie allowed her full lips to relax into something resembling a smile. Rubbing her nose, she winced. Although it was extremely sore, it felt remarkably intact. Then again, she smiled to herself, there had never been much to flatten.

Entering 217, Fuong Ba asked Mattie to wait, but she could not. Softly, softly, she turned the handle and stepped inside. Bright white, flickering fluorescents spilled their dry, brittle light from the ceiling. Not a single object, not a single mote of dust, escaped their bony grasp. The room reeked of iodine and alcohol. To her left a man tensed and raised a pistol; he relaxed as their eyes met.

Chung Soon was sitting on the floor. Between his feet, gagged, sat Ke Dong. When he saw Mattie, he let out a gurgling squeal and began to strain against his bonds. With a sharp snap of his wrist, Chung Soon caught Ke Dong across the side of the face with the barrel of his gun. Ke Dong drew a quick breath through the rag, then hunched his shoulders, casting a malevolent glance at Mattie. "He's over there," Chung Soon said, without qualification, nodding toward the far corner of the room.

Mattie frowned. Without hesitation, yet without haste, she walked toward the bed. Jumong lay on his back. Like pure, white wax, the skin of his face and hands shone. Pure and perfect, as if poured from a vessel of flawless crystal, his hair lay flat against his head, shining from perspiration.

By his side sat a man, obviously a doctor or nurse from the whites he wore. But the man did not turn around as Mattie approached. He simply sat, stroking Jumong's forehead. "What have you done?" Mattie asked, with an evident restraint that belied the thoughts raging behind the words.

Blood soaked the sheets that covered Jumong's legs. Red. Red. Red. Mattie closed her eyes for a moment and thought of her dream; rivers of blood, spreading, soaking Jumong's legs.

"I asked you a question," Mattie said softly; but the man did not move. Now Fuong Ba stood at her side. Grabbing the man by the shoulder, he whirled him about, raising his other hand as if to strike.

"No, Fuong Ba, don't!" Chung Soon shouted. "He didn't do it. Ke Dong did."

The doctor stared up at Fuong Ba and Mattie. His lower lip was split open and he was missing several teeth. Dried blood sat on his chin and was spattered all over the front of his coat. The man's eyes, small and sad and brown, like leaves of late autumn, began to fill with tears. "I wouldn't do it. He tried to make me but I wouldn't!" he said with a lisp, small flecks of red foam flying from his lips. "I tried to fix it, the best I could, but … oh, the butcher." The doctor shook his fist at Ke Dong, who seemed to recoil. "You see," he said, talking in small bursts of air between sobs, "there was nothing I …" He gestured toward a metal table at the foot of the bed. On it lay a scalpel smeared with blood and a small stained cloth that covered a little pile, soft and rounded.

Mattie and Fuong Ba turned to Ke Dong. Eyes wide, he began to struggle. Chung Soon shoved his pistol into Ke Dong's right ear and cocked the trigger. Ke Dong shut his eyes tightly. "Not yet," Fuong Ba signed. Chung Soon nodded.

Lifting Jumong's hand to her lips, Mattie kissed it. "Please," the doctor said, rising to vacate the chair that sat by Jumong's head.

"Thank you," Mattie said. Perhaps it was the sound of Mattie's voice, or perhaps it was simply that the sedation had begun to wear off, but Jumong's eyes fluttered, then opened.

"Mattie," he whispered, a smile playing at the corners of his mouth, as his hand pressed hers lightly. As his eyes roamed across her face, his smile faded. "What's happened to you? To your nose? Fuong Ba," he said, in a louder voice, "I thought I told you to—"

Placing a finger to Jumong's lips, Mattie hushed him. A look of puzzlement crossed Jumong's face as his eyes focused on Mattie's. She lowered her head. "I'm sorry," she said. "I should have told you, shown you." From her pocket, Mattie pulled out her contacts. "I suppose I should—"

"No," Jumong said, the strength returning to his voice.

"Jumong, I love you," Mattie said.

"And I love you. Now. Put them over on that little table at the foot of the bed. It seems as if we'll both leave some pieces of ourselves behind tonight."

Shuddering as she set her white prostheses on the table, Mattie resisted an impulse to lift the cloth that covered Jumong's testicles. She knew, however, that if she did, she would tear Ke Dong to pieces. *First things first.* "We need to get Jumong out of here and get him out now. Kang's forces may have seized control of the whole complex," she said in a cool, matter-of-fact tone.

Chung Soon smiled. "You go on ahead. I'll take care of this slime—" Chung Soon wrapped his free hand around Ke Dong's left ear and pulled slowly. Ke Dong squealed as the flesh peeled away from his head. A small lesion, a small scream. Chung Soon withdrew his revolver from Ke Dong's other ear and scratched his cheek with the muzzle. "So, if Kang is in control, how in hell do we get out of here?"

"Kang's not in complete control yet. Except for the command center," Fuong Ba signed.

"Kang?" Jumong said, his voice rising.

"Please," Mattie said, placing her hand on Jumong's chest. "Your welfare is the most important—"

"No!" Jumong roared. "Korea's welfare is the most important thing."

"Yes," Mattie said softly, "of course you're right. But you are the key to your country's future."

Jumong fell back onto his pillow. Small beads of perspiration sat in his upper lip. "Tell me about Kang."

Mattie ran her fingers through her hair. "Kang had planned a coup. He had your father killed. But his coup was not to be radical. With your father dead, Kang knew that power would transfer to you and to you only. No one else would be acceptable. But he wanted to run the show from behind the scenes. And he wanted his genes to control the next generation of Korea's leadership."

"What?" Jumong whispered. "Insanity. I would have shared everything with him. Given it to him if he'd waited, and if I could."

"He knew that. That's why he knew his plan would work," Mattie said.

"Knew?" Jumong said. "Where is he now?"

"Dead," Mattie said. Jumong's eyes narrowed. "I killed him."

"You? Why?"

"Because." Mattie swallowed hard. Lying was something very foreign to her. "Because he meant to join the launch tonight against Necros. To blackmail the West into letting North Korea join. His motives weren't entirely evil. He simply wanted respect."

"So—" Jumong drew a sharp breath and winced.

"I'll give you some Dilaudid," the doctor said.

"No, wait, please, until we've finished," Jumong said in a raspy voice. "Mattie, I don't understand. If all that's true, why did you have to kill him?"

"Because his calculations were wrong and he wouldn't listen to me," Mattie said, averting her gaze for a moment.

"And now?" Jumong said quietly.

"We've reprogrammed the missile. Actually, it will help. The West was wrong, too. Without our payload, the asteroid would have punched a hole in North America."

Jumong raised his hand and the look in his eyes told Mattie that he was taking charge. "Fuong Ba," Jumong closed eyes and waved his idea off. "No. You're too conspicuous. Chung Soon, not everyone will recognize you. Go quickly and identify friendly forces. Get to their commander. Perhaps Colonel Im. Get a message directly to the White House. Military channels will be too cumbersome. And contact the Secretary General of the U.N. Tell them to check their numbers. If we're wrong they'll have time to shoot down our warhead. If not ..."

Holstering his pistol, Chung Soon stood up, while Fuong Ba walked over to take charge of Ke Dong. "Identify friendly forces," Chung Soon said hesitantly. Without the hint of a smile, Jumong nodded.

With a crash, the door burst open and a half dozen soldiers stormed in, automatics raised. Directly behind them, an officer entered, sidearm unholstered. Calmly, the officer surveyed the scene. The only motion was the flickering of the fluorescents, the only sound their hive-like hum.

Mattie knew that a single thought sat stamped on the brains of everyone in the room. *Friendly or not.* If she'd wanted, she might have listened to their thoughts, but she was gaining a different perspective on the peculiar state of uncertainty enjoyed by humans. A state she had only recently shared. She thought of the Indian. Though God might not play dice, with its boring predictability over time, she was beginning to understand why Joe bet on football.

Quite suddenly, the officer holstered his gun and saluted Jumong. Mattie could see the tension drain from the faces of Fuong Ba and Chung Soon. "Liuteant Chung," the officer said.

"Yes, General Yi."

"Is this the only gangster here?"

"Yes, sir."

General Yi nodded, then ordered his troops out of the room. With his eyes riveted on the bloodstained sheets that covered Jumong's legs, the general strode quickly over to the bedside. "Sir," he said in a tight voice, "we are rounding up all of Kang's men. Of course, they will be shot."

"No," Jumong said. "They will not."

"But—" Yi began.

"They will not," Jumong said quietly. Jumong closed his eyes for a moment, small folds of skin spreading into tiny fans at their corners, as he kept them pinched shut. His hair had begun to soak once again in his own sweat.

Gently, Mattie wiped his forehead with a towel. "You have to rest, Jumong."

"I will, when I've finished. I appreciate your concern. All of you." Slowly, Jumong let his gaze fall on each of them. "So. General Yi."

"Yes, sir," the general replied, snapping his body to attention.

"A leader will always acquire new enemies, but a country can never recover the loss of valuable men.

"My brother's followers will be rounded up. Their heads will be shaved; they will be branded on the cheek with the characters of my name," Jumong paused and glanced briefly at the surgical table, "and my brother's, and they will be dressed in uniforms of black. All to remind them of their treachery. They will drill every day of the year, for at least twelve hours a day, and they will become the best fighting unit in our army. Their loyalty will be to the country and to me alone. They will be my personal guard and will await my return. These are my orders."

Though his jaw line tightened, General Yi did not say a word but simply saluted.

"Your return?" Chung said and Fuong signed simultaneously.

"Yes. It's my fault that I failed to anticipate this crisis. I was blind to Kang. I must withdraw and prepare myself to be a better leader."

"But, sir," General Yi said, breaking his silence at last, "when the people learn of Kang's treachery, without you there will be chaos."

"If the nation were to learn of treachery within the ruling family, there would be doubts in any event, and doubts lead to discontent and discontent would lead eventually to chaos," Jumong said. "But you make an excellent point, General, and that is why the nation will not learn about Kang. That is why you will address his men alone. If any of them break their silence about his night, then you may shoot them."

Jumong continued, turning to Mattie with a slight smile on his lips. "Kang, like all of us, was neither all good nor all bad. We'll forgive the bad, for it was personal, and elevate the good. He did, after all, have the peoples', and the planet's, interests at heart. Didn't he, Mattie?" She nodded hesitantly. "So, we will use a little 'spin,'" Jumong finished, breaking into English.

"A coup was averted tonight. My father was killed and my brother died bravely in our country's defense. I was wounded but am recovering. In the meantime you, General Yi, are in charge."

"Sir, please," the general said, bowing deeply," the country will accept no one but you as successor to your father and, after tonight, no one in your place. *Please.*"

With a touch of pure masculine affection, Jumong laid his hand on Yi's arm. "You're right again, of course. So, I am declaring myself General Secretary, for life. You will be First Deputy General Secretary and will lead during my penance," Jumong paused while Chung and Fuong grumbled. "My absence and my convalescence. I will address the people soon about this incident and afterwards will address them regularly. When I return, we, all of us, you, the people, Kang's gang and especially myself, will be stronger and better for it. Now—" Jumong allowed himself to fall back onto his pillow. Suddenly his color drained and a large, damp stain began to spread across the pillowcase. "Now, I must rest and we must leave, Mattie."

"Leave? Where to?"

"Why, to the Indian, of course," Jumong said.

CHAPTER X

———

With a broad smile, Mattie touched Jumong's face with the back of her hand. "You will become a great teacher. But don't deceive yourself; you're already a great leader."

"Deception? Remember, I don't believe in false behavior of any kind, including modesty." At the word false, Mattie lowered her eyes. "Do you have something to tell me?"

Lifting her chin, her eyes bright and bottomless black, she regarded Jumong for a moment. "I have a great deal to tell you. But now you need to sleep."

"You're right, of course," Jumong said, his voice now thin and hoarse. "Doctor, the shot please." While the doctor prepared the injection, Jumong spoke to his bodyguard. "*Captain* Chung. Kang's corps, my guard, will need a commander."

Opening his mouth, Chung hesitated and then said simply, "Yes, sir."

"Good. It's all settled, then. Fuong Ba, you're with me."

Fuong Ba inclined his head slightly.

"Mr. Secretary," General Yi said.

"Yes, Mr. Deputy Secretary?" Jumong said, his eyelids already beginning to droop. "Please make it quick."

"What about Ke Dong? Shall I leave him to, uh, Captain Chung?"

Chung smiled a large, toothy smile, but whether it was because of the field promotion or because he was to be given Ke, it was impossible to tell.

"No," Jumong said, with some effort, settling the question. Chung's smile evaporated. "He's to make his men as loyal to me as they were disloyal tonight. And he can't begin by killing one of them."

"But, sir," the general said, raising his voice, "you can't allow Ke Dong to join your guard. Not after—" The general waved his hand in the direction of the little bundle, his face bright purple, his eyes wet.

"I agree, General. So. Fuong Ba, I leave him to you."

At that, Ke Dong began to struggle and strain against the cords that bound his hands and feet. Muffled screams escaped from around the rag that was stuffed in his mouth and his eyes rolled back in his head, looking like two bloodshot boiled eggs.

"Untie him, please, Chung," Jumong said. "Before—" Jumong closed his eyes and took a deep breath. Above the hum of the fluorescents, his tongue could be heard to cluck as he stripped it off his palate. "Before," Jumong continued, "I leave, I want to hear why he did this thing to me."

With one fluid motion, Chung pulled a knife from his boot and cut the cords that held Ke Dong's wrists and ankles fast, very deliberately making short, deep cuts in his flesh as well. He untied the cloth stuffed in Ke's mouth and dropped it quickly, as if to insure that he would not be infected by the words that would come from Ke Dong's mouth.

Awkwardly, Ke Dong pushed himself to his feet, then rubbed his wrists for a moment. "Please, I beg you," he began.

"I asked for an explanation, not an appeal," Jumong said in a quiet voice.

"Yes. Yes, sir." As Ke Dong stepped forward toward Jumong, Chung Soon grabbed him by the collar, stopping him in mid-stride.

"Let him come, Chung Soon," Jumong said.

Chung shook his head. "I've never disobeyed you before, sir, and I probably never will again, but I will not let him any closer."

Jumong swallowed hard, waved a hand, and drew another deep breath. "I asked you a question, Ke Dong."

"Yes, sir. I, I was only following orders. Kang's orders. The doctor wouldn't do it. So, so I—"

"That's admirable, Ke Dong. And now you will follow another. Tonight, you will die for the people. It will be told how you died trying to defend me against the sedition. Everyone will know, will always remember."

Like a child, Ke Dong began to whimper. "Please, I was only following—"

"Fuong Ba, he's yours. I need rest now." Jumong closed his eyes. "Mattie," he whispered, "tell the general where we are going, where—" And with that, Jumong fell into a deep sleep.

"General," Mattie said, "we'll be returning to the Myohyang. We—"

"I don't understand!" Yi said. "It's nothing but wilderness."

"Trust us."

The general shook his head. "You know, in our early history, another Yi, Yi Song-gye, disobeyed his king and, in an act of treachery, stole the throne for himself. Don't you see, I must betray Jumong, too. Not to steal a throne, but to save the country. Help me. Please."

Mattie smiled and laid her hand on Yi's arm. Without so much as the smallest hesitation, Yi looked into Mattie's eyes. Dove into them, in hope, perhaps, of some minor redemption. Softly, the scar that sat, smooth and shiny, on Mattie's side began to coo softly, then spread a slick of warmth across the surface of her skin. Yi loved Jumong as much as she. Differently, but in his own way, as much. And, in accepting her eyes, he was accepting her as well. Love. That was the reason she had chosen to live out the remainder of her existence as a human in the first place, wasn't it?

"General," she began. "Yi Song-gye also established one of the longest ruling dynasties in your country's history. I know it's not your intention to steal power. But as King Taejo, Yi Song-gye also ushered in one of the longest periods of power and prosperity. Help Jumong do this thing."

General Yi nodded. "Take care of him," he said, addressing Fuong Ba as well. "We're all depending on you." Briefly, Yi shot a glance at Jumong, whose breathing was shallow but steady. As his eyes began once again to fill with tears, he turned away and cleared his throat quietly. "What will you need?"

"A litter, that's all. Fuong Ba and I will handle everything else," Mattie said, signing as she spoke. "Won't we?" she finished, her eyes locked on Ke Dong, who began to mewl softly, all the while sucking on his loathsome tooth. Fuong Ba nodded. "General? Would you leave us please? We'll be right along. It will take a few minutes to get Jumong settled and comfortable." The general bowed to both of them and left the room, shutting the door softly behind him, as if in counterpoise to what he must have known would happen next.

Deliberately but quickly, Fuong Ba bound Ke Dong's hands and feet once again.

"What are you going to do?" Ke Dong asked, his pleading tone strangling the words in his throat. "Please, be quick! I said what—" and as his voice began to rise, Fuong Ba stuffed the rag back in his mouth. All that could be heard was a small, sick, sucking sound.

Fuong Ba walked over to the surgical table and pulled a pair of latex gloves from a box that sat on its lower shelf. Then, looking at Ke Dong all the while, he lifted the knife that Ke Dong had used to castrate Jumong and tested its tip with his thumb.

With an inarticulate but thoroughly understandable hand gesture, Fuong Ba indicated that Mattie should stretch Ke out on the floor and hold him down by the shoulders. Kneeling, Fuong Ba pinned Ke's legs to the floor. Ke's chest began to heave and he threw his head from side to side.

Quite unexpectedly, Fuong Ba tore open Ke's shirt rather than his trousers. In an instant, Ke became quiet and a look of fear, fueled by the unknown rather than the known, began to fill his eyes, which sat wide and flat beneath his black brows. Even Mattie cocked her head.

With a quick, efficient thrust, Fuong Ba drove the scalpel into Ke Dong's flesh, just above the pubic bone; then, with one deft movement, sliced the skin up to the sternum. Alternately squealing and sucking, Ke writhed beneath Mattie's hands. Another cut, across the abdomen and perpendicular to the first, and Ke's body started to shake uncontrollably and involuntarily, small, rapid tremors coursing through his entire frame. Briefly, he looked into Mattie's face, but apparently finding no mercy there, shut his eyes and began to squeal.

Deftly, Fuong Ba plunged his left hand into Ke's belly and pulled out a handful of small intestine. Three or four feet were removed and then, after he lay the scalpel aside, Fuong Ba evacuated the contents of the bowel, squeezing them like a tube of paste with his hands.

Wide-eyed in shock, Ke Dong lay quite still now, except for a few tremors that wracked his frame irregularly. Fuong Ba rose and took a step forward, then, straddling Ke's torso, bent and wrapped the gut around Ke's neck and began to tighten the coil. Consciousness returned to Ke's eyes and he rolled them about, searching, apparently, for the redemption that he must have known would never come.

Suddenly, Fuong Ba stopped and dropped the piece of intestine. He looked at Mattie. "I saw Kang," he signed. "I don't know what happened, what it was you did, but respectfully, I give you Ke Dong if you want him."

For a moment, Mattie was quiet. "I can't," she said, looking directly at Fuong Ba. "I, I shouldn't."

"Your secret will be safe," Fuong Ba signed. "I promise you my life on that. Take him if you need to."

"I?" I don't need to. But—" Mattie touched her belly lightly with the tips of her fingers, "perhaps someone else does. And besides, I may not need to kill him but I do want to kill him."

Fuong Ba bowed. Then his face went white and he, himself, began to shake in synchrony with Ke Dong. A face that had never known fear, its flesh experiencing an unfamiliar emotion, began to stretch and twist awkwardly. A nasty clicking sound split the sudden silence. For a moment, just enough time to face the full horror of what he had done, Ke Dong regained consciousness. Sucking madly, face wild with fear, he spit out the bloody rag stuffed in his mouth and started to scream. But Tiamat was too fast, and then the only sound was a deep, slow suck that matched the ebb of Ke Dong's life blood from his body.

As Mattie and Fuong Ba left Room 217, Mattie turned to one of the three young guards Yi had stationed outside the door. "Take Colonel Ke's body to the morgue. We tried our best but we couldn't save him. He died bravely defending the General Secretary. You two bring Secretary Jumong with us." The soldiers saluted and Mattie walked slowly down the corridor to the waiting ambulance, holding Fuong Ba firmly by his upper arm, for his legs were still a bit wobbly.

CHAPTER XI

In all directions the night sky throbbed, coke-oven red. Even mother moon wore a dab of rouge. Necros filled half the heavens. A fine mist fell, as if the crimson satellite's heat were squeezing moisture from the very air.

"I wish Jumong were awake to watch this," Mattie signed after a few moments of pure silence.

"And I wish that I could stand here for as long as I wanted, letting the warm rain wash the salt and sweat from my face, and with them the fear I live with every day …"

"Fear?" Mattie signed.

Fuong chuckled, a fat, silent chuckle, his tiny lips pursed, his cheeks puffed like Buddha's. "Not for myself," he signed, his fingers flying in the bright gloom like small red balloons. "But for everything I love," he finished softly, as if his hands had learned how to whisper. "My country. This wilderness. Look! Look at the black maw of the Myohyang valley below us. Look at its teeth, the mountains that ring it, onyx-toothed, piercing the blood-red sky, ready to swallow us whole. And I love Jumong. And I love you, too."

"Me?" Mattie signed. "How? You don't know me."

Fuong Ba shrugged. "You love Jumong. That's enough. Besides, I think I know you better than most. Better than Jumong, maybe."

"But I thought I frightened you and you said you wished to be free from fear."

Fuong Ba shook his head. "What you are startled me, that's all." Fuong Ba lowered his gaze, then spat into his palms and stooped to raise Jumong's litter.

"No, wait. He's resting quietly and, besides, we're almost there. Just a few moments more and we'll see the world change forever. It'll make one of those peculiar, perpendicular turns for which this universe is so famous."

"But—" Fuong Ba began.

"Watch," Mattie whispered, "right about—"

Like a hundred suns, the planet's armada exploded directly in front of its target. All around, the scene lit up for several long seconds, electric-white. Jumong stirred. Mattie knelt down beside the litter and stroked his head. "Was Kang right? Was he?" Jumong whispered.

Like the weightless, round rain itself, Mattie's hand smoothed Jumong's hair. "We'll see."

Subtly, but abruptly, Necros veered, its vector given a nasty slap by the shock wave of the explosion. Like the bright tip of a cigarette burning through silk, the planetoid bored through the earth's atmosphere.

"Mattie—" Jumong tried to push himself up onto his elbows and Fuong Ba, now kneeling by his side, propped him up gently.

"We'll see," Mattie repeated simply. Then, "Yes. His instinct was correct," as Necros dropped dead straight down beneath Polaris. A flash erupted just above the surface of the planet. Fuong Ba and Jumong covered their faces. Mattie stared straight ahead, witnessing a scene she had seen countless times over the eons; energy fleeing madly and with wild delight from the bonds of matter.

As the stinging glare softened, Fuong Ba and Jumong lowered their hands from their eyes. "Yes," Mattie said, "Kang was right." Jumong smiled.

"Was he?" a voice asked. All three turned toward the sound, which came from somewhere on the field of scree that separated the trail from the pine forest below. Emerging into the pale afterglow, from the mist that had now grown cold and heavy, the Indian clambered up onto the trail. "Was he?" the Indian repeated, his question clearly not rhetorical.

"He's saved millions," Mattie said.

"Tonight. But what about tomorrow, and the day after that? Can you be sure he minimized misery for the greater number? And is that a valid reason in any event?" All three were silent. "I'm not being critical. I'm simply asking a question."

"But he meant to do the right thing," Jumong said, his voice straining.

The Indian knelt and took Jumong from Fuong Ba, then lowered him gently back down onto the litter. "His intention was good and, for Kang, that's enough. For the rest of us, we'll have to see."

"Joe," Jumong said, "thank you for coming out to meet us."

"You needed me to come to you tonight, Jumong, and you've lots of hard work to do; more than you know. So rest."

"So—" Jumong began, but his eyes closed and he fell into the firm grip of sleep.

* * *

Insect sharp, the sound of Fuong Ba's axe split the clear stillness of the afternoon. Bare-chested, soaked in sweat, small salty rivers tracing their course across the surface of his yellow skin, he mouthed words to a song that played somewhere deep inside his brain, its tune a wholly private treasure.

Snaggle-toothed, the axe munched monstrously in march time on the small spruce logs Fuong Ba had cut from a large tree, making them smaller still, fit stuff for the belly of Joe's stove. With each bite, his weapon sent a spray of chips skyward, only to strike the ground after a moment or two with a soft rattle, locust-dry. But some settled on Fuong Ba's arms, or on his head, making him look as if he belonged in the Indian's garden, defending the season's crops.

Mattie put her hand over her mouth to stifle a laugh. Out of the corner of one eye, Fuong Ba must have seen her, for he stopped quite suddenly. Leaning on the bright ash handle, he signed, "Well? What?" as best he could with his free hand.

"Well," Mattie said, turning to face Fuong Ba directly so that he might read her more easily, "if you must know, I can't decide whether or not you look more like the Scarecrow, covered with all of those shavings and sawdust, or the Tin Man, with that axe."

Jumong had just come out of the Indian's cabin. "Oz," Jumong said. Fuong Ba scrunched his eyebrows together. "It's an American story about a little girl who is torn from her home and family and dropped in a strange land."

"Sound familiar, Mattie?" Joe asked, following Jumong out the door.

Although Mattie's smile evaporated, she was more puzzled by the Indian's comment than annoyed. She shrugged and turned back to Fuong Ba. "Anyway,

Jumong's right. And the little girl, Dorothy, makes friends with a tin man, a scarecrow and a lion, all of whom promise to help her get home."

"Yes," Jumong said, "but each of them has their own private quest."

"For?" Fuong Ba flicked his fingers.

"The Tin Man is looking for a heart, the Scarecrow a brain, and the Lion, courage."

Deliberately, Fuong Ba leaned his axe against the chopping block. "So," he signed, "you're saying, then, that you're not sure if I'm stupid or heartless?"

"Fuong Ba!" Mattie said. "How could you think such a thing? No, it's just, you know, you look like the characters, that's all. A little, anyway."

"Yes, and besides," Jumong said, moving easily and naturally once again as he walked over to Fuong Ba and rested his hand on his shoulder, "Dorothy's friends all possessed those qualities anyway. They simply needed to have them brought out."

Slowly, Fuong Ba's scowl stretched into a grin and he threw his head back, letting go a burst of silent laughter, a gust of air.

"Oh, Fuong Ba," Mattie said, leaping from the spot where she lay stretched on the grass and rushing to plant a kiss on Fuong Ba's cheek, "you're not mad, then?"

Fuong Ba drew a deep breath. Pitch and juniper laced the thick, moist air. Golden, syrupy light dripped through the branches and between the needles of the spruce, dappling the clearing with splats of soft, warm color. "I am happier than I have ever been," he signed, his hands moving slowly with great emphasis. "Joe! Can we stay here forever?"

"No."

"When must we leave?" Fuong Ba signed.

"Whenever you like," Joe said.

Fuong Ba shook his head. "I really have trouble understanding you, Joe. You're too smart for me. Ha!" Scooping up a handful of wood chips on the run, Fuong Ba dashed toward the Indian and playfully sprinkled him with sawdust. "There," Fuong Ba signed, "that's better. You're the one with the brain, so you must be the Scarecrow."

Carefully, the Indian brushed the spruce shavings off his shoulders and out of his hair. "No, that would be Jumong. He has a fine mind. A head for solving problems. I'm the Wizard, if anything."

"I'll say," Jumong said with a smile, making a sweeping gesture.

"So then," Fuong Ba signed, "we have the Tin Man, the Scarecrow, Dorothy," indicating Mattie, "but where our Lion? Our courage?"

"Unborn, as yet, I think," Joe said, his steel-gray eyes boring through Mattie, who averted her eyes.

After a long silence, Fuong Ba clapped his hands and spoke up, silently as well. "So, we'll have to wait for our cast to be complete. Wait for our courage. Although I don't know, really, what in hell you're talking about, Joe. By the way, what did the Wizard do? Who was he in the story?"

"He helped Dorothy get home," Joe said, signing at the same time. "He was a gatekeeper and a bit of a fraud as well. So I suppose I do fit the profile."

"Joe," Mattie said, setting her hands on her hips, "what's gotten into you?"

"Nothing, Mattie, just a little honesty. From the pocket of his shirt, Joe pulled a fresh pack of Kools and tapped one out. Then he carefully slipped the cigarette back into the pack, which he replaced in his pocket.

Mattie stamped her foot. "Oh, Joe, for Christ's sake!" She pulled at her dense black hair. "You've been edgy ever since you quit. Why'd you quit, anyway? You know you'll fire up one of these days. Jeez, talk about being honest."

Joe raised an eyebrow. "Okay, Mattie, have it your way. If you won't tell him … You've had plenty of time. And time is the one thing around here that's in unlimited supply." Joe stood up, but his face softened. "You see, Jumong, I won't smoke around pregnant women. It's not healthy." Every single blood vessel in Mattie's face must have dilated simultaneously, for she flushed deep purple.

"But how," Jumong said quietly, his face a flat mask, his tone perplexed, but his words clearly surfing on top of a deep hurt that he couldn't completely disguise.

"It's time you told him, Mattie," the Indian said. "In fact, I think it's time you told him a lot of things."

CHAPTER XII

Biting her lip, Mattie drew a breath to stifle the tears that welled up in her eyes, which seemed to ripple, deep ocean black. Joe laid a hand on her shoulder. Instinctively, she pulled away. "Come on," he said, "let's go sit in the grass." The Indian took her hand, but she resisted. "Don't worry, I'll help.

Everyone sat. Everyone, that is, except for Fuong Ba. Protection was his vocation and he stood nervously to one side, as if there were anything he could do to protect Jumong, and Mattie from what she was about to say.

"Jumong—" the Indian began, but Mattie held up her hand.

"It's all right, Joe," she said. "I'm sorry. It's just that I'm not used to crying." Sniffling lightly, Mattie dabbed a cheek with her sleeve. "But there is a first time for everything."

"And for falling in love, Mattie," the Indian said.

"Yes. You see, Jumong. Neither crying nor love was part of what I was. But Ur changed that. And so have you."

"Ur," Jumong said. Though his voice was steady, a large vein bulged at the base of his neck. "You've mentioned your sister, but you've never told me about her."

"And I shall. But first you have to hear about Kang. You've a right." Mattie crossed her legs lotus-style and snapped off a stalk of grass, its head heavy with ripe seed. Gently, she stroked the florescence between her fingers, soaking up its silky warmth through her skin. Mattie lifted her chin and stared unblinking at her lover. "I told you that I killed Kang, but I lied about the reason. His calculations were wrong. But his intentions were good. I didn't lie to you about that." For a moment, the muscles in Jumong's face relaxed. "You see, Jumong, he raped me. And when he was finished, he hit me. That's how my nose got all banged up."

Mattie gestured vaguely at her face. "I didn't do it falling down when Fuong Ba and I escaped the Command Center. Kang *hit* me. Not once, but again and again, and I couldn't control my anger. So, I killed him."

Jumong began to stroke his chin. As he did, it seemed to Mattie as if the gentle motion of his hand slowly drained the mixture of hurt and fury from his eyes. What replaced it, however, was not the flat, cold stare of detachment when one person has begun to withdraw from another. Rather than fleeing or attacking, Jumong's gaze seemed to circle Mattie. Searching.

"What is it?" Mattie asked nervously. "I thought you'd be angry, at me or at Kang. It would be a normal reaction."

"I'm hardly normal anymore."

"Don't let's start feeling sorry for ourselves now," Mattie said.

"And why not?' Jumong said. "It's a perfectly normal reaction."

Mattie sat next to Jumong and placed her hand on his knee. "I *have* felt sorry for myself," Jumong said. "I still do. And angry. But time's passed. And I don't have all the facts yet. You've only told me that Kang raped you and that you killed him. The story is incomplete because there are inconsistencies. Remember, interrogation was—is—one of my specialties. You acquire such skills in a police state, and besides, my temperament is suited to the task."

"It sounds," Mattie said, "as if you can bury your emotions. Kind of like my father. Jaq always said he could set his emotions aside and operate off his intellect."

"Very stoic."

Mattie smiled, thinking of her mother Kate.

"But that's not what I mean. To be good at convincing people to confide the truth, you must be able to truly engage them emotionally. Even if you must have them shot, you have to make them believe that there is something about them that you understand. Like, even. Otherwise, they won't trust you and you'll never learn the truth. And Mattie," Jumong said, laying the back of his hand lightly on her cheek, "I do love you."

"You may feel differently when I've finished."

"No, I'll always love you." Jumong crossed his legs and shifted his position in the grass. "That doesn't mean I won't be hurt or angry. So. Let's resolve the inconsistencies in what you just told me." Jumong cleared his throat and the suggestion of a smile played across his lips. "Kang overpowered you and raped you. Then, somehow, you were able to kill him. Kang was a sixth-degree black. How did you kill him? And if you possess martial arts skills that I am unaware of, how did he overpower you in the first place?"

Running her hand through her hair, Mattie looked deep into the forest, as if the right words sat there, suspended among the deep, green, fragrant branches of spruce and juniper, and she began to speak in a voice that sounded, to her at least, to be not entirely the one with which she had become so familiar. "I let Kang rape me," she said. "Perhaps rape is not the right word, since I not only let him, but I wanted him. But his intention was rape and so we'll call it that. No, wait. I have to qualify what I said. I wanted *you*."

"Because …" she said, looking Jumong full in the face, "because of the smell.

"Smell?"

"Pheromones. You and Kang were identical."

"In humans I would doubt pheromones to be that powerful. After all, we're not salmon. Or spiders," Jumong said.

At the word, Mattie felt a surge, hot and electric, course across the surface of her skin. She froze, afraid to look at her hand or her bare arm. "Joe?" she said, continuing to stare straight ahead, her voice deep and flat.

"Not yet, Mattie," he said. "You're doing fine."

Setting her teeth on edge, Mattie picked at a finger. Then she smiled to herself. Kate had always picked at a finger when she found herself in a difficult circumstance. "I came here, to Korea, because I love you, Jumong. Not *agape*, but the love that exists between a man and a woman. I also came because I wanted, needed, to have your child. Although I didn't realize that until that night at Command." Mattie knelt in front of Jumong and wrapped her hands around his ankles. "But don't misunderstand me. If we had never had a child and never will be able to have a child, I will still love you as much. And love only you. Do you understand?"

Jumong inclined his head. "Tell me more about this child. Why is it so important?"

"Joe? Can you help me now?" Mattie said.

"Something happened the other night that will change the world forever. Your son will be a part of that change. It's in his genes," Joe said.

"Joe—" Mattie began.

But the Indian held up a hand. "That's all I can tell you, because that's all I know. I can't see the future any more than you can." Though neither Mattie nor Jumong uttered a word, their silence belied their skepticism. The Indian cleared his throat. "Your son's genes, and Jumong's, are the scions of those carried by the Khans, directly from Temujin, Genghis, himself."

While Jumong's eyes flashed a thousand questions, Mattie knew that the Indian was finished, and saw as well that Jumong understood this. "So, we understand how, and to an extent why, you became pregnant," Jumong said, clipping the ending of "pregnant" with an unnatural emphasis. "We still don't know how you killed Kang." Jumong turned and locked Mattie's eyes with his own. "Who are you, Mattie?"

"I'll try to explain. I caught glimpses of my past the day …" Inhaling softly, Mattie touched the place near her stomach where her small scar sat, then blew her breath out, making a low, whistling sound. "When Necros exploded above the Pole, I witnessed in the nuclear fires a sight I'd seen countless times before. And I know now that I had something to do with all of that." Jumong wrinkled his forehead. Mattie cleared her throat, then began to speak more excitedly, engaging her hands quite uncharacteristically, as if she were speaking in sign, as if another vocabulary, another entirely different syntax, would help her to explain. "You see, Jumong, I made choices. I … Oh, Joe, can you help?"

With a deft, almost impossibly light movement, the Indian sprang up off of the grass and began to move away from the group.

"Joe!" Mattie said, jumping to her feet. "You said you'd help. You did!"

Pulling the pack of Kools from his shirt pocket, Joe smiled. "Don't worry, Mattie. I'm just moving downwind. I need a twag for this one." Drawing deeply on a fresh cigarette, the Indian closed his eyes, then blew the smoke out through his nose. And blew and blew. Everyone's eyes flared in astonishment.

As the shapeless plume rose in the middle of the clearing, it began to take shape. First a shoulder. Then a foot. Then an elbow. Flexed. The arm supporting a head, lips pursed like pillows, large almond-shaped lids shut in gentle repose. Flitting around and through the figure, a thousand bright insects bounced, creating the impression of subtle motion, restlessness. Golden orange, the light of the dipping sun, filtered through the haze, glazing the sculptor's figure.

Fuong Ba fell forward, plunging his face into the deep, green grass, kneeling, covering his head with his hands. Rolling the cigarette over to the corner of his mouth, the Indian walked up to Fuong Ba and lifted him gently by the shoulders,. Large, fat tears rolled down Fuong Ba's cheeks. "Buddha," Fuong Ba mouthed.

The Indian held up a finger, then signed, "Listen to me." Shaking his head, Fuong Ba straightened himself and sat down once again on the grass. Smoke from the Indian's cigarette had begun to cause his own eye to tear. He wiped it with his sleeve, took another drag, then gestured toward the figure floating in their midst.

"Buddha, Fuong Ba calls it. God, some say. Brahma—"

"Dreams a dream. So," Jumong whispered, "you're the dreamer."

"No." He took another drag, blowing the smoke downwind. "I'm just what you see before you. An old Indian who likes to smoke and gamble."

"Oh, Joe," Mattie protested. "Really—"

The Indian held up a finger. Suddenly, a light gust of wind blew out of the forest, carrying with it the perfume of damp spruce needles, and scattered the sleeping god. Mattie gasped. Jumong swallowed hard but did not make a sound. Fuong Ba began to sob again, but softly.

"An old Indian who likes to smoke and gamble," Joe continued, "but who had an idea."

"Which was?" Mattie said ingenuously.

"You," Joe said, pointing at her and grinning. "You see—" The Indian squatted down alongside Fuong Ba and rubbed his back. "You see, I'm a big picture guy. An idea man, you'd say. I needed somebody who'd make the important choices, once I laid out the options. So, Mattie, I dreamed you up, having been dreamed up myself."

"But how—" Mattie began.

The Indian waved her off. "It's not important and words don't—"

"The hell it's not important, Joe. It's important to me! You're, you're trying to explain things and you blow off—"

"No," the Indian said quietly, but in a voice which, like the deep beat of a huge drum, struck softly, descended over the group, dispelling all distractions, focusing their collective attention on a single point, a solitary word. "I told you I dreamed you up. Literally." Without uttering a word, Mattie lowered her eyes and tugged at her wild, black hair.

"You claim you dreamed her up to make choices. What kind of choices?" Jumong asked.

"Example. Suppose gravitational attraction were subject to a rule other than that of the inverse square. Say inverse cube or inverse square root. The planet we're sitting on would either be an ice cube or a cinder. Little things like that. Big little things. Do you remember, Mattie?"

Throwing her head back, Mattie crossed her legs and pulled her feet up underneath her buttocks. Overhead, a small cloud drifted across the sky, bouncing, it seemed, off the tops of the large firs and pines. Its mass pale and white, its leading edge was kissed by a soft, dark gray shadow that plowed through light eggshell blue. And then suddenly it slipped past the moon, fat and gibbous, hanging quite unexpectedly in the sky of late afternoon.

She smiled. "Yes, I remember. Not all of it, but some. And just a little bit more, it seems, all of the time." Stretching out her hand to Jumong, Mattie was pleased when he reached out and they both entwined their fingers, one with the other. "I just can't seem to remember all of the details."

"That's because of who you are today. It was another choice that you made. You ..." Suddenly, the Indian began to cough again, this time with such violence that he jumped to his feet. In an instant, Fuong Ba stood alongside, clapping him on the back and, as suddenly as it had started, the fit stopped.

Jumong wagged his finger at the Indian. "I told you those things are going to kill you."

Joe smiled and took a drag. "Someone else used to tell me that all of the time. Do you remember, Mattie?"

Out of some tiny but irresistible compulsion, Mattie lifted her shirt, exposing her midriff, and delicately touched her scar with the tip of her finger.

Closing her eyes, she saw a bright, barren plain, baked by the sun. Mattie looked up at the moon and began to speak. "A man faced me in a burning desert. My father. Or at least, the man who had raised me. Tiamat, Creatrix, myself actually, stood tall and impossibly strong in another incarnation, clad in the armor and carrying the weapons of an ancient race, the Achaeans. Why? Perhaps that had been Jaq's choice.

"I chased him, as Achilles had chased Hector millennia before, round and round. A monolith, this time, rather than the walls of Ilium. High above on a cliff, as if from the old walls of Troy itself, four people watched the battle. My mother, Kate. Or at least the woman who had raised me. A dwarf, whose name I cannot recall. My own son, Nicholas Beele. The other son of my body." Mattie glanced at Jumong but his face was a mask. Without warning, her throat tightened. Why had Beele turned against her? And what of Ur? Her sister? Her daughter? In a very practical, objective way, Tiamat was everyone's sister, everyone's mother. But who else is Ur? The woman who had taken the place that Tiamat had abandoned. Ur, the child, burning-bright cobalt eyes framed by her short, thick auburn hair, gleaming like polished copper under the devouring lunar sun.

"Tiamat cast her lance," Mattie continued, "and the cast failed. Then, Jaq was on me, bashing me in the face. 'Fucking bitch,' he was screaming. 'You stole my daughter and you stole her life,' he was screaming.

"Unable to bear anymore, Tiamat made another choice and suddenly, all six were out of the glare. "I lay on my back, my skin now hard and black and chitinous in the cool stillness of my cave. But Jaq was still screaming, and so was Kate, and then I felt him drive his weapon deep into my side."

Involuntarily, Mattie shuddered. The scar in her stomach was on fire, but a deeper pain gripped her now. Great, limpid tears welled up in her eyes. "My God, Joe," she whispered, "what did I do?"

With a deft movement, the Indian flicked his cigarette onto the grass and approached Mattie. He knelt beside her, then cupped her head in his hands and kissed her on the forehead.

"We've been friends a long, long time," he said softly. "You made all of this." The Indian swept his arms in a wide arc. "And it's very beautiful. You made choices, but often they were self-indulgent, and sometimes at the expense of others. It is simply in your character. And you and Jumong, perhaps, will just have to accept that."

"But Ur. I took her and her life."

"To learn the meaning of love. Above all, it was love you failed to grasp," Joe said.

"I owe Ur so much," Mattie said.

"Ur made her own choices. She stayed with you after the battle. She could have gone back with her parents. But she didn't, she stayed with you."

"But why?" Mattie asked.

The Indian shrugged. "Maybe she wanted your job." Mattie frowned, ashamed by the tiny twinge of jealousy that flashed somewhere inside of her. "Look. If it'll help, Ur is a very self-indulgent young lady herself. The difference is, her choices are not made solely at the expense of others."

Tears coursed over Mattie's cheeks. Licking the corners of her mouth as if to suck the bitterness back inside, she tasted only her own saltiness, which she found very pleasant. And as she began to swallow her own tears, more and more greedily, she was overcome by a sense of shame at yet another petty indulgence.

"So," she said at last. "Now you know, Jumong. What I am, what I've done, who I am. I killed my sister. I fucked your brother—" And as Mattie's voice leaned deeply into the verb, she made a fist and struck her thigh again and again. "So, how do you feel now, Jumong? About your brother, about me? I'm carrying his child—"

"Fuong Ba!" Jumong shouted, signing at the same time so his meaning could not be misunderstood.

Without being able to slip even the finest hair between his meaning and his action, Jumong drove his body off the grass with a powerful push from his legs, turned a handstand and vaulted himself into the air, throwing a vicious side kick at Fuong Ba's head. Only the warning he had given as he launched his attack gave Fuong Ba time to move his head to the side the tiniest fraction of an inch and avoid most of the force from the blow.

For several minutes, the two men fought. Neither gave nor received quarter. A roundhouse kick from Fuong Ba opened a gash over Jumong's left eye and Jumong knocked the wind from Fuong Ba with a vicious punch to ribs that split the space between their gasps with a nasty crack.

Grimacing in pain, Fuong Ba doubled over and Jumong, triumphant, hesitated a split second before sending a sidekick at the big man's jaw. The hesitation was just enough for Fuong Ba and he grabbed Jumong's ankle, flipped him crooked to the ground and wrapped his heel like some biological Gordian knot around Jumong's neck.

Both men lay on the grass, gasping. Jumong tapped Fuong Ba on the forearm and he released Jumong, who struggled to his feet, grabbed Fuong Ba by the ear and kissed him on the forehead.

Jumong ran his hand through his short, black hair, then rubbed his hand, slick with perspiration, on his shirt. "So, how do I feel? Angry. But! Not as angry as a few minutes ago. Still, if my brother Kang were here now I would kill him." Mattie shrank back at Jumong's words. Never had she seen him like this. "I would have given him anything. Except you. So, I would have killed him to keep you. And the child is mine—"

"But …" Mattie began.

"No! Don't forget that Kang and I were identical. The child is mine, genetically. Still. I am angry *at* you, but not *with* you, because you did what you had to do. What happened was not your intention." Jumong walked up to Mattie, who, for perhaps the first time in her long life, withdrew. Gently, Jumong lifted Mattie off of the grass. "I love you," he said, then kissed her tenderly on the mouth.

"Joe, if you wouldn't mind leaving us, I wish to consummate our, relationship. Then the child will be mine. Completely."

"But Jumong," Mattie said softly, "we can't delude ourselves. What happened with Kang is in the past. We can't change that."

"The past?" Jumong said, his voice bloated with false surprise. Raising his arms, he swept them in a wide arc. "Space is certainly elastic. Time is elastic. So. The child's genes are mine and I make my choice. Tonight. Now. And then it will be mine completely. That is, if you agree."

Squeezing Jumong's hand, Mattie lowered her eyes. "But, Jumong, are you able—"

"Ha!" Placing the tips of his fingers under her chin, Jumong lifted Mattie's head so that her bright, black eyes met his own. "When I say I can do a thing, believe it. Joe?" The Indian folded his arms across his chest. "You seem to claim the primacy of mind over matter. As did Mattie's foster father, Jaq, if I understand him correctly. Though you profess to have no extraordinary talents, might you have a trick up your sleeve? Is environmental enhancement in your repertoire?"

The Indian raised an eyebrow. "What'd you have in mind?"

"Something, um, corny," Jumong said, turning to Mattie, who simply stood stock still, eyes wide. "When I was in college I heard a song I was partial to, a song about love. About a girl. 'She came to me, her face flushed with the night. We walked on frosted fields of juniper and lamplight.' Do you think that you could create a frosted field of—"

Joe held up a hand and then, with a small gesture, pointed his finger at the westering sun and, it seemed, pushed it beneath the horizon. A billion bugs, bursting with cool green light, emerged from the blackness. A light lace of crystals grew across the surface of the grass and the air became thick with the smell of juniper.

"Fuong Ba," Joe signed. "It's Monday out West."

"Who's playing?" Fuong Ba signed. Although he had acquired a keen interest in the American game that fascinated the Indian, he still had trouble following all of the teams.

"Redskins, Titans," Joe said laconically.

"I like the Titans," Fuong Ba said. "What's the line?"

"Titans minus two-and-a-half," Joe said, looking at the ground and scuffing his toe in the frosty grass.

"Bullshit," Fuong Ba signed, "but I'll take the Titans anyway." And they disappeared into the cabin.

Taking Mattie's hand, Jumong led her a few steps toward the edge of the forest, then stopped and drew her slowly to the ground. To her surprise, the grass was neither cool nor wet but felt like soft, warm sugar. Jumong undressed and Mattie's eyes widened as she took in his naked form for the first time. Jumong unbuttoned Mattie's shirt, then kissed her sweetly on her small scar. Then on the mouth. Naked, skin pressed tightly against skin, they rolled in the sweet, frosted grass while fireflies blinked their own silent message.

Mattie gasped. Jumong was nothing that she had ever anticipated.

As they lay on their backs, hands clasped, drinking in the thick warmth of the evening glowing coolly beneath the fat, waxing gibbous moon, it was Jumong who spoke first.

"So. When will you show this other self, Tiamat, to me?"

"Never. She's in the past."

"And you're the future?" Jumong said.

"No. We are the present. Our son is the future," Mattie said.

"Yes. Our son."

From the cabin came a loud roar. The Titans, it turned out, were at home. "How could he miss that chip shot," Joe cried, "and with no time left on the clock!" Huge gusts of silent laughter poured out of the hut's small windows.

"Joe's lost again," Mattie said, and she and Jumong began to laugh and laugh and laugh.

INTERMEZZO- NEW SPALL

Like yellow cream poured from a bright blue pitcher fashioned from sky, sunlight streamed through tall windows inset into three walls of the parlor room. The dark walnut floors glowed like melted caramel. Ur stood, leaning over a grand piano and tracing a finger idly across its shiny ebony surface.

"Does my music not please you, my lady?" Mozart said.

"Oh, Herr Mozart, of course you know it does. I was just____"

"Please, please! I believe we've passed that point in our relationship where we can dispense with such formalities."

"Forgive me. Wolfgang," Ur said.

"Wolfie."

"Wolfie." Ur sighed. "I still find it difficult to assess social context appropriately. So I err on the conservative side."

"Not unwise. But still…"

Ur continued to avert her gaze and to trace intricate figures on the piano. "A penny for your thoughts," Mozart said.

"Pennies from heaven," Frankie Howard sang, as she opened the parlor doors and entered the room. "I think Herr Mozart that you'd be paying too dear a price, since we all know what is on Ur's mind when she's pensive and distracted.

"Oh!" Ur exclaimed, standing up straight. "Pensive, yes; but distracted, never! I've learned that there is too much at stake if I become distracted. We all know what happened when Tiamat lost focus. No, I am actually quite good at compartmentalizing. Still…" Ur leaned over the piano once again.

"Well, I'll play something that might help. In a time of trouble only Tamino's tune will do!" Mozart said.

"Now you're making fun of me! That's what you told Kak Zhal and you know he's the reason I'm a bit melancholy," Ur said.

Mozart ignored her and began to play the tune from the Magic Flute anyway. Ur folded her arms and stared out through the windowpanes, sparkling like ribbon candy. Abruptly, Mozart played a bridge and then three chords. As the room settled deeply into silence the sweet voice of a flute was heard, drifting in from the porch that fronted the house.

"Kak Zhal!" Ur shouted. "At last!" Running out of the room, her bare feet slapped pleasantly against the planks of walnut.

Ur pulled up and stood quite still when she reached the front door. Kak Zhal lowered his flute. "Oooh!" was all she could say; then she dropped to her knees and opened her arms as Kak Zhal stepped toward her.

For a few long moments they held an embrace. "Why have you stayed away so long?" Ur asked.

"Phew, well…" Kak Zhal began. He scratched his nose, which looked like a lumpy turnip and pulled on an ear that an elephant would envy. Straightening himself up, so his eyes met hers directly, as she kneeled on the porch, he pointed and said simply, "Was him!"

Ur turned. Arms crossed, standing next to Grandma Kattie and Granny Jen was Nicholas Marduk Beele. "Why ever would you have kept him from me?"

"Kak Zhal would have been a distraction," Beele said.

"Distraction from what?" Ur demanded.

"From your lessons. Your history. While you comprehend the present of all possible worldlines and all futures but your own, the past is something that is out of your experience and so you must master it. And then there's your Latin," Nick said.

"Bene Latinam linguam dicere et legere possum!" Ur said peevishly.

"Ita. Still… All of that is beside the point. Kak Zhal is here. That is a gift. Embrace it. And he came playing Tamino's tune, so?"

"So what is the danger?" Ur asked.

"There's a storm comin'," Grannie Jen said.

"But I doubt it will clear the air," Grandma Kattie said.

"And it must have something to do with me, since I have not anticipated it," Ur said, picking at a finger.

"Don't worry that finger!" Grannie Jen said sternly. "It'll start to smart. You picked that up from your mother I expect."

Mozart had come onto the porch with Frankie. "Picked up___"

"Picking at a finger!" Kak Zhal finished. And with that he and Mozart began to howl with glee.

"Oh," Nick said closing his eyes and rubbing the bridge of his nose. "Must they *always*!"

Frankie had walked over to Nick and draped her arm around his shoulder. "Now, Nicholas, don't be a spoil sport."

Nick smiled and kissed Frankie on the forehead.

"I do love you all so, but what is going on? You know I struggle with complicated social interaction. I think you're making fun of me," Ur said.

Nick walked over to Ur and held her hands in his own.

"We would never try to shame you. Consider our behavior simply unaffected by any attempt on our part to structure an artificial lesson for you. No, heuristics are always best." Nick smiled and cupped Ur's head in his hands. "Your new hairstyle becomes you. I quite like it short, don't you?" Nick said, turning to the little band on the porch. Nods of approval and statements of affirmation were heard. "Why are you blushing?"

Ur sighed. "Oh, I don't know. It's…There are times I just feel odd."

Nick was quiet but looked over at the two Grandmas who simply nodded.

"But you asked a serious question. What is the danger? Consider your original worldline and observe."

Ur closed her eyes, then gasped. "Oh, my!"

"Oh, my, indeed," Nick said.

"But what can it mean? An asteroid smashing into Earth? It landed in a remote area called Greenland, I think. Nearly uninhabited," Ur said.

"This is where history comes in," Nick said, turning to Kak Zhal, who cleared his throat.

"Well, ya see, having spent a good deal of time of late underground, so to speak, bein' dead and all, I took an interest in Geology. Maybe it's part o' what I am, too. Mr. Tolkien read me his Ring story and I felt a sense of *identification* with them dwarves, seein' as how I'm put together," Kak Zhal said.

Ur raised an eyebrow.

"Ah, and Dr Samuel Johnson has helped me with my vocabulary."

"That is admirable," Ur said.

"Thank you. Anyways, while there is no library in Hades, you have call on what ya might say is original source material. So I found me a geologist or two among the crowd down there and began learnin' the field. Learned a lot about Earth, which interested me greatly since it was your original home and you interest me greatly." Kak Zhal smiled and Ur flashed her toothy grin. "Still workin' on the smile thing I see." Ur nodded.

"Well, your Ice Ages caught my fancy since it's so cold at Old Spall so much o' the time. Turns out there was a period about ten thousand Earth years ago called the Dryas. A big lake by the name of Agassiz in Canada busted through an ice dam when the climate warmed up-like and spilled fresh water into an ocean called the Atlantic."

"Yes, I know of it," Ur said.

"Well, fresh water is lighter than salt and when it hit a current called the Gulf Stream it shut down the conveyor of warm water from the south to the North and started a __"

"Big Freeze!" Ur said, her cobalt eyes flashing.

"Right. Now not as much water melted off the ice cap on Greenland when the meteor struck than was in old Agassiz, but enough to probably bollix things up for a hundred years or so. Plus, Earth is a much more complicated place with humans in the picture than it was when there was only big hairy elephants and what not. So, that's the problem and __"

"Yes, I see the problem now. The world will turn upside down, metaphorically speaking. Socially, politically and economically, since Earth's Southern Hemisphere will be relatively unaffected. And it is my home after all. " Ur picked at a finger.

She lifted her chin. "I must go."

"But Ur," Frankie exclaimed, "there's danger if you interfere."

"Oh, I understand that," Ur said, walking over to Frankie and taking her hands in her own. "But I'll have time to think. My consideration of the evolution of worldlines indicates that the optimal time for me to go would be about twenty years from now on Earth, which given differential relativistic effects means about four years here. I will be twenty then and also more, mature."

"Good!" Kak Zhal said, waving his flute. "I knew you'd want to help."

"Thank you, Kak Zhal. Can you stay? For just a little while," Ur asked.

"Yup. C'mon in and me and Herr Mozart here… Herr__"

"Here!" Mozart shouted and the two began to laugh and laugh as they went back toward the parlor.

Frankie and Nick followed and Nick simply turned and smiled at Ur, nodding approval.

Ur frowned and looked at the sky, as if she would find an answer there to some question that was gnawing at her.

"What is it, girl?" Grannie Jen asked.

"Well, I can't see my own worldline of course, but there is someone else. I can't make them out," Ur said. She sighed.

"You said you've been feeling odd," Grandma Kattie said. "Do men strike you as different?"

"Well…" Ur stomped a heel on the porch. "Yes! They used to be just people. Now I don't really understand them."

"Come over here, girl," Granny Jen said. "Ah!" Frankie had just walked back onto the porch. Lovely notes in duet floated out behind her. "You're just the person to have a talk with Ur. She seems to be growin' up."

"And your approach to the birds and bees might be more…*modern*," Grandma Kattie said.

"Oh," Ur whispered. Then she laughed and all of the long leaves of rye in the field around the house swayed and seemed to make a sound as if they were made of the most delicate sheets of copper. "I think I see. But I understand all of that. The act of sexual reproduction is__"

"Ur!" Frankie said, firmly but with a smile. "Men are far more complicated than that." The grannies nodded. "So, the first thing you need to know about men is…"

PART TWO – BRAZIL

Twenty Years Later

CHAPTER I

———

"Tall and tan and long and lovely, the—"

"Young and lovely," Buford corrected.

"Long, Bu," Carmine said.

"Young, Minnie. Trust me."

Carmine stared at Buford for a moment. "I do trust you. That's why you're here."

"Your parents trust me. That's why I'm here." Carmine's full lips, almost feminine, a gift from his father Vinnie, puffed into a pout. "I trust you, Bu. And you fucking-A know it."

All along the shore xenon lights blazed. Klick after klick, deeper and deeper into the night, the locals were playing volleyball on the beach. "My God!" Carmine said in a whisper. "Did you see that one?" Carmine came up out of his seat. "And that one! Bu, I'm in love."

"You're in Rio, Minnie. You're in Ipanema."

Carmine nodded, his eyes glued to the sand strip that lay just across the road. "Long and lovely. My God, those legs look as if they go on forever!"

"Yep, son. Right down into the sand and straight through to China." Buford took a long drag on his cigarette and exhaled slowly out the window. "Carioca. Most beautiful people in the world and the most beautiful language. Too bad they're all mulattos and mongrels." Buford, his pale blue eyes twinkling, cast a furtive glance at Carmine.

"Goddammit, Bu, cut that shit out. You don't really believe that stuff. Do you?"

"'Course I do. I'm a citizen in good standing of the Rocky Mountain Republic. Have to believe it or they'd kick my ass out."

"Aw, bullshit. My Uncle Jaq's still there."

"Nah. Ran his ass out six months ago."

"They did like hell," Carmine said.

"How would you know? You haven't been out to see him in what, five years? Six?"

Carmine shifted uncomfortably. "But what about all of that stuff about mongrels and, well, you know, niggers and all. We hear some brutal shit back East."

"All propaganda. We ran the Nazis out a long time ago. They're all holed up near Sandpoint. Too fucking cold for them to cause any trouble up there. Got their hands full just staying warm. Besides, your Aunt Tia's holding down the fort for the pinkos. Still runs the plant store in Ketchum and nobody messes with her." Buford grunted and pounded the steering wheel lightly a couple of times with his fist. "Nobody would dare. Old school Maoist."

"What about Mattie?"

Buford shrugged. "Hasn't been home in twenty years. Hardly heard from. Still in Mongolia or some other god-forsaken place, as far as I know."

"Does that bother Uncle Jaq?"

"I don't really know. Funny relationship they had. But I'll tell you one thing he misses. That's your Aunt Kate. He's never been the same since she went down in the Big Lost, fishing during runoff. They never did find her body ..." Buford's voice trailed off.

"Anyway, you should visit. Jaq's pretty old. Besides, things are getting better in Idaho. Glaciers stop at Coeur d'Alene. Hell, sometimes it'll hit fifty in the summer." Carmine eyed Buford suspiciously. "Almost, anyways."

"Maybe I will." Carmine smiled. "Sounds like heaven. It's getting better back East, too, but they still kept Wollman Rink open 'til June last year."

Buford Stemp turned the red Mustang into a gravel lot in front of a low, white building lit eerily orange by mercury vapor lamps. A pathetic, pink neon relic buzzed on the bar's single window, hissing something about 'Brahma'. A young woman with long, light brown hair and caramel skin, wearing a silver thong, was leaving the bar. She was swinging a six-pack, most likely for her team across the street on the beach. Carmine whistled, long and low. "Bet they don't dress like that in Idaho."

"Freeze their tits off," Buford said, hopping out of the car. "And remember, I took you here to bowl, not ball." Buford took a drag on his cigarette and ran his fingers through his short, gray hair. He scratched the light stubble on his cheek with the butt, then flicked it onto the ground. "Just keep your pistol holstered."

"Okay, okay." Carmine paused at the entrance. "You're a fuckin' cornball, you know that?" He turned back toward the beach, closing his eyes and taking a deep lungful of the soft, salt air. Carmine rubbed his bare arms and was almost astonished to find no gooseflesh. "Ipa-fucking-nema," he whispered.

Buford disappeared.

The joint was cramped. Low ceilings. Fourteen narrow bowling lanes. In a corner near the bar sat seven small, battered tables, four of them occupied. Threading the air was the pungent, sickly sweet smell of cigarette smoke. Turkish. Carmine wrinkled his nose. Another odor wafted over the top of the smoke. Churrasco. By the beer taps, a large haunch turned on a spit, glistening with fat. His stomach growled. He licked his lips.

Buford clapped his hand on Carmine's shoulder. "Checking out the barmaids or you just hungry?"

Carmine started. "Jeez, Bu, don't do that, huh?" Carmine frowned as he let Buford steer him toward one of the tables by the bar. "Ay, where you been, anyway?"

"Kid, when you're my age you'll get it. Got kidneys the size of watermelons and a bladder the size of a walnut."

Carmine shook his head. "How come they gave me an old fart like you for a bodyguard? Sure as shit, botta boom! Someone'll whack me while you're in the can."

Buford fumbled for a Lucky and lit it hastily. "Look, kid, I'm not the friggin' Secret Service and I'm sure as hell not your mother. We're not supposed to be joined at the hip. My only job is—"

"Yeah, yeah. I know. Is to make sure I get home alive." Carmine twirled the ashtray on the table. "Say, why did you take this job anyway. You're a Class A spook. Navy Seal, CIA__"

"Back when there was a CIA."

"Yeah, well, God knows what the fuck else you've been. My point is, this is like penny ante private eye shit," Carmine said.

"I took the job because your parents asked me to and because I like 'em a whole hell of a lot. And I'm sort of in between work now anyways," Buford said.

"And all you gotta do is make sure you get me home in one piece."

"That's right. And breathin'," Buford said, setting his cigarette down in the grubby ashtray. Leaning forward in his chair and glancing quickly around the room, Buford whispered, "C'mere." Carmine inched his chair toward Stemp. Buford's right arm shot out and he drove it underneath the table, catching Carmine square in the midsection.

Almost imperceptibly, Carmine drew in a short gasp of air through his nose, but he kept his eyes fixed on Buford's, unblinking.

Buford flexed his fingers then reached across the table to grab his cigarette. Casually, he flicked off the long ash and took a quick drag; then he leaned back in his chair. "That was good, Minnie. Good reflexes. And you've stayed in shape. Just like I told you."

"Ay, not all of us New Yorkers are pussies. Send some of your cowboys to Brooklyn sometime." Carmine smiled. "I watched your eyes. Just like you told me."

"Yeah, well …" Buford scratched his cheek with the butt of his cigarette. "But you shouldn't have let me reach you at all."

"But I wanted to leave both hands free. One, *botta bing!*, to turn the table over. Kind of catch you off guard. The other, *botta boom!*, to smack you square in the kisser."

"Good plan, good plan," Buford said casually. "But—" His hand reached out and he wrapped it around Carmine's forearm. "Don't ever, I mean never, let anyone get that close to a vital spot."

Carmine pouted. "But Bu, I had a plan. I was gonna use the table. Catch you—"

"I would have eviscerated you before you had the chance." Pouting more deeply, Carmine made a fist and sat staring at his knuckles.

Buford pinched Carmine's cheek, then gave it a friendly smack. "It's been a long time, Minnie. You were just a kid when I taught you. I can't expect you to remember everything. And I haven't exactly made the effort I should've to get back East. No. You did good. Real good, son. That was just a little refresher. Speaking of refreshers—" Buford's hand shot up into the air, catching the attention of a waiter. "Favor," he shouted, "Brahma Chopp!" and held up two fingers.

Carmine's pout evaporated and his face broke into a grin. "Well, just keep refreshing me," he said. "I don't make it home in one piece my mom'll be *really* pissed off."

"That, young fella, is my greatest incentive. Clara knows there's gonna be trouble at this conference and it's my job to make sure you stay out of it."

"She told me the same thing. But how does she know there's going to be trouble?"

Buford shrugged and took a drag. "There's always trouble at these things. People don't agree, there's trouble."

"Yeah," Carmine said, "but we know she thinks this one'll be trouble, trouble."

"Your mom's a trader. Best, probably, in the business. She's got intuition and—"

But Carmine wasn't listening. He was staring at a woman with blue-black skin and almond eyes. He blinked a few times. "She looks like one of those fucking Queens of Egypt at the Brooklyn Museum."

Buford glanced over his shoulder. Carmine's obvious interest in the woman had caught the attention of the man seated next to her, who rose and approached their table. "Speaking of trouble, here it comes. I'm telling ya, ya gotta stop thinking with your cock, son."

The man was tallish with black, wavy hair sprinkled liberally with gray. His biceps stretched the short sleeves of his shirt. Stopping a foot from Carmine, he began to speak angrily in Portuguese and in a voice that was very loud.

"Now just a second, friend," Buford Stemp said, smiling. "He didn't mean—"

The man turned abruptly to face Stemp. "Shut up, old man," he said.

"So, you kapeesh the English, huh?" Stemp said.

With an almost audible snap, the man wheeled about to face Stemp. "I said, shut up, old man." His upper lip curled in a snarl. "Or I'll take you outside, too."

Buford grinned and rubbed his cheek. "Now, now, no one's going outside. I said my friend here didn't mean—"

"And I said, shut up, old man!" The man grabbed Buford by the front of the shirt. Carmine began to rise, but Buford's eyes said 'no,' and he sat back down.

With a small smile still sitting serenely on his face, Buford Stemp grabbed the stranger's shirt and sunk his fingers into his pectoral muscle. He made the move slowly and gently. Then, even more slowly, he began to squeeze.

The man's eyes flared. "Hey—"

"Shh, shh, shh," Buford hushed softly. "You shouldn't let the hair fool ya." Buford reached for his cigarette with his free hand, took a short drag, then began to squeeze a little harder.

Small beads of perspiration erupted on the man's upper lip. "But—" he began.

"Let me finish," Stemp said quietly. "Darn it, you just won't let me finish. I've tried a couple o' times." Buford applied just a little more pressure and the man fell completely silent. "That's better. Thank you. *Obrigado.* Now, as I was saying, the boy here didn't mean—"

"Boy? Bu!"

"Minnie, you shut the hell up or somebody *will* be goin' outside. An' it'll be you and I'll wup yer ass." Carmine swallowed hard and averted his gaze. "Now, as I was tryin' to say, the boy here didn't mean anything rude by his attentions and he wants to apologize. Don't you, Minnie?" Refusing to look up, Carmine stayed silent. "Don't you!" Stemp shouted, his voice shattering the inchoate din of the bowling alley like a sledgehammer. Not a sound followed, except for the click of a few stray pins falling. Above the polished alleys, the fluorescents buzzed like mindless insects, and in the lounge the smoke seemed to curl into ever more fantastic shapes, upward through the thick, yellow atmosphere, snaking around the recessed lights in the tin ceiling.

"Yes, sir," Carmine said quietly. "Mister, I'm sorry. I didn't mean any disrespect. Your, um, lady—"

"My wife," the man snapped.

"Sorry, your wife. I didn't know. She's very beautiful. I'm, um, only human. I apologize. *Perdao.*"

For a second, the man was silent. Then he nodded, the possibility of a smile insinuating itself at the corners of his mouth. Buford Stemp relaxed his grip, then extended the same hand. The man accepted and shook it. "Polite *and* brave," he said. "Quite the rare combination for NOHMs."

"You'd be surprised," Buford said. "Some of us are all right." The man's face broke into a grin and with that the general babble resumed. "You look thirsty, *senhor.*" Buford motioned to the waiter to send a pitcher of beer to the man's table. With a subtle bow, he returned to his wife.

"Say, what in hell is a NOHM?" Carmine asked.

"Acronym for Northern Hemisphere. It's what they call us."

"Oh." Carmine chewed that one over for a minute. "Anyway, I'm sorry, Bu."

"Look, there'll be trouble enough this next week without inventing any more." Buford tapped his forehead. "Start using this. I know you're young. Was once myself, believe it or not. But you can't always be thinkin' with the old perdork."

As the waiter set down two bottles of Brahma Chopp, Carmine laughed aloud. "It's not that, Bu—"

"The hell! You've been sniffin' like an old mutt in rut ever since we got here. Can't exactly blame you. But listen—"

"No, Bu, you listen to me." Buford narrowed his eyes. "Please. I'm a lot like my dad. I've got some talent with numbers."

"Some? He's like fucking Ramanujan. And you aren't far behind."

"No. I'm not. A little, but not very. But I'm also like my mom. A little. I have some of her intuition. And my intuition tells me that I'm going to meet someone down here. I'm not a pussy hound, Bu. Honest. Not a hundred percent, anyway. I just want to make sure I don't miss her."

"The way you're goin' you couldn't possibly miss her." Buford drained half of his beer in three gulps, motioned for two more and lit up another Lucky.

"Hey, what about you, Bu? You ever meet somebody special?" Carmine said.

"Me? Old dumb ass cowboy?"

Carmine chuckled. "C'mon. You're tall-ish. Ripped. Lean and mean." Carmine grabbed Buford by a bicep. "For your age. I mean you got that grey lid and all, but still. You didn't always. Square jaw, blue eyes." Carmine leaned closer to Buford. "I mean, I could take a run at you myself if I were into that shit." Buford chucked Carmine on the cheek.

"But seriously, was there never that special someone?"

Buford shrugged. "Oh, one night stands, even short sprints. But no. It's hard in my business. Besides, I never really did meet that special someone. Kinda wish I could o' though."

Carmine exhaled and nodded his head slowly. "Maybe you still will." Buford took another deep drag on his Lucky. "Bu," Carmine said, "don't you think you ought to ease up on those things?"

"Hell, no. What with all the coal we burn out West, our lungs are shot anyways. Nobody lives much past seventy. Shit, I'm almost on borrowed time anyway."

The waiter set down two more bottles of Brahma. "Ya hungry, kid?" Buford asked.

"I was, but all the excitement kind of took the edge off my appetite."

"How about a couple o' games." Buford nodded in the direction of the bowling lanes. "I was here in the teens. Place hasn't changed a bit."

"Let's roll!" Carmine jumped out of his chair and drained his beer.

"Son, you can't bowl in those things," Buford said, pointing at Carmine's feet, "anymore than I can in these shit-kickers." Buford was wearing a pair of bright yellow lizard cowboy boots.

Behind a counter that fronted several large racks containing shoes and balls of just about every imaginable color stood a small man with a glistening pate, guarded by a ring of kinky, iron gray hair. The man squinted at them through thick glasses. "*Favor. Dos zapatos*," Buford said, having exhausted his command of Portuguese earlier with *obrigado*. He pointed at his boots.

"Ah," the man said. He studied the two men and, after a few moments careful consideration, pulled two pair of bowling shoes off the shelf and handed them to Buford.

"Suppose it'd be a waste of time to try to get the right size. We'd be here all night, seeing the way I *falar* the Portuguee," Buford said. "*Dos bolos, favor.*"

"Color?" the man asked.

"*Uno negro por* me and *azul* for my *compadre*," Buford said, motioning to Carmine. "The blue one's for you."

"Very funny," Carmine said.

Buford smacked the rental fee down on the counter. "C'mon," Buford said to Carmine.

"*Momento, favor*," the attendant said. The man motioned to their feet and nodded vigorously.

"I think he wants our shoes as security," Carmine said.

"Oh sure, sure," Buford said. But Buford didn't look so sure at all when he handed his boots to the attendant, who stroked them and cooed softly to them.

"I hope to hell that guy's not a pervert." Buford said.

"What?" Carmine said.

"Did you see the way he eyed my boots? Happened to me once in New York. Sent 'em out at this fancy hotel to be shined and this bootblack … Anyways, he ruined the damned finish. Jesus, what people'll do! Say, let's take this lane, Minnie.

"Seriously, you never bowled?" Buford asked as they were putting on their shoes.

"Nope. But I used to watch it on TV on Saturday afternoons. When I was a kid. When there was a pro league."

"Yeah," Buford said, "and an NFL and the major leagues …" His voice trailed off.

"Cheer up. The scientists say it'll warm up. Eventually."

"In about a hundred years. We won't be around to see it," Buford said sourly.

Carmine shrugged. "Might not want to." Picking up his ball, he began to turn it over and over. "Say, Bu?"

"Yeah, kid?"

"Where're the holes?"

"What?"

"The holes. For our fingers," Carmine said.

"These are duckpins. Everything's kind of scaled down, like. Pins, balls, alleys." Carmine nodded thoughtfully. "Anyways, we're burnin' daylight."

"It's ten o'clock at night."

"It's an expression." Buford lined up and taking three steps, let his ball fly. "Eight," Buford shouted, rubbing his hands together briskly.

"Say, Bu," Carmine said in an overly loud voice, just as Buford was releasing his second ball, which left his hands with a wicked spin, shot across the lane and into the gutter.

"Did you have to shout just as—"

"I'm sorry." Buford glared at Carmine. "I couldn't remember how many shots you get."

A small figure dropped down from above the duckpins and collected them, her gaze fixed on Buford. "Not enough, with you yapping away."

"So take another turn," Carmine said glumly.

"Bowl," Buford growled. "You need the practice and I need a beer."

"Sure, Bu." Quickly, Carmine stepped up on the left side of the lane and, with a sharp flick of his wrist, let his ball fly to the right.

"Minnie, for Christ's sake—"

Curving sharply at first, it straightened, then slammed into the neat collection of pins, which exploded, then collapsed in a heap. Carmine's face burst into a smile. Buford sat sullenly, slumped in his chair. "A strike! That's good, huh?"

Buford took a swig on his beer. "Say, you sure you never bowled?" Carmine shook his head. "Then how in hell—"

"I just threw the ball on a trajectory that described the curve 'y' equals 'ln' to the power minus 'x'. Botta boom! Strike," Carmine said.

"Oh."

Behind the newly set triangle of tiny pins dangled a pair of tanned shins, the color of lightly browned toast. "What in hell's that?" Carmine asked, pointing at the legs hanging from a platform suspended above the alley. One foot casually scratched the instep of the other with its big toe.

"Hm? Oh, that's one of the pin boys. Or girls. Can't afford automatic pinsetters here. Never could. Never wanted to, more likely. Gives the kids from the *favelas* a way to make a few extra *cruzeiros*. Or *cruzados* or whatever the hell passes for money here nowadays." Buford scratched his cheek slowly and thoughtfully with the butt of his cigarette. "Let's see you do that again."

Carmine nodded and took one step to the right. His bright blue ball sailed down the alley and crashed into the pins lined up on the right, leaving three standing on the left.

"Losing your touch?" Buford said.

"Nah, I just shifted the 'x' axis," Carmine said, his back to Buford.

"You mean you missed on purpose."

"Spare means I get another chance and I want to see the pinsetter."

Buford grumbled something and then fumbled for another Lucky. Carmine kept his eyes riveted on the end of the alley. A slender, figure dropped down behind the pins and began to clear them away. The hair was auburn, almost copper colored, and the fingers long and fine. But the pin girl, dressed in a tight, white sleeveless top and Capris, exposing a firm, smooth calf, did not look up and, when the last downed duckpin had been gathered up, sprang lightly up and onto the little bench behind and above the polished, blond boards of the alley.

Deliberately, Carmine lined up and rolled his ball gently down the lane. The three remaining pins fell softly. Once again, the girl dropped onto the brightly varnished surface. Without looking up, she rolled Carmine's ball back to him down the gutter. When he picked it up, she stared directly into his eyes. Her own blazed bright cobalt above her thick, sensual lips. Carmine dropped his ball with a resounding thud.

"Jesus," Buford swore, spinning a Lucky slowly between his fingers. "Be careful, for Christ's sake, or I'll never get my boots back." Buford started to get up. "Well, I guess it's my—"

"Bu, can I bowl again?" Buford eyed Carmine suspiciously. "Can I?"

"Well … Oh hell, sure. If you're havin' fun. That's why we came, isn't it?" Buford took a swig of beer. "Go on."

Carmine lined up and bowled a perfect strike. Again, the girl dropped down and stared at him, her cheeks plumping almost imperceptibly. She rolled his ball back and hopped out of sight. All except for her legs.

For a moment, Carmine stood quite still, moving the fingers of his left hand slowly across its surface.

"Carmine," Buford said quietly. But Carmine did not acknowledge him. "Carmine," Buford repeated, this time louder.

"Did you see her, Bu?"

"Who? See who?"

"The pin girl. I think she smiled at me. I think I'm gonna fucking die."

"Sure, but… Shit, Carmine! I thought I told you …" But Carmine clearly was not paying attention. The features of his face were flat and flaccid, his eyes large and limpid. "Siddown," Buford said. He lined up and flicked his wrist casually. The dull, black ball snaked sluggishly toward its target, succeeding at last in knocking down only four pins. "Now see what you've done, Carmine. I've lost my mojo."

But Carmine wasn't listening. The pinsetter dropped to the floor. Carmine jumped out of his seat. "Buford! She's gone!" A small boy with black hair and blacker eyes scrambled about, gathering up the pins.

Buford shrugged. "Shift must've changed."

Carmine's eyes searched the hall frantically. "But, Bu. I gotta find her."

"Minnie, for Christ's sake, I told ya—"

"There she is!" Carmine was pointing to a side exit as a slender figure with reddish hair slipped out.

As Carmine bolted in her direction, Buford caught a glimpse of her, but this time he focused his attention. "No. It couldn't be," he said very softly. "Minnie! Wait!" he shouted. But Carmine was already out the door.

Carmine had made a noisy exit, jostling a number of bowlers and brushing past a waitress, making her lose her balance and slop some beer on the floor. Buford and Carmine had already attracted enough attention. Especially for a couple of NOHMs who weren't particularly welcome in the first place. On his way out, he stopped for a moment and handed the waitress, who was mopping the spilled beer off the floor, a fistful of *cruzeiros*. She smiled and then lowered her beautiful black eyes.

As Buford stepped out the door, the little shoe attendant raised his arm and was about to shout across the room. But he did not make a sound and simply looked longingly at Buford's boots, shrugged and smiled.

Buford slammed the palm of his hand down on the hood of the Mustang. "Dammit," he swore.

"What's the problem?" a voice said.

Stemp turned around. It was the Carioca with whom he had had the encounter earlier. "Damned kid," Buford growled. "Took off after one of the pin girls."

"Your friend has quite the appetite," the man said.

"Maybe. Although," Buford said, as he ran his hand through the gray stubble that covered his head, "this may be different."

"Different? How different?"

Buford scuffed some gravel with the toe of his shoe and pounded his fist a few times lightly on the fender of his car. "Aw, I dunno. Anyways, I gotta find him. Or there'll be hell to pay. Problem is, I don't know which way he went."

"Perhaps I can help you. We'll split up," the man said. Buford eyed him suspiciously. "Allow me to introduce myself. I am Joao Limon. I'm with Brazilian Intelligence."

"And I'm—"

"You're Buford Stemp of the Rocky Mountain Republic. Formerly… well, let's just say we were in the same business. And your friend, Carmine, is with the delegation from the Republic of New York and Venice."

Buford pulled a Lucky from his shirt pocket and rubbed the butt against his cheek.

"I've been assigned to make sure that you and the boy arrive at the conference in Brasilia without incident. Call me Jorge, if you like."

Buford snorted. "Without incident? Then what in hell do you call that performance you put on back in there?"

"I asked you to step outside. I wanted to introduce myself."

"Funny way you had of asking. Jesus."

"That was my wife and I am, as your friend says, only human. As well as being a hot-blooded, hot-headed SOHM." Smiling, Limon shrugged. "Besides, an encounter inognito tells you a more about a man than a formal introduction."

"Very true. Good technique." Buford laughed. "I guess some of you boys from the Southern Hemisphere ain't so bad after all. You seem … how'd you put it? Polite enough."

"And brave, if the occasion demands. But we're wasting time."

"Yes, we are."

Limon glanced around. "I'm sure the boy's in no real danger. He looks Latin. But nevertheless … Anyway, he'll be on the beach. Nowhere else to go, really." Opposite the ocean, up and behind the bar, a series of low hills, black and lumpy, lay huddled behind the soft urban glow of Rio. "I'll walk south and you take the car and head north. Either way he can't have gone very far."

"Okay," Buford said. "I'll cruise a half mile or so, then double back for you."

"He should be fairly easy to spot," Limon said. "The beaches aren't very crowded this time of night."

Buford opened the car door, then stopped. "Like you said, uh, Jorge, he is Latin-looking. The girl he was chasing, though, had red hair."

"Red? That's unusual."

"Well, auburn, copper, really. Tall and lanky, kind of. White, for sure. Hint of a tan, but white." Buford cupped his hand around the end of his cigarette and lit it. "But, uh, what do you mean unusual? Uncommon, I could see that. But then again with all the mulattos and quadroons and what-not here in Brazil … well, I've seen some redheads." Limon frowned. "No offense about your racial demographics. I was just stating a fact."

Limon waived a hand. "None taken. It's just that I come here quite often and I've never seen a redhead setting pins. At least not a NOHM."

"I'm not sure she's a NOHM, exactly."

"Well, then, what *are* you sure of? Do you know her?" Limon asked.

"Maybe."

Limon raised an eyebrow and withdrew a small pistol from beneath his shirt. Stemp tensed but didn't move. Limon checked the chamber. "Is she dangerous?"

"I don't know for sure," Buford said. "But if she is, it's in a way that neither you nor I could really understand. And that," he finished, pointing at Limon's revolver, "won't do you any good at all."

"In that case," Limon said with a smile, "I'll just have to be very polite."

"And brave," Buford said.

****

Slowly, Buford Stemp cruised north, hugging the shoulder in the right-hand lane of the highway. The car's brights cut a deep slice through the darkness. A couple of times an oncoming car flashed with obvious irritation, but Buford didn't pay any attention.

Across the road, on the beach, the action had begun to thin out. Only a few teams were playing under the mercurys. Down by the water's edge, a knot of kids was hanging out. Buford made a U-turn and pulled the car into a turnout. He grabbed a pair of night vision binoculars out of the glove box and stepped out of the car. Two young men and two women, early twenties, stood talking in the green glow of the gentle surf that lapped about their ankles.

Scanning the beach, Buford swore softly. "He can't have come this far. Not in bowling shoes, anyways," he said aloud. Climbing back into the car, he tossed the binoculars onto the passenger seat and reached for the ignition. A soft tap on the trunk stopped him cold. Buford snapped his head around and reached for his gun suspended beneath the dash, but the turnout was deserted.

"I'm sorry. Did I startle you?" a voice said.

Gasping lightly but audibly, Buford looked over his left shoulder and found a pair of bright cobalt blue eyes boring into his. "Yes."

"I'm sorry," the girl said. "It wasn't my intention."

"That's all right," Buford said cautiously. "It's just that I've been trained to avoid surprises."

"But surprises provide a basis for learning," the girl said.

Buford wiped his palms on his pants, leaving two damp stains. "That's a darn good thought. So, you're a philosopher, too?" he asked, though he was not at all sure whether he wanted to hear the answer. The girl cocked her head and her short copper hair dropped below her ear and dangled above her shoulder, like a purse full of pennies poured onto the sand. "Like your father," he said, finishing the thought. Buford Stemp's shoulders slumped. He'd shot his bolt.

"Does that surprise you?" the girl asked. Buford Stemp shook his head. "It shouldn't. I am a consequence of my father."

Folding her arms and leaning up against the car door, the girl peered inside, surveying the interior carefully. She held her face very close to Buford's. So close, in fact, that he could feel her breath on his cheek. Surrounding her was a faintly metallic odor, though not at all unpleasant. Her hair perhaps? No, not metallic at all, Buford thought, rather, flinty and acrid. Almost on ancient smell. Or ageless.

"I'm looking for Carmine," Buford said.

"So am I," said the girl.

"But you—"

"Not in the same way as you are looking for him," the girl said.

"Once again, the philosopher."

"Once again and always," the girl said. "Perhaps we might help one another."

"Would you like to get in," Buford hesitated, "Ur?" he said, her name floating up his pharynx like a dry leaf rattling across a desert floor.

"My name is pronounced Oor, nor Er, cowboy. And yes," Ur said, running her hand across the bright red surface of the car door. "I would like that very much." In something like a grin, Ur stretched her lips across her teeth, but the expression lacked mirth. And yet her cobalt eyes pulsed softly. Some deep happiness, perhaps, lay behind them. Or at least the expectation of it.

"Still can't smile worth a damn, can you?" Buford ventured. Could he, should he, try to connect with this strange creature in such a personal way?

Ur stood up straight and regarded Buford thoughtfully. "No. In that area I still am …" she picked at a finger. Buford Stemp's eyes flared but he did not interrupt her. "I am functionally—autistic, you might say. A result of my birth accident. Does that make sense to you?"

"Yeeess," Buford said slowly.

"Good. I want you to know that I have done the thing, though. I've even laughed. Although that's much easier," Ur said. She peered back down the beach toward Rio. "We need to go meet up with your friend and Carmine."

"Hop in." Buford popped the passenger door. Ur sprinted around the front of the car and slid into the seat beside him. Holy shit, Buford thought.

"What are these?" Ur asked, pulling something from beneath her hip.

"Binoculars. I was looking for Carmine just before you, uh, showed up." Ur turned them over slowly in her hand, examining them casually but thoroughly. "They help me see at a distance and in the dark," Buford said, not at all sure what the lovely young creature knew of his world. Did she know anything? Or everything. "Just look through—" But Ur had already raised them to her face.

Ur surveyed the beach. "Aaah!" she exclaimed in a high, soft voice when she had trained the binoculars on the young people playing in the surf. Then she handed them casually to Buford and shook her head. "Homo prosthesis," she said.

"Huh?" Buford said, tossing the binoculars onto the back seat. Suddenly but softly, a sound filled the cab of the car, like tiny copper bells blown by a soft bright wind. Ur was laughing. Her eyes, flashing, showered him with cobalt sparks. All the tension in his frame melted under the assault and was washed away by the liquid sound of her laughter. At last, she stopped, though Buford wished she never would. He blinked and felt the space between his eyelids cushioned by the warm wet fluid of his own body.

Gently, Ur laid a hand on top of Buford's, and then with the other dabbed the corner of his eye. "Homo prosthesis," she said. "It's what my father called the species. He is a Kantian, you know?"

Ur cocked her head and waited a moment for Stemp to respond.

"Oh. Yes. I think I do. I remember now." Buford said after clearing his throat. "Kant was that eighteenth-century philosopher. Eee-pistomologist. Studied how we come to know things." Ur remained silent, waiting for him to continue. How polite of her, Buford thought, not to assume his ignorance. "Anyway, this Kant fella believed that, uh, our minds, our brains, were structured for organizing the world around us in a very specific way. Organizing the way we *look* at the world, that is. So, reality, the, uh, true nature of things, so to speak, wasn't hidden from us but was kind of presented to us by our minds in a way that was, uh, unique to us. As a species that is, to use your turn of phrase. So I guess we need help, prostheses, so we can see, um, manifestations of reality that don't come to us, natural like." Buford paused expectantly. "How was that?"

"Darn good," Ur said, wrapping the phrase in Buford's own accent and tossing it back to him. Buford chuckled. "I thought the question might be helpful in establishing a bond between us."

"You've already done that, miss," Buford said quietly.

Ur slid her hand off the top of Buford's and he swallowed hard. "Is something the matter?" she said.

"Oh, no … Oh, hell, yes. I feel kind of like that Odysseus fella your dad, Jaq, used to talk about. Had himself tied to the main mast of his ship so he could listen to the Sirens' song. Nearly went mad not bein' able to follow it. That's how I feel, a little, now. That's how I felt, too, when you stopped laughing."

Ur averted her gaze and reached back and grabbed the binoculars. "This device is interesting. It stretches the boundaries of spectrum and scale." Buford sat silently. "Is there something wrong?" Ur asked again, after a time.

"No. It's just that you sound so much like your old man."

"We've already established that as an obvious consequence of our relationship," Ur said. Buford's jaw went slack. "Is something else the matter?" Ur said.

"No. It's just that you connect … No, it's that you don't connect. I mean, no, I don't mean that either. I'm sorry, I—"

"I don't connect seamlessly?"

Reluctantly, Buford nodded. "I am sorry. I don't mean to—"

"I'm learning. Please be patient."

"How could I be anything but patient with you?" Buford said, softly. "And, besides, even if that were difficult, which it's not, I'd owe it to Jaq. He was always patient with me. I never had the mind for things, philosophical things, that is, the way he did. But I'd listen anyway. He seemed to enjoy my company, especially after Nick Beele disappeared. Everyman, he'd call me. Though I was just a kid, Jaq needed someone to talk to. Man to man." Buford shifted uncomfortably in his seat. "Shit. I didn't mean—not that Kate—"

"My mother had a far more practical turn of mind than my father, Buford

Stemp. There were times when she simply got tired of his 'philosophical bullshit,' Uncle Nick said."

"*Uncle* Nick?"

"You know him, of course."

"I know of him."

Ur paused and Buford sensed from the expression in her eyes that she understood his unasked question. "He's my teacher."

"Your—What does he teach you?"

"Latin."

"Latin?" Instinctively, Buford reached in his shirt pocket and pulled out a Lucky and rubbed the end across his cheek. It failed to surprise him when he found his hand shaking.

"And other things. Philosophical bullshit, mostly." Ur flashed her odd, toothy grin and stared directly into Buford's eyes. "Don't deceive yourself. You have the mind for the stuff. There is a difference between lack of intelligence and ignorance."

"Thank you," Buford said. "I think."

"You're welcome," Ur said. She handed the binoculars back to Buford who tossed them into the rear seat. A silence insinuated itself between Buford and Ur. Occasionally, small sounds floated in through the open windows, only to steal out again as quickly as they had come. The low roar of a passing car. A voice raised above the muffled growl of the surf breaking against the sand, then racing out to sea again, its foamy fingers wrapped around the ankles of a timid bather. Caressing it all, a warm, salt wind blew lightly, rising and falling as if the world itself were breathing, which, of course, it was.

With an emphatic jab, Buford depressed the lighter on the dash. "Mind if I smoke?" he asked.

"No. Uncle Joe smokes all the time. Though it's not at all good for him."

"You mean the Indian?"

"Yes," Ur said.

Buford lit his cigarette and then, taking in a large lungful of smoke, went to replace the lighter. But Ur took it from him and replaced it herself, then punched it on. Slowly, Buford settled back in his seat and even more slowly, exhaled. Out of the corner of his eye he observed Ur as she lit and relit the lighter, taking obvious delight in the primitive technology, her face reflecting the orange-red of the glowing coil.

"I guess we should get going," Buford said at last. "It's getting late and all and we still need to find Carmine and—"

Ur was leaning forward, running her hands over the bright black leather that covered the dashboard. "This car is lovely," she said. "Where did you get it? It must be a hundred years old."

"Eighty. There's a guy in Rio that rents antiques. I used to own one just like this when I was a kid. Bright red, black interior. Four on the floor." Buford ran his own hand over the smooth chrome knob that sat atop the gearshift. "Guess I just enjoy indulging myself a little. But I suppose it's kind of dumb, too."

"Well, maybe it is a bit dumb, but there's certainly nothing wrong with that. My father indulged himself in the same way when he moved to Idaho just after I was born. He bought a 1952 Chevy pickup and took me for a ride. I guess he was trying to … connect with me."

"Jaq still has the truck."

"Oh," Ur said, then turned away from Buford, opened the glove box and peered inside. "I don't remember very much about the ride. That was a very confusing time for me; my brain was such a wreck." Ur shut the glove box. "We should be going, Buford Stemp."

"Yes. It is getting late and—"

"That's not what I meant. Time is quite elastic. It's simply that it's time for us to go meet Carmine."

"Sure," Buford said, though the word, one simple syllable, tumbled out of his mouth in an odd, halting manner. Buford turned the ignition over and pulled slowly out onto the empty highway and aimed straight for the soft, fuzzy glow of Rio.

A mile or so past the bowling alley the beach came alive once again. With a pulsing, driving rhythm, the shouts of people, the cool blare of the old bossa nova beat, even the harsh glow of the mercury lights, easily drowned out the gentle pounding of the surf against the broad beach of Ipanema.

Ipanema blended into Copacabana and then quite suddenly, Ur told

Buford to pull into a large parking lot. Angled against the curb, the Mustang commanded a vantage of both the beach and the night skyline of Rio.

"Kind o' pretty, ain't it?" Buford said.

Ur followed his line of sight. "The city, you mean?" Buford nodded. "Oh, yes," Ur said.

"With the stars all smothered by the city lights, kinda looks like a small galaxy itself. I mean, the bright core; and then as you climb up into the hills, they're dotted with all those tiny, scattered lights. Kinda like, kinda like—"

"Spiral arms," Ur said.

"Yes. That's it," Buford said, flicking his cigarette butt out the window. "Not a bad analogy, if I do say so myself."

"It is an apt homology. The structures are comparable. But, functionally, the comparison fails."

"Yeah, and why's that?" Buford said, a bit testily. Immediately, he felt angry with himself for becoming irritated with this lovely creature. Then a small smile flicked at the corners of his mouth. After all, he thought, isn't this what relationships are all about? Connecting. Failing. Reconnecting. That's what Kate used to say, anyway. Maybe he *was* beginning to develop a relationship with this strange creature. Creature? No, he thought. Strange, yes. Maybe with this *person*.

"You see," Ur was saying, "the cores of galaxies are full of light, but quite dead. Isn't that odd? It's the arms, the neighborhoods more sparsely populated by stars that are full of life. Here it's the core, the center that's teeming with life and potential." Palm up, Ur held her gesture for a moment and for the first time Buford felt frightened, as if she held the power within that hand to wrap those long, slender fingers around Rio and mold all of the light and the life in any way she wished.

Ur turned her hand over and pointed with a finger, tracing an irregular line across the steep hills above the city proper. "But up there, in the *favelas*, people merely cling to life by the very tips of their fingers, because that's what instinct tells them to do. What do you think of that, Buford Stemp?"

"I'd say that's pretty accurate," Buford said.

"Accurate. Is that all?" Ur said.

Putting his hand over his mouth, Buford coughed lightly. Then a little harder until, at last, he turned and spat out the window. "Excuse me," he said.

"You should stop smoking. It's bad for you," Ur said.

"Well, maybe," Buford said, slumping in his seat. Slowly, he folded his arms across his chest and pursed his lips. "But it's bad for the Indian and he hasn't quit, has he?"

"It won't kill Uncle Joe."

"It won't?" Buford said.

"No, it won't. But it may kill you." Buford grunted. "You haven't answered my question," Ur said.

"Your—" Ur's eyes bored into Buford's. "Hell. Look, Ur, we don't have the resources now and—"

"You did."

Buford exhaled. "But you see, we didn't have—"

"The will."

"That's right," Buford said.

"So, you used to have the resources but not the will and now you have the will but lack the means."

"No, that's not it either, it's just that—what're you doing?" Buford said.

Carefully, Ur was testing the handle that held the convertible top in place. "May we put the top down?" Ur asked. "Does this handle release it?"

"Yes," Buford said. "It does and we may." Quickly, they unlatched the ragtop, stowed it behind the rear seat and hopped back into the car.

"So," Ur said, once they were settled back in their seats.

"Dammit, Ur." Buford pounded the steering wheel lightly with his fist. "Look, we're in a tight spot ourselves now, up North."

"Tight, but temporary," Ur said.

"Temporary?" Buford said, raising his voice slightly. "Sure, it'll warm up in a hundred years or so, but what good'll that do us now?"

"But then, what good have future generations ever done for their ancestors?" Ur said.

Buford chuckled. "Ya got a point. But they've spent the better part of the last hundred years down here chopping down rain forests, poisoning the rivers and the oceans—"

"As you all spent the better part of the previous hundred years," Ur said.

"True. But we learned from our mistakes."

"Did you?" Ur said.

"Why, hell yes, we did! We cleaned up the air and the water. We developed technology to, uh, to protect the environment. We—"

"Why, Buford Stemp, you sound like—I seem to remember Uncle Nick dropping a colorful expression, once, from the last century." Taking a deep breath, Ur threw her head back and stared for a moment at the fuzzy blackness overhead. Breathing, Buford thought. My god, she is breathing. "Tree-hugger," Ur said at last, startling Buford.

"Hmm?"

"I said you sound like a 'tree- hugger,' Buford Stemp. What must they think of you in the Rocky Mountain Republic? Aren't such ideas forbidden?" Buford blinked. Once again, and for the second time, Ur laughed and Buford felt his flesh melt into the soft night, losing a sense of definition between his own self and every other thing that surrounded him.

"We're not so bad as ya think, miss," Buford said softly.

"Nothing is either all good or all bad, Uncle Nick says. That's what makes ethical decisions so complicated."

"Right. Exactly," Buford said, sitting up, his eyes flashing. "And this just isn't a question of ethics. Hell, there is no question here. Everyone's got a right to a better life. Nobody'll argue with that."

"Won't they?"

"No. Mostly nobody, anyways."

"Anyway."

"Anyway. Right, well, mostly nobody worth a damn will argue with that. No sir! What we've got here is a practical problem, that's all. I mean, the Chinese, for example. Look at them. There's three billion of 'em and they gotta eat. Still, they spew more crap into the atmosphere every year than—"

"No, Buford Stemp. They simply burn as much coal as the old United States does right now."

"But it's only temporary," Buford said, his tone pleading now. "Look, when it warms up, things will be different than they were."

"Will they?" Ur said.

"Sure they will. All those people up there, in the favelas, gotta do is be a little patient."

"Just as they've been for the past hundred years?" Self consciously, Buford wiped a line of sweat off his upper lip. "They won't be patient, though, Buford Stemp."

"Fine. Fine. All right. So what're we supposed to do, huh? Stop burning our coal and freeze to death, stop farming their ocean and starve to death? Lie down and die? Is that what you're saying?"

"No. In fact, that is what you must not do. Your technology, your intellectual legacy is what, more than anything, they need. Without it, they'll fail to survive. Without you, they will fail."

"So, then, it's a question of how we manage—"

"No," Ur said in a voice that stifled every other ambient sound. Like a deep brass bell, its tone rocked Buford's bowels and, for the second time, he felt fear. "I am not talking about managing resources. That's not what this situation is about. Although everyone seems to think it is." Ur picked at a finger and then stared through the windshield at the *favelas* of Rio. "They won't be patient; they know they can't afford to be. It will warm up again in your hemisphere and they think they have to seize their opportunity now. They're coming, Buford Stemp, and the question will be how you will handle it when they try to kill *you* and you must kill *them*. That will be the crucial decision and it's a profoundly moral one. To save them, you'll have to save yourselves."

Buford swallowed. Hard. "Who are you?" he whispered.

Ur shrugged. "Who are you, Buford Stemp?"

Turning from Ur, Buford caught sight of his reflection in the mirror. Behind the image of his own eyes staring back at him lay another, and another, and another … Buford looked away quickly and fought for air. "What are you?" he croaked. "A god?"

"No," Ur said, picking at a finger. "Actually, I don't know. I guess you might say, like everything, I'm a work in progress." Ur opened the car door and stepped out onto the pavement. She stretched and ran her fingers through her hair, which flickered like flame in the light breeze and bright light of the lot.

"Where are you going?" Buford asked.

Ur glanced up at the hills above Rio. "To see for myself."

"But why? It sounds as if you already know what's going to happen."

"What happens in the end is up to you. All of you, that is." Gently, Ur closed the door and began to walk toward the boulevard.

"What about Carmine?" Buford said.

"He and your friend, Mr. Limon, will be here soon," Ur said.

"But I thought your whole point was—"

"Tomorrow I'd like you to drive up into the hills, into the slums, with Carmine," Ur said.

"Where exactly in the—"

"You'll know," Ur said. "Carmine will be an actor in all of this. He'll have to make up his own mind. His decisions, and the decisions of others, will determine outcomes."

"And you? Aren't you interfering? Isn't that what Mattie—" Buford bit his lip and averted his gaze.

"Yes, she did. And, no, I'm not. We're catalysts, Buford Stemp, you and I. We participate in the process, not the outcome."

"We?"

" Mattie was self-indulgent. We can't afford to be." Ur ran her hand once again over the surface of the car and smiled her strange, tight smile. "At least not at the expense of others."

Ur walked toward the highway. "But where—" Buford began.

"Just drive downtown," Ur called back without turning around.

"Ur!" Buford shouted as she walked in front of an oncoming car. But she avoided it. Or did it avoid her? With graceful nonchalance, Ur crossed the broad boulevard, walking, it seemed, not through, but precisely between the traffic and disappeared into a crowd on the other side of the street.

"Bu!" he heard a voice call. Carmine and Limon were walking toward him. "Who in hell were you shouting at?" Carmine asked.

"Oh." Buford got out of the car. "Um," he pointed vaguely across the street, "someone almost stepped in front of a bus and I, you know …" Buford pulled a cigarette out of his pocket. "Got any fire?" he said to Limon, patting the sides of his shirt. Limon lit the cigarette for him. As Buford pulled it from his lips, Limon shot him a puzzled look. Buford's hand was trembling slightly. "Guess it shook me up a little. That woman stepping into the street and all."

"Shook *you* up?" Limon said.

Smiling sheepishly, Buford shrugged. "Say, Minnie, any luck finding the girl?"

"Not yet. But she's gotta be out there. I never saw anyone like her," Carmine said.

"No. I'd expect you hadn't," Buford said. "But it's late and we've got that early meeting with Faddle and the delegation tomorrow."

"Aw, Bu!"

"Minnie, we'll look for her tomorrow if you like. Give you a chance to see Rio before we head off to Brasilia."

Carmine scuffed his toe on the asphalt. "Awright. But shouldn't we at least go back to the bowling alley? You gotta get your boots back."

"Naw. Think I'll let that little fella keep my kicks. He fancied 'em and, uh, I got plenty more." Buford took a drag and glanced up at the sparse lights scattered across the *favelas*. "More'n him, anyways." He threw the butt down and ground it into the pavement.

"But Mr. Limon here probably needs a lift. His wife's probably wondering what happened to him," Carmine said.

"She knows what happened to me. She's used to this kind of thing. By now I'm sure she's home taking off her makeup," Limon said.

In front of the Copacabana, Limon hailed a cab. "I'll see you in the morning," he said.

"What'd he mean, he'll see us in the morning?" Carmine asked as the taxi drove away.

"Just doing his job," Buford said.

"His job?"

"I'll explain," Buford said, handing his keys to the valet, and gazing one last time that night at Rio. Somehow, the lights that twinkled sparsely in the hills above the city seemed to Buford to be burning just a little brighter.

CHAPTER II

———

"Minnie," Buford said, as he hurried into Carmine's room, "c'mon. You know how John gets when somebody's late for a meeting."

"Yeah, I know. 'Carpe diem.' Or 'Time's money," Carmine said, slouching in his chair at a small breakfast table on a porch overlooking the beach. "Did you ever know anyone who could reel off more clichés than Uncle John?"

"Aphorisms."

Carmine draped an arm over the back of his chair and regarded Buford Stemp with interest.

"You heard me. Aphorisms. Concise formulations of basic truths or opinions."

"Who are you, Daniel Webster?" Carmine quipped, his eyes wide above a subtle smirk.

"Don't get smart with me, Minnie," Buford said, surprised at how much Carmine's comment had stung him. "I'm not as dumb as I sound sometimes." Buford pulled a pack of Luckys from his pocket and smacked it against the pad of his thumb. "Besides. I know you're a math genius and all, but you really shouldn't neglect other parts of your education."

Carmine's face fell and he blinked. "What in hell's gotten into you?"

Searching around for a moment, Buford spotted a pack of matches on a side table, stamped simply, "Copacabana," pulled a fag and fired up. "Nothin'," Buford snapped. "It's just that John Faddle is one hell of a man. And whether people think they're clichés or aphorisms or friggin' bullshit, I never met anyone in my life who lived by what he said the way John has. Or as he would say—"

"Practiced what he preached," Carmine finished. Both men smiled broadly.

"Yeah," Buford said, "that's right. Now, let's go or—"

"Bu. Come over here and sit down. We got—" Carmine glanced at his watch, "ten minutes."

"Minnie—"

"C'mon, Bu. It's just so beautiful, especially in the morning. Know what I mean?"

Buford's thoughts trailed their way back to the previous night, leaving tiny tracks in time, and Buford Stemp heard the sound of small, bright copper bells. "Yes," Buford said, sitting down at the dining table covered with crisp white linen and plates that flashed vivid tropical fruits. "I think I do. Guess it won't hurt."

"Gotta 'stop and smell the roses' once in awhile," Carmine said.

"As Uncle John would say."

Spread below them across the boulevard was the great beach of Copacabana and, beyond that, the gleaming gray-blue of the South Atlantic. Thick yellow light, the color of small birds that flitted brightly onto and off of the slender porch railing in search of crumbs from the breakfast table, bathed the narrow balcony.

"Sure feels good, doesn't it, Bu." Carmine said. "When's the last time you felt the sun soak into your bones like this?"

"In 2018. '19, maybe."

Carmine nodded. Deftly with the tip of his spoon, he picked up a shiny black seed out of the papaya that squatted, burnt orange, on his breakfast plate, and cocking the spoon like a catapult, fired the tiny missile off the porch. With extraordinary skill, a big, red bird picked the seed out of midair and flew off toward the beach, chirping madly.

"That's just how everyone at this conference needs to behave," Buford said. "Like that bird, we all need to exercise our technical resources and we need to be opportunistic."

"First you're a goddamned philologist and now you're a philosopher," Carmine said.

"Philologist?" Buford said, feeling just a bit inadequate. He'd never felt inadequate before. He'd always been perfectly centered. A gust of wind racing in off the ocean slammed into the cream-white louvered doors that guarded the room, rattling them violently. Buford shuddered in syncopation.

"Carpe semen," Carmine said.

Buford thumped his palm on the table, rattling the breakfast dishes. "Goddammit, boy! Can't you keep your mind on anything but—"

"Easy, Bu. It means 'seize the seed.' A little, you know, play on words. It's Latin. I mean, it's not declined properly but ..." Carmine popped a piece of mango into his mouth. "See? I didn't neglect my education like you thought."

"I guess you didn't at that," Buford said, crushing his cigarette butt against the heel of his boot.

"Where do you suppose she is, Bu?" Carmine asked.

"She's out there, all right," Buford said.

Leaning forward, Carmine planted his elbows on the table. "You know something I don't? Do you know who she is?" Carmine said, his voice rising.

"Maybe. Maybe not. I'm not really sure what I know." Buford shrugged. "Say, Minnie, flick another one of those seeds at that palm."

"Huh?"

"Just do it."

Carmine shrugged and flicked a seed off his spoon. With one fluid movement, Buford whipped what looked like a pen from his shirt pocket, aimed and a blue ray shot from the tip of the pen and incinerated the seed.

"Bu!" Carmine exclaimed, "what the fuck was that?"

"I dunno. Some goddamned toy invented by Professor Corey Irwin."

"*The* Corey Irwin?" Carmine said.

"Yup. An X-ray laser. Xaser he calls it. I haven't had a chance to practice with it much. Anyway, up, go, vamoose. The old man'll be plenty pissed as it is." Sullenly, Carmine picked up a whole spoonful of papaya seeds and launched them at the top of a tree that grew just below the porch, sending a half dozen birds airborne in a screeching, tweeting panic. "After the meeting, Carmine, we'll drive into Rio. We'll find her. Or she'll find us."

* * *

"And so—" As hard as they had tried to be discreet, Carmine and Buford's entrance into the committee meeting had stopped John Faddle in mid-sentence.

It was as if someone had thrown a cold, damp towel over everyone in the room. Beneath eyebrows that bristled like steel wool over his thick, black glasses, the great John Faddle's gray-green eyes tossed about like a nasty sea and washed over them like stormy surf. "Goddammit!" Faddle shouted, pounding his fist on the table and sending a bowl of sliced mango splattering all over the pure white, starched tablecloth. "Out whoring around last night, I expect, all over the Copacabana, Carmine? Eh?"

"Actually, it was Ipanema, Uncle John," Carmine said.

"Don't get smart with me," Faddle said in a tight whisper. "And don't try to soft soap me with that Uncle John crap!" Buford Stemp marveled at the man's masterful use of histrionics. No wonder he'd been such a great salesman, then a great politician in the world's toughest, though arguably most idiosyncratic, city—New York.

"Early bird catches the worm," Faddle said, "early bird catches the worm," then glanced at his watch. "Only five minutes late this morning, Carmine. That's an improvement." Wrapping his great hands around the arms of his wheelchair, Faddle peered over the tops of his glasses, his eyes now flat and placid like a pond at dawn. All around the conference table shoulders slumped, jaws slackened. A woman stretched her neck then took off her jacket, folded it carefully and draped it over the back of her chair. A man stifled a yawn. For what seemed like a very long time Faddle did not speak, nor did anyone dare to break the silence he had imposed with his own.

At last and as one, the table began to breathe, chests rising and falling in unison, nostrils flaring. Once, over a few bourbons, Buford had asked Faddle how he'd gotten to be so goddamned effective at pitching people. "Lots o' tricks up my sleeve. Lots o' tricks." he'd said. "But once they start to breathe together, you know you got 'em."

The sun slipped over the top of a large grove of palms that sat alongside a walkway outside the meeting room. A cool, gentle breeze lifted the curtains that framed the sliding doors and brushed everyone's cheek. The woman blinked. A man rubbed his neck.

"Improvement," Faddle said, slowly and softly. "That's what we're after. Small gains. Just like our Minnie here." Carmine winced. "Used to be he'd miss meetings entirely. Then he'd be twenty minutes late. Now it's five. Would I have liked to toss him out on his ass? You bet. But Carmine has value, and so I maximized his resources subject to the constraints of his character."

"But John," said Harold Krumpp, a delegate from the Heartland Confederation, "if the Mexicans don't ease their immigration restrictions sufficiently, we'll simply be left with too many people. They'll either freeze or starve."

"Now, now, Harold," Faddle said gently, "no one's gonna freeze to death. We've got plenty of coal to keep that from happening and—"

"And as for starvin'," said Elmer Pitkin of the Rocky Mountain Republic, "there's still plenty o' game. All you gotta do is shoot it. Or is that too offensive for some of your constituents, Harold?"

"Now, listen here, Daniel Boone—" Krumpp began.

"Yeah, that's all well and good for you," shouted Q'peesha Parks from the Atlantic Seaboard States, "but y'all got only six million people out there in those godforsaken hills and poor Harold here, he's got sixty!"

"Fine," said Elmer Pitkin, "then why don't you start shipping some Care Packages full of your precious Bull-Kelp?"

"'Cause the water's too goddamned cold to grow enough for our own people, that's why," said Q'peesha, the large gold rings that hung from her ears swaying in time with her voice. Abruptly, she turned and began shaking her finger at Faddle. "And that also is why you gotta tell these motherfuckin' jungle bunnies down here that either they give us a million hectares off the coast to farm Bull-Kelp or we'll take it!"

"Why Ms. Parks," said Elmer Pitkin in a tone of mock surprise, "I never realized. I may recommend you for Honorary Colonel in the Rocky Mountain Militia." Q'peesha Parks harrumphed.

John Faddle tsked, shaking his massive head, wreathed in old age by a small garland of steel-gray hair. "*Jungle bunnies.* My, how the shoe that pinched for so long seems to fit the other foot so well. Shoe's on the other foot now. That's what's happened. Shoe's on the other foot. The Southern Hemisphere now has something that we need. Not just something we want, like cheap labor and raw materials. But something we need." Faddle leaned forward and folded his arms on the table in front of him. "Desperately. They have room for our surplus population. Not in the cities, that's for sure. But they have land that's *warm*. And they have warm oceans to grow the food we need."

"And they've got oil," said Elmer Pitkin.

"And we've got coal," Faddle shot back.

"Which they'll tell us we have to stop burning," said Harold Krumpp. "That's a hot one," Krumpp finished, laughing weakly. "We told the Chinese that earlier in the century while we encouraged the Latins to burn down the whole goddamned Amazon." "Chinkies don't give a shit about anybody but themselves," Pitkin grumbled, then spat a wad of dip into his coffee cup.

Faddle regarded Elmer Pitkin for a moment until he began to fidget. "Shoe's on the other foot now," Faddle said again. "Yessir, shoe's on the other foot."

"Doesn't sound like the old John Faddle to me," Elmer Pitkin said. "Why, twenty years ago you would've gone into the Middle East with both guns blazing."

"Just like your Minute Men or Soldiers of Christ or whatever the hell they called themselves did just about ten years ago. A dozen of them air-dropped into Riyadh with a small nuclear device strapped to the chest of their fearless commander."

"Now, John, be careful. Tubbs was a brave man," Elmer said.

"Yes, he was. And just a little bit foolish," Faddle said gently. "The TNT blew but the SND malfunctioned. A dozen good men, or pieces of them, scattered over ten square miles of Saudi desert."

"Because of you," Pitkin said, pointing a finger at Faddle, his hand trembling slightly, his face beginning to glow a very bright shade of crimson against his very blond hair. "Because of you and all of your lily-livered East Coast pinkos."

"As for lily-livered, you're right, Elmer. Which is why we were given what was left of the nuclear arsenal. Two subs. The Twin Towers. Only to be used in extremis. Only in extremis."

"And what in hell do you call our situation now, if it ain't *extremis*?" said Q'peesha Parks.

"We're converting oil and gas plants to coal as fast as we can. And nobody's freezin'," Faddle said, glancing at Harold Krumpp. "We've got enough Bull-Kelp, barely, but enough, along with whatever surplus the New Confederate States will sell, to feed our populations. And the Californians are building desalination plants to cope with the drought." Faddle's face was tickled by a small smile. "Where in hell are the Californians, anyway?"

"The beach. Where else? I reminded them at least a half-dozen times about this meeting, but of course, they forgot," said Brian O'Reilly from New England and the Rhode Island and Providence Plantations.

"There are people," Faddle said, with a chuckle, "that are sensible in their complete insensibility. You have to love their motto, 'What Ice Age?' Why, they've all thrown away their surfboards and turned them in for snowboards."

"They're screwballs," Pitkin said. "Dangerous screwballs."

Faddle shrugged. "Maybe. But they're adaptable. Which is what we need to be. Adaptable and willing to build on marginal gains. The Californians are like the grasshopper and we're like the ant. Yessir. But they've found a way to beat the winter. They simply pretend it doesn't exist. We need to think like grasshoppers and behave like ants. That's it. That's the formula."

"I'll tell you what the problem is," Harold Krumpp said. "You are the *old* John Faddle. Too old."

With that, Faddle wrapped his hands around the edge of the table and pushed himself away. Slowly, he lifted himself out of his wheelchair. "Uncle John!" Carmine began, making a move in Faddle's direction.

"Siddown," Faddle said. "I'll tell you when I need help." A cloud passed in front of the sun. The room dimmed for a brief moment, and a chill breeze cut through the palms along the promenade. Q'peesha Parks put her jacket back on.

"You all listen to me," Faddle said. "I may be old and I may not be the brightest bulb on the tree. Probably not by half. But I'll tell you one thing. There's no U.S. of A. anymore, but if we don't pull together there never will be again." Faddle looked at Pitkin. "'Don't tread on me'? *'Join or Die!'* I say. If we only follow our own narrow interests we're done. That's why we need to speak with one voice. That's why they put someone in charge. That someone's me and I'll tell ya what we're doing.

"We're gonna ask for easing of immigration restrictions in South America and we're going to ask for a million hectares of ocean, Q'peesha. And we're gonna take what we get and then come back next year and ask for more.

"And we're going to give them some of our gold and we're gonna give them our technology. And do you know why? Because when people have something to live for they don't want to fight.

"And we are going to ask them for oil and if they don't sell it to us, or give it to us, we'll burn all the coal we need to burn and to hell with them. 'Cause if *we* die, *they* die. They cannot succeed without us.

"That's it." Faddle eased himself back down into his wheelchair with a grunt. "The planes leave at 7:00 a.m. tomorrow. Don't miss them."

Carmine got up and moved carefully but quickly to Faddle's side. "Uncle John, can I take you—"

"No. You go out and enjoy yourself, Minnie. You're young," Faddle said with a gentle smile. "Explore Rio. And soak up some sun; it'll be your last for a while."

"Okay, Uncle John, but if there's anything—"

"Go, go," Faddle said gruffly.

Buford was leaning against the wall and watching the members of the delegation file out. "Well, Bu, let's go," Carmine said.

"Sure. Let's," Buford said, frowning.

"What's wrong?"

"Oh, nothing. Let's go find that girl." Carmine grinned broadly.

To be young again, Buford thought, smiling a small, private smile somewhere deep within. But then a dark thought flattened it. To hell nothing's wrong. He had heard Parks and O'Reilly as they filed out. "Who's gonna tell him?" Parks had asked. "I'll do it," O'Reilly said. And Buford Stemp had also noticed that each member of the committee breathed alone.

CHAPTER III

In front of the Copacabana, under a large, low portico offset against the hotel's grand front staircase, vans and limos and taxis scooted noisily into and out of its deep shade. Buford Stemp gestured toward his red Mustang, parked against a yellow brick curb opposite the valet stand. With a satisfied smile, the valet exchanged the keys for a fistful of crumpled *cruzeiros.*

"Let's drop the top and catch some rays," Carmine said.

"Or look at the stars," Buford replied, staring vaguely at a spot across the Avenida Atlantica and hard by the beach.

"Bu, what in hell's with you?" Carmine said, shaking his head as he rolled back the ragtop.

"May I help?" a voice said before Buford could answer.

"Ay, Jorge! Good morning," Carmine said cheerfully. "I guess you're our escort today, huh?"

"Escort, guide …" Limon fingered a bulge under his shirt. "Protection. Take your pick. Or all three."

"Morning, Jorge," Buford said laconically. Limon nodded.

"Say, Jorge. Why don't you hop in front?" Carmine said.

"I wouldn't be able to do my job. And this way I'll be able to keep an eye on both of you."

Carmine chuckled. "Yeah, or plug us both." Neither Stemp nor Limon moved a single facial muscle. Carmine cleared his throat and smiled a thin, nervous smile. "So, you checked him out, right, Bu?"

"Sure, kid. I checked him out."

"Carmine," Limon said, "the politics of our country, of the entire region, are very complicated right now. Some people wish to see the North, and especially what was once America, destroyed because of what they were, because of the simple passive arrogance of your former wealth and power. Others support you because if you collapse, a paradigm for their future collapses with you. And others, more pragmatic perhaps, simply view us as one nipple on the oil tit of the Islamic Axis. They'll do anything Al-NoSide tells them to do. It's not simply that there are factions. Things are *very* unstable. Constituencies are temporary. So, trust no one implicitly. Use your instincts." In silence, Limon helped Carmine snap the boot in place. "But, it is a lovely day and I believe we might even have some fun searching for the mysterious and beautiful redhead, eh?"

"Auburn," Carmine said, putting on his shades and turning back toward Limon. "Gotta get our description right if you're playing cops and robbers."

"Thank you. *Auburn*, an important qualification," Limon said.

Slowly, Buford followed a ragged caravan of taxis and vans trundling down the wide drive that led away from the Copacabana. The intersection with the Avenida Atlantica was gorged with flowers, brilliant bunches of reds and yellows and pinks that spilled over the curb. Buford smiled. Buford blinked. *What in hell is with you, anyway, Stemp? The kid's right. One minute I'm fillin' up, ready to burst, the next I'm dead squashed flat. Feel like a fucking accordion.*

The light was green and Buford decided that he wasn't going to miss it. Dropping the gearshift into second, he popped the clutch and squealed out into traffic, leaving a five-meter strip of rubber, dusting the lumbering buses and barely, just barely, taking the corner on all four wheels.

Carmine squeaked, grabbed the chrome frame of the windshield.

"Ain't these old cars somethin'," Buford shouted above the roar of the engine. "None of those bullshit titanium dioxide batteries or propane horseshit that'll take you from zero to sixty in ten minutes."

"This is a magnificent machine," said Limon.

As Buford shifted smoothly into third, he caught Carmine out of the corner of his eye, fumbling around the sides of his seat. "Whatcha lookin' for, boy?" Buford said. "Your balls?"

"Funny, Bu," Carmine said, his head buried between his seat and the door. Carmine held up a short strap. "What do you do with this?"

"Old-fashioned engineering. Goes around your waist. Here, let me help you," Buford said.

"That's okay. I can—" with that, Buford dropped the car back into second and jammed the accelerator to the floor, throwing Carmine flat against the seat. In a flash, Carmine secured the buckle.

"What the hell was that for?" Carmine shouted irritably.

"Necessity, boy. The great mother of us all," Buford said. "Didn't you ever study mechanics, boy? Gravity—"

"Is equivalent to acceleration," Limon chimed in.

"That's right," Buford said, smiling. "Imagine. Here you are, Minnie. A goddamned *bona fiday* fuckin' math prodigy. And two old broken-down spooks gotta instruct you on the very goddamned basics of fucking physics. Pathetic." Buford pulled a cigarette from his shirt pocket and scratched his cheek with the butt end. "Hit the lighter for me, will ya, Minnie?" Sullenly, Carmine punched the lighter with his thumb. "I was just tryin' to help. Make ya more stable-like. Whaddaya figure, Jorge? Added a couple of kilos—"

"Five, at least," said Limon.

"Right. Five kilos to that candy ass of yours." Buford chuckled as he stuck the Lucky in his mouth. The lighter popped up. "Say, light this for me, will ya, Minnie? Wouldn't want to take my hands off the wheel. Too dangerous." Buford drew in a large lungful of smoke and exhaled it through his nose. Blue-gray wisps sailed over his head to mingle with the fumes that swirled above the roadway.

"Call me Chocolate Cheeks, but how about cruising into the right-hand lane. The slow lane, Bu."

"Sure thing—" Buford hesitated, taking another drag on his cigarette. "Chocolate Cheeks." The two older men laughed coarsely above the road noise and Buford flipped his turn signal and eased the car over in front of a fat orange bus that lumbered along on the local route, most likely.

"Laugh if you like," Carmine said, "but I've got *no* interest in having my brains splattered all over Copacabana beach."

"Goddammit, Candy, didn't you know that your pa used to ride his Harley all the hell over Idaho when he was courting Clara? And Vinnie never wore any candy ass helmet. Even in the winter."

"No self-respecting Brooklyn Guinea would think of messing up his hair. Say, Bu, give me a—"

Buford pulled the pack from his shirt pocket and offered Carmine a cigarette. "When did you start smoking?" Buford said.

"I just smoke when I'm nervous. Or hammered," Carmine said.

"Ya nervous?" Buford asked with a sly smile.

"Dunno." Carmine fired up. "Say, Joe," Carmine turned around and draped his arm casually over the back of his seat, "speaking of candy, what in hell is that sweet smell in the air?"

"Candy," Limon said laconically.

"Huh?"

"Sugar, young man. In Brazil, there is sugar in everything. In the gasoline, in our liquor. It's even said the women drip sugar, if you know where to tap the tree. We even named that mountain after it," Limon said, pointing at Sugarloaf, bursting out of the sea and into the yellow sunshine like a great gray whale.

More slowly now, Buford steered the car through the gentle curve of the long, wide boulevard that bordered the beach. A single strip of median, lush with jade-green grass and planted with palms, fruit trees and thick, low broadleaf bushes, seemed to nudge them toward the sea.

In silence, the men smoked and began to breathe as one. Settling back in his seat, Buford gulped a large draught of air. "God, Minnie, smell that air, will you? There is no air on the planet, not anywhere I've been leastways, and I've been around, that smells like Rio's. Isn't that so, Jorge?" Buford asked rhetorically, gripping the wheel tightly with both hands. "I mean, it's all sugar and, and salt— Minnie, can you taste the brine? You could lick it off your lips. Yessir, sugar and salt and, and ..."

"And pussy," Limon added. "There are no women like the Carioca."

"By God, you're right, Jorge!" Buford shouted. "There are no women like the Carioca. Mostly." Buford relaxed his grip on the wheel and his shoulders slumped slightly. "And no air either. Sugar and salt and damp, moist earth. Not like Idaho. There the dust slices your nose like a knife. The air is acrid, like flint. It bites." Suddenly the hairs stood up on the back of his neck. A remembered smell launched from his memory, and it was not just the odor of Idaho.

What in hell is with you, Buford Stemp? All morning his feelings had flipped wildly. Clara, one of the Street's legendary traders, once told him that when markets are ready to make a big move they often get skittish, vacillating wildly but narrowly until—

"Bu!" Carmine shook Buford free of his thought. "We've been talking to you. Jorge says we're coming up on a main intersection in a mile or so and we have to make up our minds. We can either stay on the Atlantica and sail out to the end of the beach," Carmine said, describing a soft, slow arc with his arm, "or bail out and head downtown." Buford shifted in his seat, moving his head gently from side to side, listening to a sound only he could hear. The delicate sound of his vertebrae grinding and snapping in his ears.

"You know where she is, don't you, Bu," Carmine said, flipping his cigarette out of the car, where it hit the roadway, bouncing and rolling and sending up a hundred tiny red-orange sparks. "You saw her last night, didn't you."

Buford slowed the car a little and hung his arm over the door. Behind them, the fat orange bus began to blow its horn. "Well, Minnie, which way'll it be? You decide," Buford said on a hunch.

Carmine looked over his shoulder at the gleaming white mass of Rio, all concrete and stucco and glass; then, almost cautiously it seemed to Buford, he let his eyes track up the hillsides, unspoiled and luscious green a century before, now covered with cardboard and tar paper and tin, glowing dully under the morning sun. But Carmine glanced away quickly and stared straight ahead and up the beach. His features relaxed. "I don't think she's up there," Carmine said, waving vaguely at the *favelas*. She belongs out there on the point. Solitary. Beautiful. Let's—"

With a roar, the fat orange bus lumbered by, nearly clipping the Mustang's rear fender. The driver was hot, screaming at Buford as he passed.

"What's he saying, Jorge?" Buford asked. "I got the *merda* but—"

"Bu, look!" Wildly, Carmine shook his finger at a figure sitting by a rear window. Auburn hair, catching rays of the sun, burst into flame. Brilliant cobalt eyes crackled and a soft smile insinuated itself across her full, pale lips.

As the bus bellowed by, Buford swallowed hard. Quickly, he pulled into the middle lane, feeling himself drawn along by the mysterious creature whose hair flamed like a torch through the back window. "Well, Carmine, the great thing about life is that most of the time, it makes your decisions for you. Whether you know it or not." With a snap of his wrist, Buford flicked the turn signal and followed their future into downtown Rio.

But following the large orange omnibus and its copper-topped cargo turned out to be a greater challenge than Buford Stemp had expected. The Rio of the Forties turned out to be a far more complicated affair than he remembered.

Or was his memory faulty? Or worn smooth in spots? Buford glanced in the rearview mirror. A pair of blue eyes, pale but piercing, stared back, each one surrounded by a fan of folds. A short, thick mat of gray-white hair bristled above them at attention, standing sentinel. But over what? Did the skin and the hair belie the eyes? Or was it the other way around?

Buford grabbed his sunglasses off the dash and slapped them irritably against his face.

"Bu! Watch it!" Carmine shouted.

Just in time Buford noticed the taillights of the taxi in front of them flicker and he stomped on the brake pedal, narrowly avoiding being sandwiched between the cab and a van that sat behind them, inches from their bumper, its horn blowing madly. Was he losing his skill as well?

"Jesus, that was close," Carmine said. "C'mon! We're losing her." The bus sat at a stop a full block ahead.

"I haven't lost anything." The red Mustang screeched around the taxi. Quickly, efficiently, Buford swerved from lane to lane, picking up a half-block on the bus.

As they drove through and were drawn along by the thickening traffic, Buford slowly gained on their target until after several blocks, he sat on its tail staring at the back of Ur's head, blazing like a penny in the sun one moment, glowing dully in the deep shade of a building the next.

Ur turned and regarded them; but this time she did not smile. Then she turned away.

"She saw us," Carmine said excitedly. "The bus should stop at the next corner. Pull over, okay?"

"Sure, kid," Buford said.

Carmine unbuckled himself hurriedly and vaulted over the door and onto the street, making for the bus at a sprint.

Queuing up behind an old lady, her face as black as the asphalt that paved the street, her head covered in a kerchief the color of ripe, red apples, Carmine rocked back and forth from foot to foot as the old woman struggled to lift her bags, filled with food, fruit and loot, up onto the first step of the bus.

"Is the boy blind?" Limon said.

"Preoccupied," Buford said.

"Or self-centered," Limon said dryly.

As if he'd heard their conversation, Carmine stooped over and helped the old woman with her bags. She turned and shot him a toothless smile. Limon and Buford laughed.

"So," Limon said. "Perhaps all is not lost. A selfless gesture."

Just as Carmine pulled himself up to the first step of the bus, the doors closed behind him. And as they did, the rear doors flew open and down stepped Ur onto the curb. Her movement must have caught Carmine's attention, for only a moment before the rubber stops on his door kissed, he saw her and his eyes opened like two hands from whose grasp something incomparably precious had slipped.

Ur was not wearing the Capris she had had on last night, Buford observed, but rather a short simple black dress with narrow straps across the shoulders and back. Buford was not sure he had ever seen something as lovely. Then he frowned. *Dirty old man.*

Ur slid into the crowd and allowed herself to be carried along by its momentum. Yawing as it pulled away from the curb, the fat orange bus tooted its way back into traffic and as it did, Buford laughed as he saw its front doors shaking, pounded in great futility by Carmine's fists.

"You watch the girl," Limon said tersely. I'll take the kid, in case there's trouble." Buford shot him a questioning look. "He'll bolt at the next stop. It's only a block away." Limon hopped out of the car.

Buford's frame tensed as he followed Ur's progress down the street. Focus, he thought. All of his instincts were on alert, flicked on automatically from decades of practice. Bobbing about like a bright autumn leaf on the surface of a stream, her head traced a desultory route across the width of the sidewalk until at last, as if grabbed by a powerful eddy, she swirled across the crowd and away from the street, ending up, in patient repose in front of a *churrascaria*.

Buford's ears pricked up and his nostrils flared. Liquid and musical, like a stream itself, the soft sounds of Carioca babbled brightly, bouncing off the buildings that contained the course of the crowd and, like steep canyon walls, reflected the voices back above the deep rumbling river of the street.

An open-air stand, its bins of fruit lolling on the sidewalk like a mottled tongue, belched, and its sweet breath perfumed the air with the scent of melons and mangoes and cherimoya. Nearby, Ur stood patiently. Pork, beef and lamb turned slowly on their spits. Randomly, bits of fat crackled and spattered, sending their scents curling through the crowd.

Buford's mouth began to water. Then once again, another odor pierced his nose. He winced at the smell of dust and dry bones. His stomach tightened and tiny rivulets of sweat coursed from his armpits, down his sides and across his ribs. Dust and dry bones and flint. And steel. The smells of battle. Often, he had accepted his own fear as simply another variable to be considered in a tight spot. For the first time in his life, Buford Stemp wanted to run.

Ur bit into her sandwich and her blue eyes flared. Chewing slowly at first, and then luxuriously, a tight smile flickered across her face. She gulped down the rest of the sandwich and sucked at her fingers greedily. Who is this creature, Buford wondered. Was she learning or was she leavening knowledge with experience?

As he watched her lick the last of the juice from the tips of her fingers, Buford felt his fear collapse. At that moment, he wished very much to close his eyes and listen to her sweet laughter, tinkling like tiny copper bells. But he knew his craft well enough and knew that he could not permit himself that indulgence.

As she dropped the small, greasy paper wrapper in a trash can, Ur laughed. Above the wild cacophony of downtown Rio, the sound reached Buford's ears and he knew he would never run away.

CHAPTER IV

———

Ponderously, the orange omnibus carrying Carmine rolled into the next stop.
Another bus, pulsing parakeet yellow, pulled up in front of the Mustang, belching
a thick, territorial cloud of blue-brown diesel and obstructing Buford's view of
Carmine and Limon.

Buford tried to crane his body across the passenger seat but realized that
the angle would obscure Ur from his field of view. Frowning, he looked directly
at Ur. She stared back, raising her eyebrows and shrugging her shoulders. Buford
allowed himself a subtle, wry smile. They weren't following her, for Christ's sake,
she was leading them.

Buford grabbed a pair of binoculars from the glove box and searched
quickly for Limon and Carmine. Limon had been right about trouble. Carmine
stood on the curb of the next block, arguing with a small gang, three to be
precise, of Rio street toughs.

Buford let go a long, low whistle. Their bodies were not merely tattooed,
but every square centimeter of skin had been dyed. One, deep feldspar red.
The second, cockatoo blue. The third, bright black. Against the background
were all manner of figures—dragons, snakes, spiders, piranhas—and slogans—
Fuck, Shit, I Eat Rita. Buford scowled. He knew enough Portuguese to figure
out NOHMS DIE, scrawled in silver on black across the chest of the tallest of
the three.

The hoodlums were shoving Carmine and he, intelligently and
surprisingly, Buford thought, was merely shouting back. Limon was negotiating
his way across the side street. He'd reach Carmine in time, Buford hoped. That
bunch looked especially nasty. Besides the graffiti, the boys sported eight-inch

spiked Mohawks and a piece of body jewelry Buford hadn't seen in the briefing clips. A small semicircular loop of thin wire was attached from earlobe to earlobe and behind their necks.

Limon stepped up onto the curb and burst through the bunch from behind, then turned to confront them, shielding Carmine with his own body. For a split second the horde advanced. Limon was talking. Fast. Soon and slowly, the three reached behind their heads and unfastened their garrotes.

For another long minute Limon alternately talked and listened, then nodded, grabbed Carmine by the arm and walked off the curb and back toward Buford. Cockatoo blue gave Carmine a parting shot, cuffing his skull with the back of his hand, the fingers studded with rings of all sizes and shapes. Carmine wheeled but Limon caught him and pulled him through the intersection. The last thing Buford saw was a black shoulder blade with the silver graffiti NOHMS DIE disappear into the crowd. For a few seconds the spiked Mohawks bobbed about, then dove into the crowd and disappeared.

Buford exhaled loudly and dragged his hand across his chin. Turning back toward Ur, Buford watched her down the last of a fresh juice, pale pink and orange. Papaya, most likely, and grapefruit. Ur licked her lips, set the cup back on the counter and cut effortlessly across the grain of the crowd, just as she had done the previous night on the Avenida Atlantica; just as Nick Beele had one winter afternoon in Sun Valley. Or so Jaq had told him.

Without so much as a casual glance at Buford, Ur stepped off the curb and into traffic. Carmine was yelling and gesticulating wildly. Having broken free at last of Limon's grip, he bolted across the intersection but slammed into the crowd as soon as he stepped onto the curb. From there on it was slow going. Carmine was swimming upstream.

Casually, Buford settled back in his seat to follow Ur's progress. With perfect aplomb, she strode across the street. Neither she nor the traffic deviated the smallest fraction of a centimeter from their trajectories. Ur stepped up onto the median, looking back down the street at oncoming traffic, and raised her arm.

"Bu!" Carmine was yelling, "Don't lose her!"

"Calm down, Minnie. No way we're going to lose her in that," Buford shouted back, cocking his wrist and casting a thumb in Ur's direction. Traffic had stopped dead behind a shocking pink Volkswagen, with fuzzy seats to match, that had pulled up to the median. More shockingly, all of the cars behind the pink VW waited patiently for Ur to get inside. No shouting, no honking, not the slightest indication of any effort to drive around the taxi. In respectful silence, almost in reverence, traffic in the other lanes rolled slowly by. The street became eerily quiet. Ur closed the door. The taxi blew its horn, a few bars of "The Girl From Ipanema," zoomed off and all hell broke loose again.

"What was all that about?" Carmine asked.

"Copper top seems to have that effect on traffic," Buford said.

"As does the Whore," Limon said.

"I'm sorry?" Buford said.

"Her cabbie. The Whore of Pavao," Limon said.

"What in hell does *she* do?" Buford said.

"As I just told you. Or so they say. And drive a taxi. Nobody fucks with her. At least, not when she's driving," Limon said.

"Bu, c'mon," Carmine said, jumping into the car. "Let's cut the bullshit. We'll lose her."

Buford checked the rearview mirror briefly and gunned it around the bus. "I don't think so, Minnie. Not unless she wants us to."

Amidst the yak of horns and the squeal of brakes, Buford squeezed the car into the middle lane. "All right, Candy Ass," Buford said, "we're in position for a perfect tail. Don't take your eyes off her."

Carmine turned and nodded at Buford. Buford's right hand shot out and snapped Carmine's head back around. "I told you not to take your eyes off her. Ya fucking deaf?"

Limon tsked. "Rookies."

Like feeder streams, the side streets continued to pour cars onto the Avenida Rio Branco, packing it ever more tightly. Buildings, gleaming white beneath the late summer sun, swam but refused to melt in their own reflected heat.

"So, Jorge, what was with the punks back there?" Buford asked.

"Just that. Punks. The new breed. They were cruising. A lot of delegates from the North are in town until the conference starts in the capital, and the kids pick them out. Rob a few. Maybe kill a few. Harass all of them. But these guys were different."

"I noticed. What was with the body jewelry?" Buford said.

"I didn't mean different in that way. But for your information, those wires are razor sharp. Cut your hand off if you grab them. They're daring you to jump them from behind.

"Anyway, something's up with those guys. They're going to Brasilia."

"How'd you get that out of them?" Buford asked.

"Same way I got them to give Carmine back to me. I told them exactly who I was and that I was merely keeping Carmine alive until we got to the conference. Kind of like a prize pig being saved for slaughter."

"A what?" Carmine squeaked.

"Keep your eyes on that car, Minnie!" Buford snapped.

"Anyway, they bought it." Limon finished.

"What else?" Buford said, looking at Limon in the rearview mirror. But Limon's face revealed nothing, and his eyes were hidden by dark glasses. Buford frowned.

"Nothing else," Limon said. But Buford did not believe him. "You'll have to be very careful, my friend." That, Buford believed.

"Bu, she's got her turn signal on!" Carmine cried. The street had split a few blocks back around the old Bolsa and had become a broad, one-way thoroughfare, lined with graceful palms. Buford eased over into the far left lane.

A few blocks ahead the pink taxi sat patiently at a red light. Seeing the light at his own intersection flash amber, he hit the gas. A cop, outfitted in paratrooper boots, a sub-machine gun slung casually across his back, stepped off the curb and snapped his arm up. Buford hit the brakes and screeched to a stop just short of the crosswalk.

"Glad you're wearin' your seat belt, Candy?" Buford said.

"I'm glad as shit right now. Hey! The taxi's turning the corner. We're gonna lose it! Let's go," Carmine said.

"We're not going anywhere," Buford said. The cop glared at them, twitched as if he was going to approach their car, then apparently changed his mind and waved the pedestrians onto the crosswalk.

Carmine slammed his palm against the car door. "Fuck shit!"

In the midst of the crowd were two more street toughs, one yellow, one orange. Almost casually, they slipped out of the crowd and approached the red Mustang. In tow was an altogether different pair, middle-aged, close-cropped black hair, nondescript casual clothes, sunglasses; and very large.

The pedestrians had finished filing across the street but the cop failed to signal the traffic to move on. It became very still. A solitary horn barked from someplace in the line behind Buford. The cop pointed his finger, adjusted his weapon and stepped out of the crosswalk, passing Buford without so much as a glance.

For a moment, the four toughs slouched sullenly against the car. Yellow hoisted himself up over the fender and sat on the hood. He said something to Buford. Buford shrugged and reflexively reached his fingers under the dash. His gun hung patiently, suspended by its clips. *Too risky.*

Yellow began to jabber at Limon. He couldn't make out much but "fuck" and "kill." Buford fumbled for a cigarette. He felt the xaser but left it alone. The 'toy' seemed as if it could be pretty handy, but he wouldn't be able to take out all four.

Orange circled around the front of the car and walked up to Carmine. His body was covered with all manner of black figures in bold relief against an orange background—jaguars, sharks, skulls, as well as graceful arabesques that were almost touchingly delicate. Almost.

Orange fingered Carmine's tropical shirt and smiled viciously, revealing something less than a full set of choppers. "Looks like a fuckin' pumpkin, eh Minnie?" Buford said, trying to break the tension. It worked. Carmine laughed. Orange didn't get it and grabbed Carmine's cheek between his fingers and squeezed the smile into a pout that matched his own.

Carmine flinched and Buford barked at him to sit still. He needn't have bothered. Limon froze everyone as he cocked the hammer of his pistol. Especially Buford, when he felt the cold metal of the barrel slip behind his right ear and up against his skull. The fingers of Buford's right hand twitched, but other than that he did not move.

As Limon talked the four thugs relaxed, nodding grimly all the time.

"We'll see you in Brasilia, then," Orange said. At least Buford was pretty sure that's what he said. As walked away, Limon lowered the gun.

Buford gasped audibly. "I don't know what the fuck that was all about, but thanks, Jorge. I think."

The cop strode past the car and up to the crosswalk, turned and glared once more at Buford.

"You're welcome, Buford Stemp. Now let's get the hell out of here. Fast," Limon snapped.

"So what the fuck was up with that?" Buford asked as he sped to the next light.

"Same shit as before with Carmine," Limon said. "Something's up."

"What'd you tell them?" Buford said.

"I told them the truth. I'm a government agent, I'm guarding you guys until we get to Brasilia and then I told them I was going to kill you. But if they wanted proof I'd blow your head off right then and there. And then I'd blow their heads off for fucking with me."

"Okay," Buford said, drumming the wheel with his fingers while the Mustang growled and bucked impatiently at the light. "Now which part of what you just said was the truth, Limon?"

Limon laughed as he pocketed his pistol. "None of it."

"So you're not an agent then?" Buford said.

"Oh, I'm an agent all right. It's just that with all of the doubling and tripling I get confused as to who I'm working for," Limon said.

"Know what you mean," Buford said. But he didn't. Not really.

"Bu, let's blow this light," Carmine said with a whine, squirming in his seat.

"Boy, you have a one-track mind. Say, light this fag for me, will ya?" Buford inhaled deeply. "Your old Uncle Buford almost got his brains splattered all over the windshield, Peter fucking Pumpkin Eater might have decapitated you with his earring and all you can think about is pussy." A green arrow blinked and Buford turned the car sharply, through the curve sweetly, away from downtown and up the side street that led into the hills.

The street lay open and oddly empty before him. The contrast with the broad flow of life through downtown came as something of a shock. Buford snorted a short, shallow burst of air into his lungs and involuntarily blinked hard. He lifted his left hand off the wheel and stroked the top of his head. What felt like tiny tendrils, warm, blue and electric, flowed through his fingers and down his arm. Casually, he draped the arm over the door.

Buford started to tell Carmine to search the side streets for the pink taxi but stopped himself when he saw the boy lifting himself off his seat, craning his neck and straining to stretch his gaze to its limits. Buford glanced in the rearview. Limon sat silently, his head lowered, polishing his pistol with the tail of his shirt.

An occasional car passed, but otherwise the way remained deserted, while to either side the narrow streets bulged with all types of traffic. Shoppers and hawkers swore and haggled. Cars poured into the street from behind, but ahead lay nothing. While yellow-white sunshine, Easter bright, lit the side streets, his own lay in light shadow, the buildings tilting, it seemed, falling toward one another. Another of Ur's tricks? Was she a trickster, as Mattie had been? Or, more precisely, Tiamat?

Steeper and steeper the street rose before him, until at last Buford could not see what lay beyond the crest. He settled back into his seat and smiled. *Well, well.* "Kinda makes Frisco seem like a pancake, doesn't it?"

"Bu, don't you think we ought to turn the car around?" Carmine said, breaking the silence, his voice squirming.

"Yes, the boy is right. We should turn around. Now," Limon echoed. His words, though, were rubbed raw by some unexpressed anxiety. Perhaps Limon was not as interested in finding Ur as he was in avoiding something that lay ahead of them, Buford thought.

A cranky horn tooted behind them and, with the irritating buzz of a lawnmower engine, the pink VW zoomed past —*"Tall and tan and young and ..."* Briefly, Ur turned and shot them her strange smile—teeth clenched—as the taxi roared up the hill.

"That settles that," Buford said laconically as he downshifted the car.

At the top of the hill, which was only the bottom of the next, they burst out of the shadows and into the sunlight, which cut across the road clean as a knife. Once more the buildings glistened glacier white.

Soon, the streets began to twist and turn. Stucco was peeling off the sides of the buildings in great chunks, like lesions caused by a lazy pathogen that slowly, but systematically, was destroying its host. Shops began to disappear, the bazaars below gone altogether, as if commerce were afraid of heights. Here and there the lone bodega sat squat, burrowed deeply into the sides of the buildings, as if frightened of something. Bits of paper blew about like ghosts whose teeth were set on edge by some awful anxiety, while everywhere shards of broken glass lay strewn about, sparkling like cheap zircons.

Little by little the vacuum was filled up with children. Children of every description, every size, shape and color. Hollow-eyed, bright-eyed. Wasted, fat. Barefoot, shod. They were there, then gone. Virtual children popping into and out of the void. But with every meter they climbed, always more.

Slowly the buildings began to lose elevation and clusters of tropical trees sprouted along the streets. Into and out of the dappled shade the red car raced, hot with fever on the scent of its elusive pink prey.

More and more aggressively, the roads began to twist and turn. Slowing through a turn, they were ambushed by a half dozen children, all snot-nosed and screaming, their grubby fists punching the air, yelling, "Presentes! Presentes!" Buford downshifted through the turn and left them behind, standing mute and perfectly still, but for their eyes which snapped greedily.

"We should turn around. Now," Limon said.

"What in hell for?" Buford asked.

"It's not safe."

"Safe? Since when is our job ever safe?" Buford said.

"You should listen more carefully. It is dangerous up here," Limon said.

"Tell ya what, another five minutes and we'll haul down our flag and head for home," Buford said.

"Aw, Bu," Carmine whined.

"Quiet, Candy, we're in charge of security," Buford said.

Around the next bend, all tall vegetation disappeared. Every square meter was packed with houses, hovels, shacks and shanties. A hundred meters beyond, the road ended abruptly, like a parched tongue, black and swollen, lolling in the dust. Cracked and crumbling asphalt gave way to simple dirt. Huts of baked mud and rude shelters made of tarpaper and tin lined the rutted, rocky path.

The Whore's VW sat at the end of the pavement. Ur was absent, but a tall woman with straight, striking brunette hair was entering the last house at the end of the street. A low, simple structure, it was nevertheless covered with a fresh coat of cream-colored stucco and resembled a mansion in comparison with the rest of the neighborhood.

Buford pulled up behind the taxi and set the emergency brake, which made a nasty, crunching sound. Glancing in the rearview, he saw Limon scrunched up, eyes averted, staring blankly across the road.

"Well, let's go introduce ourselves," Buford said, flicking his cigarette butt onto the blacktop. "C'mon, Minnie." Carmine was smoothing his hair, checking himself out in the vanity mirror. "C'mon, Jorge."

"I'll stay here if you don't mind," Limon said sullenly.

"Like hell. You're security. What if we're ambushed?" Buford said.

Reluctantly, Limon climbed out of the back seat. A group of children had already begun to gather around the cars. Buford reached in his pocket for loose change.

"Don't," Limon said, "don't encourage them." The children were smiling. They seemed to know Limon. He barked at them. They stopped as if startled, but only for a moment. Once again they advanced, girls giggling and boys yelling. Limon pulled out his pistol and waved it menacingly in the air. Buford frowned. Limon shouted angrily at the children and they backed away, then scattered, slowly, looking more hurt than scared.

Limon shoved his revolver back into his belt. "All right," he said, "you want to be introduced, I'll introduce you." He barged through the front door without knocking.

When Buford entered the house, he found himself at once in the living area. The space was very dark. Few windows had invaded the walls. All of them were small and most were shuttered; protection against the heat.

Buford's eyes struggled to adjust to the low level of light. A knot of four people stood in the center of the room. Ur and the Whore stood with their backs to Buford and Carmine. They were chatting in low but pleasant tones with the couple that, he assumed, owned the house. The woman was quite tall, the man at least a head shorter, and they were framed by double doors that led to a small, bright patio. The high glare of the equatorial late morning obliterated their features with brutal, brilliant backlighting. Jorge stood off to one side, arms folded, almost petulantly.

"Ah, Jorgezinho, would you be kind enough to introduce us to your friends?" the man said in impeccable English, but in a tone that felt overly formal.

"Certainly, Father," Limon said. Buford raised an eyebrow. "May I present Buford Stemp and Carmine." Limon gestured back toward his father., "Senhor Joao Limon, my mother Camilla, my sister Donna, the..." he winced, "and, I'm sorry, miss," Limon said, addressing Ur, "as you are aware you have me at a disadvantage ..."

Ur laughed. A light, sweet laugh like the sound of aspens rustling, tickling the wind with leaves made of pure, impossibly thin copper. "Of course," she said, "I am the one who should be sorry." Ur's laugh had slipped out beneath the patio doors. "My name is Ur." Carmine cocked his head and frowned. Then he shrugged and smoothed an eyebrow.

"Just Ur?" Camilla said. "One name. That's very Brazilian, you know. Oh! And are you Brazilian, Carmine?"

"No, ma'am," Carmine answered politely.

Buford's vision was adjusting to the light. Something about the elder Limon seemed familiar. The voice?

"Well, then," Limon said, "now that we have observed the formalities, I think we should be going. Will you come with us then, Ur? Carmine is most anxious not only to meet you, but also to spend the day with you."

"And I am even more interested in meeting him," Ur said.

"You are?" Carmine said, grinning not only from ear-to-ear, but from his hairline to his neck. Buford rolled his eyes. "Well, let's go, then," Carmine said, smacking his hands together and rubbing them briskly.

"I'm afraid I can't do that," Ur said. Carmine's face contorted, as if she'd just chopped off his right hand. "But I'd like to talk to you."

"Yes," Camilla said gaily, "let's do talk. It is so nice to have guests. I'll get some juice. Do you all like fresh juice? The papaya is wonderful this time of year."

"Yes, ma'am," Buford said.

"No, really, Buford—" Limon began

"So, what is it Jorgezinho? Eh?" Senhor Limon snapped. "Ashamed of us, of our home, where we live? Like always. You rarely come to visit and you never bring friends. It's always, 'No, I can't. Meet me in Rio here, meet me in Rio there.' Eh?" His voice was shaking.

Glaring at his father, Jorge clenched his fists but did not say a single word.

"Please, please, *caritos*," Camilla said, taking her husband's hand in her own, "don't argue. You always argue. If you must, save it for another time. We have guests. I'm sorry, *senhores*, we've been very rude."

Buford smiled. "Don't mention it, ma'am. I come from a large family and somebody was always yelling at somebody. There was lots of love, but that's not always where the strong feelings stopped."

"Buford, please, stay out of this," Limon said in a polite but firm tone, "and let's get out of this…this place," he finished, waving his hand vaguely, his words soaked through by some bitter, inchoate thought.

"There! There, you see?" the elder Limon shouted, "you are ashamed. Of us, of our home. Come on, admit it. You are ashamed. Just a little, no?" Limon did not answer but simply looked away.

"You two. All the time the same argument. Class warfare every time you step into the same room," Camilla scolded. Then with a gentle smile, she turned to Buford. Her eyes bored into his, but she did not say a word.

Buford rubbed his cheek and, drawing a deep breath, glanced around. The room was furnished simply, the walls a light, nondescript shade and empty but for a small picture that hung over a simple sofa covered with coarse, dark red fabric. Buford did a quick double-take at the picture, which showed an old woman, black as ink, squatting among baskets of fruit. She sported a bright red bandana and wore a toothless grin, just like the old woman that Carmine had helped at the bus stop.

Maybe all this old world needs is a simple act of kindness on occasion, Buford thought. *Kindness? Whatever is getting into you, Buford Stemp?*

At either end of the sofa sat a large armchair and a straight-back wooden rocker. Against the opposite wall a small television sat on a tiny table. The Virgin Mary cast a benign gaze on the TV from a small pedestal affixed to the wall.

A table and chairs sat offset against the doors leading to the patio, guarding the entrance to the cooking area. Gently, Buford sniffed and caught a whiff of yeast, a telltale that betrayed Senhora Limon's prowess in the kitchen. On the table sat a small laptop. Probably a rarity at this social elevation, Buford thought.

"I think it's very smart, ma'am," Buford said to Camilla. "Kind of reminds me of a place back home, in Idaho. Belonged to a good friend of mine. Name's Joe. Anyway, he likes things kind of simple. So do I, for that matter. Keeps the mind clear." Everyone stood stock still. No one made a sound. Buford wasn't at all sure anyone was breathing. "And, uh—" He glanced down. "There! This carpet. He's got one almost like it. More than one, actually. He collects them. Sells them, too. Indian Joe, they call him."

"You're right, Buford," Ur said. "This is very much like Uncle Joe's place, except for all the scratch sheets lying around."

"Scratch sheets? I'm sorry … " the elder Limon said.

"Um, they're, uh—never mind," Buford said. "Anyway, this place is neat. Yessir. Smart and neat and, uh—" Buford punched his left hand lightly, "straightforward." He'd shot his bolt.

"Keeps the mind clear. I like that," Camilla said.

"Oh, *favor*. Neat? Smart?" Limon said, his voice rising. "Thank you for being so polite, Buford Stemp, but look at this place. Why, the goddammed floors are dirt. Jesus, why do you live up here? You don't have to, you know. I told you that you could move down into the city any time. I'd take care of you."

"We don't need you to take care of us," Camilla said, throwing her shoulders back. "We can do that very well." She smiled. "This is all very interesting, you know, Senhor Stemp. Very pleasant. Usually, everyone ends up crying and running away. I find this talk most con, con—"

"Constructive, ma'am?" Buford ventured.

"Yes, that's it exactly. Constructive." Camilla walked up to Buford and took his hand in hers and patted it lightly.

Buford studied Camilla for a moment. Her eyes were jaguar black and her skin light caramel with few wrinkles. Her hair was black as well, streaked with gray. She still had a figure. Camilla must have been very beautiful once, he thought. Buford smiled. Bullshit, Buford Stemp, she still is.

"And you, Carmine?" Camilla said.

"Yes?" Carmine said.

"We haven't heard much from you yet. We need another opinion. They will be having their conference in the capital. We will have ours here. Maybe we can settle everything once and for all."

"Senhora," Buford said, "I think they could use you in Brasilia."

"Perhaps they will," Camilla said. Jorge shot her a puzzled look. "Plain talk. That's what is needed. Honesty. Not political *merda*. Excuse me. Things, *ideas*, differences need to be tossed into the air, you know? So, Carmine, please tell us, what do you think of our dirt floors and our neighborhood?"

Clearing his throat and drawing small circles on the carpet with his toe, Carmine squirmed.

"Yes, Carmine," Ur said, clenching her teeth in a smile. Drawn to her voice, Carmine looked up at Ur. For an instant only, a startled expression gripped his features, as if he'd just seen the girl of his dreams for the first time, only to discover that she had a wooden leg. Buford stifled a snigger. Carmine recovered. "Please, tell us," Ur continued, "what you think of the Limon's floor which, you understand, is only a metaphor, and what you think of their neighborhood. Which, you understand, is most certainly not."

Carmine's jaw hung slackly. He blinked. He closed his mouth. "Well," Carmine said, "The floors are dirty, but they're clean. I mean neat. You know." Carmine exhaled loudly. "Ay, fuggedaboutit. This is really a really nice place, you know. But …"

"But?" Camilla prompted.

"Well, you know, I think Jorge has a point about the neighborhood. I mean, it's, well, I mean, your house is beautiful compared with, you know—"

"There, you see?" Limon said, snapping his fingers. "Carmine agrees with me."

"I don't see," Ur said, and Limon appeared a bit crestfallen. "You said, Carmine, that their house is beautiful compared with—what?"

"Well, with, you know—" Carmine muttered.

"I don't know. And I'd like you to tell us. That's why I brought you here,"

Ur said, in a voice that grabbed the group by their collective throat. Flat, broad, sonorous. Startled, everyone looked at Ur and then, very slowly, turned their attention to Carmine.

"Look," Carmine said, standing stiffly, "I really don't feel comfortable about this."

"But why not?" Camilla said, placing her hands on her hips and smiling a very warm, very comforting, smile.

"Because," Carmine said, "I'm a guest in your home and you've asked me to comment on something that's of a personal nature."

"That's correct," Camilla said, "but I asked you, so the risk of your answer is mine."

"Yes," Carmine said, "that's true, but I think that the answer is also, um, political. And I'm a guest in your country and I'm not sure I have the right to comment on matters of class here." Carmine shrugged, satisfied that his argument had carried the day.

"Ah," Camilla said, "but you'll be talking about exactly that in the capital for the next week, no?" Carmine began to protest but Camilla held up her hand. "Besides, these are political times. None of us can escape them. And most great political events are driven by class, are they not? Often, class distinctions are disguised as racial or ethnic problems. But at the bottom of it all is the problem of wealth and, perhaps more importantly, the *opportunity* to create and acquire wealth.

"You know, you Anglos started something very important. A long time ago common people cornered a king and made him sign his name to a piece of paper that elevated their status. Then, much later, you came up with the brilliant but dangerous idea that all men are created equal. The last few hundred years have been spent expanding the very definition of 'men,' although many of your own people and most of the rest of the world have been dragged along kicking and screaming to accept a definition that grows broader by the year.

"So, Senhor Carmine, you cannot run from the question because the question of how my husband and I should stand in relation to our neighbors is one we can't avoid. It is embedded in our daily lives and it frames our entire existence. It has established the, the—ah, Senhor Stemp. Excuse me, Buford. Could you? I am just a simple person."

Jesus Fucking H Christ. What in hell is going on? "Excuse me, ma'am," he said, "but if you're simple then I'm the Pope. I think context is the word."

"Thank you, Buford. Yes, Carmine, politics is the context of our times just as it was a hundred years ago and a hundred years before that. Fascism, communism. They were both solutions, poor ones, it turned out, to problems of class and wealth and poverty. So—"

"What can I say?" Carmine said, shrugging his shoulders.

"You can answer my question," Camilla said, her black eyes, pouring like hot pitch over Carmine, cradled incongruously in the embrace of a sweet smile,.

Carmine cleared his throat and wiped a simple strip of sweat from his upper lip. "When we drove up to your house, it, well, it stuck out like, you know, a sore thumb. Or, or maybe it stuck out like a healthy thumb surrounded by a bunch of sore fingers. It's poor up here, Senhora. Very poor. If you can leave, why shouldn't you?"

"So," Camilla said, "do you not have poverty where you come from? Do you not know poor people?"

"Yes," Carmine said, "we do have poverty, but it's temporary. At least I think it is. And, no, I really don't know any poor people. But that's not the point."

"Isn't it?" Ur said, cocking her head to one side.

"I dunno," Carmine said. "But I do know that it's scary."

"Scary? Yes, it is scary," Camilla said.

"Right," Carmine said, his voice gaining courage. "I mean, the problem's so big. You stand outside your home, Senhora, at the end of the pavement, and look up the hill. Look left, look right—fuggedaboutit! As far as you can see—almost, anyway—nothing but shacks. And, from some research I did before we came, they just keep creeping up the hill, year after year.

"But more than that, it's the kids. Did you see those kids out there? Bu, did you see them?" Carmine asked. "Some tall, some short, but all skinny. I mean, like emaciated. Some kids had sores, all of them were filthy. Their clothes, rags really, you know, were filthy. But all of them, I mean all, had this hungry look. Like the ghost of Christmas Future."

"Ah, Dickens," Camilla said. Buford just stared at her in wonder.

"Right," Carmine continued. "He opened up his robes and two kids stood there. Eyes wide. Hungry. One was Ignorance and one was Want. That's what I see when I look at those kids. Jeez!" Carmine visibly shivered.

"You don't think we should try to help?" Camilla asked. "Even in a small way?"

Carmine shook his head. "The problem's too big. Get out. Jorge's right. Just get out."

"If we move off the mountain, the *favelas* will eventually slide down the slope and bury us. Get out? Walk away from the problem?" Camilla said. "Just as the North has done for centuries? Well, that time is over. Now the problem, I'm afraid, is about to walk right up to *you*."

Buford saw Carmine's hand shaking slightly. In the cool, soft silence of the room, all that could be heard were the sounds of breathing. Not in unison, but each according to its own, regular rhythm. "Carmine," Ur said at last, walking up to him and taking his hand in hers, "let's take a walk."

"Sure," he said softly.

"Ah," Ur said, "just a moment. Senhora Limon, may I speak with you?"

"Of course," Camilla said.

Beneath the serene gaze of the Virgin and off to the side, the two women spoke in low voices. "But, I couldn't," Camilla was heard to say.

"That, as you know, is not accurate," Ur said, in that commanding tone. "You are able to. The question is *will* you. It can be arranged. Jorge will do it." Limon's eyes flared but, interestingly, he did not object, Buford observed. You should understand that it will be dangerous. So, you—" And once again the women's voices dove several decibels.

"I will talk to my husband and son," Camilla said. They frowned.

"I'll stay here?" Buford asked rhetorically, suspecting his role.

"Thank you, Buford Stemp," Ur said, taking Carmine's hand once again.

Silently, Buford watched as they walked out of the house with Donna, the Whore, in train. Everyone, it struck Buford, seemed to know what to do.

The front doorway framed a crucible of withering, white heat. Buford blinked and squinted through the glare until at last the three were swallowed up by the blinding light and the door closed quietly behind them.

CHAPTER IV

———

"Whoa," Carmine croaked as he fumbled for his shades, "I don't know which is worse, the light or the heat." Carmine squinted, even through his dark glasses, at the sunlight reflecting off the dry dust, and the white tin that seemed to be stretched taut over the hills that sprawled above and about them.

"Why, Carmine," Ur said, "I would have thought this would have been a welcome change from your climate."

"Yeah," Carmine said, chuckling, "so would I. Guess you have to be careful about what you wish for."

"Yes. You do. That's a good thought, Carmine. Remember it," Ur said, stepping off the pavement and onto the dirt path that wound through the shanties.

"Where're we going?" Carmine asked, his toes nailed to the edge of the asphalt. From behind buildings and around corners, the children stared. Dark eyes, like blinds drawn over deep secrets.

"Come," Ur said gently.

Swallowing hard, Carmine stepped onto the path, sending up tiny clouds of bright dust. Suddenly, from all directions, the children emerged into the sunlight, some even dropping like ripe fruit from trees stunted by the wind and poor soil. Carmine began to retreat. "Don't you think—" he said.

"Donna!" Ur shouted. At the top of her lungs, the Whore began bellowing at the children in a voice without malice but with clear consequences. Slowly at first, and then faster, faster, the children began to gather around her. Black eyes brightened, hollow, hungry holes burst into broad smiles in chain reaction.

The Whore tossed a few pieces of candy into the air and the taller boys caught them all. The Whore glared at them, her eyes flashing, but like her voice, without malice. With reluctance, but also gently, they offered the candy to the younger boys and girls, who accepted it with smiles and the high, soft hum of "*obrigados.*"

Donna glanced at Ur, nodded, and tossed her head and her gaze up the road. Once more, Ur took Carmine's hand and together they walked slowly up the dirt track that cut through the *favela.*

With no particular urgency, Ur and Carmine ambled up the road in silence, crossing from one side of the road to the other to benefit from the shade of vegetation that hadn't been cleared. As they climbed, children popped out of the shanties, but paid no attention to Ur or Carmine as they ran past, screaming and giggling to join the crowd collecting around the Whore, who lagged a few tens of meters behind.

Carmine stopped, his nose wrinkling. "What's that?" he asked.

"The wind's changed," Ur said, then pointed down a narrow alley between two rows of shacks. Fifty meters away the space opened up. "A midden," Ur said, pointing at a large pile of trash. "It's worse when they burn it."

Carmine looked around. "Where do they get their water?"

"Ah," Ur said, "do I detect some interest in conditions up here?"

"Just intellectual curiosity," he said edgily.

Pressing her lips together, Ur nodded. "Here," she said, stooping over and lifting the plywood cover off a shallow, galvanized aluminum tub. "Rain."

Carmine turned away and exhaled. "Jeez," he said, "the smell's not too bad but what in heck is the green slime floating on top?"

"Just some algae. Doesn't seem to cause any serious problems. Their guts are pretty well used to it. If it doesn't rain for a while, that's another issue. The dysentery gets pretty bad. Many die, especially children and the old ones. This stuff is probably okay, but I wouldn't suggest you try it."

"Don't worry," Carmine said.

A few meters farther on they approached a small hill. "Come," Ur said, taking both of Carmine's hands in hers and leading him to the crest. Standing beneath a squat palm, she gazed out over the *favelas* from their modest vantage. "What do you see?"

"You," Carmine said, turning Ur around to face him and staring deeply into her impossibly wide cobalt eyes. Letting one hand fall softly, he placed it on her buttocks and drew her toward him, then, even more softly, pressed his lips to hers and held them there for a long, lingering moment. At last, he drew back, sucking in a large breath of air, and turned away, as if he could no longer bear the intensity of her gaze. "Well?" he said, looking beyond the *favela* at the sparkling sea.

"Well?" Ur replied, sounding slightly puzzled.

Carmine turned to her. "Well, did you like it?" he asked in a chafing tone.

Ur pursed her lips and picked at a finger. "Yes," she said.

Carmine's face burst into a grin as he placed his hands on Ur's shoulders. "Step two," he said.

Ur took Carmine's hands off her shoulders. "Step two?"

Carmine frowned and fidgeted. "Well, yeah. You know."

"I don't."

"Well—" Carmine cleared his throat. "I, I've always kind of looked at love making as a do-it-yourself kit. You know. Step one. Step two. You know. Then, botta bing!"

"Botta bing?"

"Yeah. Botta boom, botta bing. It's an old Brooklyn expression. It means—"

"I understand," Ur said.

"You do?"

"Certainly, I do. Love is like an Erector set," Ur said, glancing down at Carmine's trousers.

Self-consciously, Carmine thrust his hands into his pockets. "Erector set?" he mumbled, avoiding Ur's eyes.

"Yes. It's an old-fashioned toy. Strips of metal and nuts and bolts. Uncle Nick gave me one. He told me that it would be good for visualization."

"Oh, Uncle Nick." Nicholas Beele. A tiny cloud floated across Carmine's consciousness. "But you liked, um, the kiss?" Carmine asked, his intonation rising along with all of his other expectations.

Ur cocked her head and appeared to consider his question for a moment. "No."

"No? But you already said you liked it," Carmine said.

"It was pleasant, yes. But no. In the sense you mean, no, I didn't like it," Ur said. Carmine frowned deeply. "I'm sorry. I do like you, you know, and the kiss was very pleasant. I told you that."

"Pleasant? Great," Carmine said. "That's a start."

"Carmine, is it uncommon in your experience to be refused by women when you attempt to convince them to have sexual intercourse with you?"

"You get right to the point, don't you? Yeah, all right, it's uncommon. In fact, it's fuckin'—I'm sorry." Carmine's face flushed crimson. "It's, uh, unprecedented." Grinning sheepishly, he shrugged his shoulders. "Almost, anyway."

"Well," Ur said, "I can understand why. You're very good looking."

Carmine's eyes widened. "So, there's hope then?"

"Why, Carmine, your language anticipates a Shakespearian turn of phrase, I think" Ur said.

"You know Shakespeare?"

"Oh, yes. He's very nice," Ur said.

"He's—what?" Carmine said.

"Carmine," Ur said, taking his hand. "Look out there." In a great arc Ur swept her arm across the entire scene that lay sprawling before them. "What do you see?"

"I see you," Carmine said. He hadn't taken his eyes off her.

"That's very nice, Carmine, but what do you see—out there?"

Thrusting his hands more deeply into his pockets, Carmine turned away from Ur, set his jaw and squinted. "Well, I see—the sea." He laughed weakly. Ur did not respond. "And, um, Sugarloaf and, uh—" he turned back to face Ur, "and you."

"That's it?"

"Yeah, that's it," Carmine said.

With a very graceful movement, Ur ran her fingers through her short, auburn hair. Carmine stared at her hand as it passed over her head. The fingers were delicate and very, very long. "All right, then, Carmine. Tell me about the *favela* that's sitting right in front of us."

"Look" Carmine said, "if this is about that conversation we had back at the Limons'—"

"That's exactly what this is all about," Ur said, her voice flat and cold and gray as the roof of tin that lay below them in the shade of a tree. "In fact, in a very short while everything will be about this *favela*. Metaphorically speaking, of course. Or perhaps it would be more accurate to refer to this neighborhood as a synecdoche." Ur looked directly at Carmine. His jaw hung slack. "A synecdoche is—"

"I know what a synecdoche is. I've read the classics," Carmine said.

"Good. Uncle Nick would be pleased."

Carmine gave his head a shake, as if everything had suddenly gone slightly out of focus and he was trying to get it back. "And you're a pinsetter," he said.

"Among other things," Ur said. Carmine rubbed his hand over his jaw, making a raspy sound as the hand ran against the grain of his beard. "Now, please, Carmine, indulge me." Gently but firmly, she placed her long, slender fingers on Carmine's shoulders and spun him around to face the *favela*.

With a peculiar movement of the head—up, across, down, across— Carmine breathed deeply and scanned the shacks. Briefly, his eyes darted back and forth. "There are two hundred and sixty-two structures in the two sections I'm able to count. Up to the next major road, if that's what it deserves to be called. Beyond that, I can only estimate because the land falls away and I can't distinguish discrete buildings."

"That's very good, Carmine. You have your father's talent," Ur said.

"Not exactly. He wouldn't have had to bisect the area," Carmine said. "But, say, how do you know about my father?"

"Oh, come now, Carmine, he's very famous, you know. Most humans can only identify five or six objects in a group. They call him Snowman, now, don't they?" Ur flashed her very worst smile.

Carmine grimaced. "Ever since the weather changed," he said.

"So," Ur said, "two hundred and sixty-two cardboard shanties. That's all you see?"

With a great, loud exhalation, Carmine dropped his arms to his sides, clenching his fists. "Shit," he said. "Look, I know what you want me to say."

"How could you, if I myself don't know? Understand me. I'm not trying to lead you to any specific conclusion. We're discussing a very large problem, and all I'm trying to do is to get you to talk about the facts from your own unique perspective. And it is unique, you know, in the most narrowly defined sense of the word. You are remarkable, epistemologically, as I'm sure you understand."

"Facts?" he said, making a fist. "I gave you facts. Two hundred and sixty-two of them."

"The fact was uninformative because it was presented without context. It led nowhere."

"Oh, yeah?" Carmine said, smacking his fist into his palm, his upper body fidgeting in a series of asynchronous movements. "Use your imagination. Two hundred and sixty-two shacks, sitting right in front of us in an area no bigger than a few hundred miserable square meters. And then beyond that, there're another two hundred and sixty-two and, then, over the hill another two hundred and sixty-two. There are two hundred and sixty-two above us and another two sixty-two beyond that. And another and another. And, oh yeah, behind us. Fuggedaboutit! And this is just one neighborhood in Rio. Of course there's Sao Paolo and Belize and, well, that's just Brazil. Then there's Bolivia. There's La Paz and then, of course, there's Lima. Then all of Peru. And we haven't even finished with South America, let alone Central America and Mexico. Oh, and, uh, we forgot to mention Africa, or what's left of it, and Central Asia and, and, and … Gives you a headache just thinking about it all."

"And what do you do when you have a headache?" Ur asked.

Carmine blinked. Ur did not. "Well, I take an aspirin."

"So you treat the symptom," Ur said.

"Well, yeah." Carmine scuffed the toe of his shoe in the dirt. "But, uh, it seems like in the context of this discussion—you know, what we're really talking about here—that treating the symptom is a cop-out."

"Is it really?" Ur said. "Fever is a symptom that fights infection, but fever can kill. Besides, in this case the symptoms are foul water, lack of sanitation, inadequate shelter—do I need to continue? As you would say, we're talking about a fucking big aspirin."

"That's right!" Carmine said, his voice rising. "One fucking big aspirin. Too big. That's what I'm saying here. That's what I was saying back there at the Limons'. The problem's too big. And life's too short."

"So, you walk away. Leave them all like this?" Ur said.

"Oh, and who are you? Miss Bleeding Heart? Look, we got problems up North, too. Besides, cleaning up this mess isn't exactly like sweeping out your garage. You can't just haul all of this shit away and burn it."

"Why not?" Ur said.

"Whadda you mean, why not?" Carmine said.

"I mean, you've still got the nukes," Ur said. "Botta boom! Out of sight, out of mind."

"Now you're being facetious," Carmine said. "Snotty facetious, too."

"No, I'm not. I'm simply stating one of the options. It may come to that, anyway," Ur said.

"It? What's *it*?" Carmine said.

"So," Ur said, turning away, "you lack the resources to deal with the symptoms of this type of poverty and, in any event, the problem might be too large, logistically, to tackle. And you won't burn the infection out. So, you walk away?"

"Okay, okay!" Carmine shouted. "No!" Carmine grabbed her by the arm and spun her around to face the *favela*. "Look. It goes on and on. Want to end it? They should stop fucking!"

"Interesting," Ur said. "The Chinese have taken that approach for almost a hundred years. It's not a final solution but it's kept the problem manageable. It allowed them to make progress on other fronts."

"I didn't say control it," Carmine said, "I said stop it!"

"Carmine," Ur said gently, "when you consider your own motives in following me today, wouldn't you say that stopping the fucking is an unrealistic expectation?"

With some deep resignation kneading his features softly, Carmine turned his gaze away from Ur. But this time his eyes did not travel as far as the brilliant

Atlantic. It settled instead directly in front of them on the *favela*. Suddenly, children's laughter drifted up the road through the thick, lazy air. The Whore sat under a tree, surrounded now by low chatter and giggles, telling a story, most likely.

"It seems as if, this morning at least, the Whore is dealing with Ignorance," Ur said.

"But what of Want?" Carmine said softly.

Slapping her hand in Carmine's, Ur began to walk down the bank. "Come on," she said, "we have a little further to go."

"You mean farther, don't you?" Carmine said, smiling at his own clever remark.

"That, too," Ur said. Carmine's smile vanished.

As they strolled up the road in silence, their footfalls made pleasant, scraping sounds in the dry dust. From behind, the voices of the children grew louder, even as they put more distance between them. Ignorance, it appeared, continued to be shouted down.

Carmine stopped, tugging at Ur and pulling her back toward him. Across his lips, a faint smile flickered.

"What is it?" Ur said, resisting slightly.

"Nah, not that." With a casual nod, Carmine indicated a shack that stood opposite along the roadside. Roof and sides were an irregular patchwork of metal: steel plates, corrugated tin; thin, gray sheet metal. The door had been hacked from plywood. A window faced the street. Inset was a piece of brilliant, colored glass. Bottomless blue, like the Atlantic off Copacabana in the deep afternoon. "Can you believe that anyone here would even have the imagination to try?"

With an unusually determined stride, Ur walked across the road and sat down opposite the shack beneath a small fruit tree, its limes pale and pinched like withered, green gonads. Carmine followed and settled beside Ur. "There are more wonders yet," Ur said, pointing. "Do you see the child in that house?"

Behind an open window, shaded by an overhang trimmed decoratively with palm fronds, sat a small child. A female. With great concentration, she was poring over a book, her cheek cradled in her palm.

"How come she's not out with the other kids?" Carmine asked.

"Perhaps she's beyond them in the battle against Ignorance and is tackling Want," Ur said.

"So let me guess," Carmine said. "She's studying to be a doctor and will take an exam that will get her a scholarship that will get her the hell out of here, and she'll become a famous brain surgeon and save thousands of lives."

"Now you're being facetious," Ur said. Carmine pressed his lips together and adjusted his sunglasses. "Although it's possible. Actually," Ur leaned against the tree and folded her arms on top of her breasts, "she loves science and dreams of becoming a nurse but will become a phlebotomist instead." Once again, Carmine stared at Ur's long, slender fingers, each positioned perfectly, cradling her forearms that glowed cinnamon brown against her black dress. "You're not paying attention."

"I am too," Carmine said.

"To what I'm saying," Ur said.

"Sure I am! Phlebotomist. The kid's gonna be a phlebotomist. Uh, hypothetically, right?"

Ur laughed, but very softly, and the leaves of the little lime trembled, although the air sat perfectly still, its eyes shut, its lips pressed together, and the girl, although she could not possibly have heard, sat up and searched about for a moment. "No, not hypothetically, but conditionally."

"Conditionally?"

"That's right. She might become pregnant in a few years or, perhaps, simply drink the water when she shouldn't, fall ill and die," Ur said.

"Jeez. Ya think?" Carmine's eyes wandered over the tops of the homes, tin and tarpaper, reflecting, absorbing.

"Carmine," Ur said, wrapping her hand gently around his bicep, "while those possibilities are sad, they don't constitute the point. My mother used to say that, in matters of mortality, nature fails to distinguish between the drug dealer and the concert pianist. She said that after I died."

"After you what?"

"Died. In my original worldline." Withdrawing her hand from Carmine's arm, Ur examined it for a brief moment before letting it fall and come to rest on her hip. "Simply, the quiddities of existence up here dictate different circumstances from your own, but the outcome is the same."

"Yeah, I see," Carmine said, although he quite clearly did not, and he tried to collect himself. "You've got a point, only the distribution of outcomes is different here than, um, up North. It's severely, and negatively skewed."

"Distribution?" Ur asked, although her eyes failed to look puzzled.

Carmine cocked his head. "Are you just jerkin' me off here? I mean, okay, I get the point of this little hike, but have you got all the answers?" Ur shook her head. Carmine exhaled. "All right, it's just that up here, the standard deviation of death is a lot smaller, when measured against age. And, like I said, it's severely skewed."

"Good," Ur said. "Now we have an objectifiable goal. Increase the standard deviation of death and normalize the distribution."

"Say," Carmine said, "what in hell are you, anyway? You're no pinsetter."

"Of course, I am." Ur picked at a finger. "Among other things."

"Okay, but what are you, really? Who are you?"

"Those are two related but separate questions," Ur said.

"Aw, c'mon. Cut the philosophical bullshit, will you? For Christ's—"

Ur placed a finger over Carmine's lips. His eyes flared and his respiration quickened. Beads of sweat began to trickle down his face. "I'm a catalyst," Ur said simply.

"Buh," Carmine mumbled through her finger.

"Shhh," Ur said. "Watch," her eyes indicating once again the little girl's home.

Bent over the rain tub, the girl most carefully ladled out a small amount of water into an old tin can. Her shiny, black, braided hair glowed under the glare of the sun. On her feet were sandals, the soles cut from tires, fastened to her feet by bits of thin rope. Face and hands appeared freshly scrubbed and her dress, hanging down to her knees, most probably an older sister's, carried the old splotches and stains of play but sparkled white and clean, its scattered, bright blue flowers faded now to a soft, subtle cornflower color.

Carrying herself with quiet dignity, the child walked to a patch of ground beneath her window and, as if administering a sacrament, poured the water slowly and carefully on a clutch of varicolored flowers, as gangly but as lovely as herself. Placing the can carefully against the side of her house, she turned and drew in a deep breath, then picked a blossom, impossibly orange, and stuck it in a braid, then went back inside and back to her book. Once she lifted her head and stared for a moment at her garden and smiled.

"So, do we save her alone because there are simply too many to save altogether? Or do we save as many as we can, as best we can, because our resources are limited? Or is there another way, perhaps?"

With an uncharacteristically delicate movement, Carmine lowered Ur's hand from his mouth. Carmine took off his sunglasses and wiped his face with his sleeve. "How do we get her out?" he asked, his voice moving anxiously across a razor's edge.

"Make her your project. But understand, it will take many of your resources and much of your time," Ur said.

Loud laughter stunned the still air once more. Carmine turned and looked back down the road. The Whore was laughing as well. "And them?"

"They would require all of your resources and all of your time," Ur said.

Carmine chewed on his lip and swiveled his head around. The *favelas* sprawled over the flanks of the mountain in every direction, seemingly forever. One last time he glanced at the girl, absorbed completely in her lessons.

"Let's go," Ur said. "It's time." Smiling her terribly toothy smile, Ur waved to the Whore, who rose, smiling back warmly. Jumping up, the children ran toward Carmine and Ur. This time, however, Carmine did not flinch. Spreading his arms wide, he bent down and scooped up one grubby urchin.

As Carmine's mouth exploded in a grin, his nose wrinkled. The smell, at once sweet and sour, was that bad. In one black fist, she held a hard candy. At the corners of her mouth were smeared the ruins of a chocolate she'd devoured; her eyes shone like soft brown caramel. For no reason, Carmine belted out "Volare," off pitch. The children laughed and screamed. Carmine, undaunted, energized even, sang louder. Soon, the kids had not only picked up the tune, but gently forced the music on key and the beat morphed into a samba. Laughing and singing and dancing, they snaked back down the hill.

"What if they don't get out and they don't die?" Carmine shouted to Ur over the din. Ur pointed to a shanty. An old man stood at the door, mouth agape, his eyes hollow and hungry. Suddenly, they filled with tears and his hands began to shake and his body swayed, all in time to the samba. Carmine swallowed hard, pressed the girl closer and sang even louder.

At the pavement's edge, Carmine set the child down, who ran off, skipping and squealing into the crowd of kids that flowed back into the *favela*, like a river running dry and disappearing into the desert. Outside the door to the Limons' home stood Buford, Camilla and the two Joes.

Neither of the Joes appeared to be especially pleased. Yet Camilla's smile stretched all the way to Sugarloaf and was as warm as the Brazilian sun in December. At her feet sat a small valise.

"Howdy," Buford said. "Have a nice walk, kid? Talk? Walk-talk?"

"Ay, yo," Carmine said. "Sure. You could learn a lot up there, Buford."

"I expect you could, Minnie," Buford said.

"Now then," Camilla said, folding her hands. "Senhor Carmine, should we stay here, or go, like Jorgezinho says?"

With a gentle smile on his face, Carmine walked up to Camilla and took her hands in his. "I still think you should go, Mrs. Limon."

Camilla's eyes flashed and her smile evaporated. Slowly, she raised her chin and then, as if she'd been struck, threw her head back. Buford glanced at the Joes. Senhor Limon's cheeks were being dragged down by an ugly frown. Jorge was smiling and nodding approvingly.

"I see," Camilla said abruptly, withdrawing her hands from Carmine's. "However, I—"

"Excuse me, Mrs. Limon. Excuse me for interrupting but I need to finish." Carmine fidgeted with the frame of his sunglasses. "Look down there," he said, his arm sweeping across the series of great bays that tucked Rio in and up against the mountains. "It's so beautiful and life is so short." Carmine cleared his throat and glanced back at Ur. Buford followed his gaze. Did Carmine know? Buford winced. Ur's eyes were filled with some terrible sorrow that tugged at their corners like an immense weight. Was it for herself or for Camilla, he wondered? "But don't forget the people up here. Maybe all any of us can do is make small differences. Your daughter, Donna, she's a real hero. You shoulda' seen her with those kids."

Camilla was beginning to smile again. Donna tsked while she flapped a wrist. "I'm no hero. Just, how do you call it, a Paid Peeper." Buford bit his tongue and held his breath. He wasn't at all sure whether to shit or wind his watch.

"What an accurate turn of phrase, my sister," Jorge Limon said.

Buford swallowed a great gulp of air, then exhaled it slowly. The crisis had passed. "I think you mean Pied Piper, Miss Donna," he said.

"Pied Piper," Carmine echoed. "Yeah, you're that. But you're also a teacher, 'cause those kids aren't rats to be led *away* from the opportunity down there, in the city. You're helping them back *down*. Helping them fight against the social gravity of this place." Carmine shrugged. "Anyway, I guess that's it."

Sweetly, Camilla kissed Carmine on the cheek, then patted the place lightly. "You're a good boy." Camilla drew herself up. "Now we must go."

"Jeez, I thought it was a good speech and all, but I didn't know I could be that persuasive," said Carmine, chuckling somewhat superciliously. "Maybe I should make a speech at the conference? Whaddya think, Bu?"

"It was a very nice speech," Camilla said.

"But Senhora Limon will be the one speaking in Brasilia," Ur said.

Somewhat crestfallen, Carmine nodded. Then he brightened. "Yeah. Yeah! That was pretty powerful stuff you said awhile ago, Mrs. Limon. And you know what? It'll do all of those egomaniacs good to hear it from one of the people." Carmine pumped his fists. "Botta boom, botta bing." Ur winced. Buford noticed and frowned.

"We'll see," Camilla said. "Jorgezinho, please. Put my bag in Donna's car."

"But mother—"

"We've already discussed the matter. It's settled. You'll arrange it?" Camilla said.

"Mother, I really don't know—" Limon began.

Camilla held up a hand. "Twenty years in Brazilian intelligence. Stop. You can, how do you say, pull it off. Correct, Buford?" Camilla said.

"Yes, ma'am."

Reluctantly, Limon grabbed Camilla's suitcase and put it in the truck of the pink VW.

"Ay, why don't you and Donna come with us on the plane? There's room and—" Carmine began.

"Because I'd like to see the jungle," Ur said.

"You're going too?" Carmine said.

"I've lived most of my life in a desert. I need the experience," Ur said.

"Desert? How … you don't look … There's so little I know about you, Ur." Carmine paused. "Ur," he said again, thoughtfully. Carmine smacked his forehead. "*Marone!* Sometimes I got a clear head. What a coincidence. I've got an uncle, sort of, who had a daughter and her name was Ur. Remember you said like father like son with me and numbers? With your line of philosophical bullshit, and boy does Uncle Jaq love philosophy, you could've been his daughter."

"I am," Ur said.

Carmine's eyes flared and his mouth dropped. "So what your mother said about you—"

Ur kissed him on the cheek. "See you in Brasilia," she said as she climbed into the back seat of the pink taxi.

Without a word, Camilla hugged her husband and son. Donna kissed her father and then regarded her brother. With great dignity, he stepped forward and wrapped his arms around her and kissed her hard on the forehead. "I love you, too," Donna said.

Donna and Camilla piled into the taxi, which disappeared around the first corner in a booming ball of hot pink.

Carmine was standing in a small spot of shade, but he was sweating profusely. "Bu? Can I—"

"Later," Buford snapped. He smacked his hands together and forced his best shit-eating grin. "Looks like we got ourselves a kitchen pass."

"I'm sorry?" Senhor Limon said.

"Boys' night out," Carmine said. "Or day. Or day and night. You know, a few beers, maybe some women."

The elder Limon raised his hands. "No, no, I'm happily married. I—"

"So window shop," Carmine said.

Though he opened his mouth to protest, the protest turned into a grin. "Of course, window shop!"

"You're all invited down to my place on the beach," Jorge said. "The Brahma Chopp is ice cold and the *churrasca* melts in your mouth. Senhor Carmine, you can ogle my wife, but only when I'm not looking. Later, we can bowl a little. Maybe a little game. What do you call it? Some action. Eh?"

Buford narrowed his eyes, as if that would help him focus. Slowly, he let them wander down to the elder Limon's feet. He looked up and pointed. "I thought you looked familiar. You're—"

"Ah, yes. Well, you see, I never got the bowling shoes back … But, here, let me return these to you now." Senhor Limon stooped and began to tug at the boot.

"No, no," Buford said. "Keep 'em. Looks like they fit for sure."

Without the slightest protest, Senhor Limon straightened. "Thank you! They sure are—" he paused—"sweet kicks!" The men laughed heartily. Even Jorgezinho.

"All right, boys," Buford said, "let's go, we're burnin' daylight!"
***

"We'll be down in a minute," Buford said to the valet in front of the Copacabana Rio Hotel, and handed him the keys to the red Mustang. "C'mon, Carmine."

"Ur," was the only word Carmine said as they rode the elevator to their rooms to pick up their bowling shoes.

Buford cleared his throat and chuckled nervously. "Damndest name, huh, kid?"

"Bu, cut the crap, okay? She set the whole thing up. She set me up. And, well, Bu, you may be a great spy and all but you're fuckin' lousy at lying to me. You saw her last night, so you set me up too."

The elevator door opened. "Well, maybe. A little. But I trust her. And you've gotta go with your instincts about people. In my business you do, anyways, especially when you're right about people most of the time."

"Oh, yeah? What makes you think you're right most of the time?" Carmine said.

"'Cause I'm still alive."

Carmine was still sweating, as Buford clapped a hand on his shoulder and led him into his room. He had been perspiring ever since they'd gotten back to the Copacabana and Buford had finally allowed him to ask. "So you're telling me she was Jaq and Kate's kid. What's with that shit? Their daughter's dead."

"Was," Buford said.

"Was? C'mon, Bu!"

"Go get your shoes, kid," Buford said.

Buford greeted him with a full glass of scotch. Neat. "This'll take a few minutes."

With a loud slurp, Carmine drained the last of his whiskey. "So Ur, that girl, woman, whatever, died, was abducted to the moon in some parallel universe by Mattie, and was rescued by Uncle Jaq and Aunt Kate? What's she up to?"

"In training, I guess," Buford said.

"For what?"

Buford sipped his scotch and shrugged. "For Mattie's old job. Or Tiamat's, or whatever she was called back then. Holdin' the universe together requires a little savvy, I'd expect. And my guess is she's developing her own … style."

"Crazy shit," Carmine said. "Bu, hit me again."

"Take it easy, kid. It's gonna be a long day," Buford said as he poured a full finger.

"Already has been," Carmine said. "You know, though, I'd still like to fuck her."

Gently, Buford placed his hand on the side of Carmine's neck, then began to squeeze the boy's flesh. "Don't even think about it. Not her."

"Ow! Bu! Jeez," Carmine said, pushing Buford's hand away from his throat. "Fuggedaboutit." Carmine massaged his throat and coughed. "Besides, I think she can take care of herself."

Buford drained his glass. "I expect you're right about that." He patted Carmine on the shoulder and smiled. "Let's go. Our boy's probably wonderin' where we've got to."

"I expect you're right about that," Carmine said with a cowboy drawl. Buford laughed and Carmine joined him. But Buford could see that Carmine's eyes weren't laughing. They appeared neither angry nor fearful, but, rather, curious. Did Carmine suspect him, Buford wondered.

"Let's light a shuck outta here, kid. We're burnin' daylight," Buford said.

CHAPTER V

———

"Look at it! Just look!" Faddle boomed, banging his fist on the armrest of his seat. "Just goes on and on as far as the eye can see. Yessir! Far as the eye can see."

Glancing over Carmine's shoulder, whose face was pressed against the window, Buford Stemp took a long, deep slurp of air, as if drinking in the beauty of it all. Below and beyond the jungle stretched to the horizon. Beneath the low but brilliant morning sun, the forest canopy shimmered and danced, reflecting dozens of dazzling shades of green. At the forest's feet was spread a carpet of soil, stained a deep, rich orange by minerals and time, like an exotic fruit that grew beneath rather than on the trees.

"There it is! I can just make it out," Carmine shouted. Buford leaned over again and in the bright distance, could see the clearing that contained the capital of the Republic. Here and there the tops of buildings caught the morning light.

"We're approaching Brasilia," a voice said calmly over the intercom. "We will begin fuel-efficiency maneuvers in preparation for our descent. Please fasten your shoulder restraints securely."

"Fuck, I hate this part, Bu," Carmine said. The engines roared and the jet abruptly inclined to vertical and began to accelerate. "Aw, shitfuck," Carmine said, in a small squeaky voice, his eyes squeezed shut.

"Here, Candy," Buford said, shoving a bag into Carmine's hand. Without opening his eyes, Carmine clutched it tightly in a white fist drained of blood.

At dead vertical, the plane lurched slightly and spun in a tight loop. A few retching noises were heard but Buford couldn't smell any vomit. A good sign.

With one last, deep growl, the jet dove. Several seconds passed, though they felt like long grinding minutes, before the engines were cut. All that could be heard was the soft whoosh of the plane gliding through the thin atmosphere at sixty thousand feet.

"We're approximately two hundred klicks from the capital. We should be on the ground in approximately twenty-five minutes. Please keep your restraints fastened for landing loops," the pilot said.

"I never liked the sound of 'on the ground'. Couldn't he just say 'land'?" Carmine stuffed the airsick bag between his seat and the fuselage.

"Don't you think you ought to keep that thing handy until we land?" Buford said, chuckling.

"Fuck you, Bu," Carmine said, laughing along with him.

Gently, the jet began to bank, then settled into a series of large, lazy loops as it circled the capital. Even from their elevation, Buford could sense the heightened level of activity on the ground. Vehicles, most of them military, buzzed around the new roundabout dedicated to the Amazon Basin. Buford grunted. At its base, he could just make out a knot of people with protest placards.

"What is it?" Carmine asked.

"Oh, there're some demonstrators down there. Club o' Rome, I expect. Funny how they thought scarce resources would be an unmanageable problem for the twenty-first century. That goddamned meteor took care of that. If you can't produce you can't consume. I guess they're keeping their intellectual motors running, pushing for population control."

"Well, they don't have to worry about the North. It's too cold to fuck back home," Carmine said.

"For some, maybe," Buford said. Carmine smiled sheepishly.

Long lines of limousines stood in front of the gleaming white government ministries, all in the modern, neoclassical expressionist style of the nineteen-sixties when Brasilia was built. Looks like ancient Greece, Buford thought. All it needs is a Trojan Horse. Darkly, an inchoate thought settled over Buford. The hairs on his hand stood up. He settled back into his seat and watched as taxis buzzed into and out of stands near the hotels.

"Bu, do you think there'll be trouble?" Carmine asked.

"I dunno, but I always anticipate it," Buford said. "That's what I'm paid to do. But say—" Buford tapped Limon, who sat in the aisle seat opposite, on the shoulder.

Limon started from a deep nap. "We there?" he asked hoarsely.

"Almost, Jorge. Anyways, the kid here wants to know if you think there'll be trouble," Buford said.

Limon rubbed his eyes. "Trouble." He stared at Buford and Carmine. "Yeah, there'll be trouble." Calmly, Limon folded his hands across his stomach. In seconds he was snoring. "There you go, Minnie."

The pilot deftly trimmed the plane and, like a leaf buffeted by a light breeze, it floated flawlessly onto the runway.

A soft thump told Buford they'd landed. Battery power kicked in and the jet followed a signalman on the runway to a large, open space at the end of the tarmac where it came to a stop. Seatbelts snapped like a swarm of crickets. The delegation began to collect their computers and briefcases.

"Hold your horses! Just hold your horses," Faddle growled. Abruptly, the clatter stopped. Buford noticed O'Reilly glance at Q'peesha Parks, his eyes pinched like grapes surprised by their own sourness.

With great effort, and even greater grunting, John Faddle hauled himself out of his seat, turning to face the delegates while bracing himself against the aisle seats. "Uncle John, can I—" Carmine began.

"Siddown, kid,"

For a long moment, the passenger cabin stayed quite still as Faddle raised one of his great, meaty paws, then, most delicately and with only two fingers, wiped a sparkling fluorescence of sweat from his forehead. "Well, kids, I've saved your bacon again. Yup. Saved your bacon. Got here just in time to miss the insufferable opening session," he said, chuckling. No one so much as smiled. No one moved. The group barely breathed. Faddle raised an eyebrow, which arched like a big, black serpent ready to strike. "All right. All right, then. Here's the deal," he boomed.

"No, John," O'Reilly said, stepping forward to face Faddle. "We're going it alone."

Faddle nodded, his lips pressed tightly into a thin line of light pink flesh. But Buford thought he saw a light twinkling from somewhere deep within the man, reflected only dimly in his eyes. "All right, O'Reilly." Faddle shrugged. "New England's no big deal, as far as I'm concerned. Do what you like. Cut your own deal."

"John," O'Reilly said, quietly, "I mean *we're* going it alone. We, all of us, not just we, New England." O'Reilly's voice was dry and pinched.

"Ah, so that's how it is," Faddle said softly.

"John, goddammit, we're just not comfortable with your position. You're just too, too *dovish*," O'Reilly said.

"Oooh," Faddle cooed in a high falsetto. Suppressing a smile, Buford could only think, *Here it comes.*

"I mean, it's all right for you," Harold Krumpp said. "New York's got, well, position. Stature. You're still the world's financial capital. You've got intellectual assets and you've got gold. Can you believe it?" Krumpp laughed nervously in a failed attempt to break the tension. "You can't eat gold and you can't burn it, but everybody wants it."

"That's right, John," O'Reilly said, his voice clearly regaining some of its lost courage. "Think about it. You've got gold, so you can afford to be more conciliatory, more dovish, like I said. And we understand you've got to think about your own constituency. They're—"

"They're a bunch o' lily-livered pinkos, John. Shit, that's why we gave you the nukes. Knew you'd never use 'em except as a last resort, like," Elmer Pitkin said.

"And you've got Venice, John," Q'peesha Park added. "Lord knows what in hell *that* is all about. That she-bitch Maria, Doge or whatever she calls herself, keeps creepin' around doin' Lord knows what, tradin' with them sand niggers. Probably gets you all the oil you need for—"

"Q'peesha, we've never hoarded a single barrel of crude. We've always shared what we buy. And at a fair price," Faddle said calmly.

"Bullshit!" Q'peesha shouted. "You got gold to buy food, you got oil to keep warm, you got nukes to kick ass. Bullshit, bullshit, bull—"

"Q'peesha!" Faddle bellowed in a voice so deep, so loud, and yet so focused, Buford actually raised a hand and covered one of his ears. "I thought you of all people would've had the balls to tell me all of this back in Rio."

Blinking slowly and deliberately, Q'peesha drew herself more erect. "Mr. John Faddle, I resent that kind of antediluvian, sexist—"

"Cut the crap, Q'peesha," Faddle said, his intonation scraping the warm, stuffy air in the cabin like a curette. "We've had a woman president and a black president. Now, if we ever get out of this Necrotic mess and put Humpty Dumpty back together, we might have a black woman president." Faddle smiled beatifically.

"Now, John, it's too late to turn on your charm. We've made up our minds. And, and we have that right," Harold Krumpp ventured cautiously.

"Yes, Harold, you do. You all are delegates plenipotentiary," Faddle said. Very deliberately, he cast his gaze over all of the members of the delegation. *What's up?* Buford wondered. This was not like John Faddle. "Run along, now," Faddle finished.

"Well, then. I guess that's settled," O'Reilly said cautiously.

"Yes. I guess it is. Harold here is very persuasive. Minister plenipotentiary. Yessir. That's a clincher. Can't argue with that," Faddle said.

"Why, thank you, John," Harold Krumpp said. "May we help you off first?"

"No. No. But thank you very much," Faddle said. "I think I'll just sit down right here." Removing his hand from the aisle seat opposite, Faddle began to totter precariously, like a great boulder. Subconsciously, the metaphor must not have been lost on the delegation, for instinctively, they withdrew a pace.

Krumpp, however, advanced, offering a hand. "Get away! Leave me alone," Faddle said, his soft sirocco suddenly snapping with an icy bite. Slowly, huffing, Faddle lowered his great bulk back into his seat. "Yes," he said, "I think I'll sit down right here."

"All right, then, John," O'Reilly said. "We'll send someone back for you and—"

"I said I'm staying right here."

"John, come on, you know how it would look if New York isn't represented," O'Reilly said.

"New York'll be represented just fine. Carmine's come a long way. Haven't you, Carmine?" Faddle said. Carmine simply looked at Buford, his eyes wide. Buford winked.

"Goddammit, John, don't be childish, for Christ's—" O'Reilly began.

"Get off my plane," Faddle whispered.

"John," O'Reilly attempted once again.

"Get the fuck off my plane!" Faddle roared. Oceanus Faddlensis cleared the beach. Silently, averting their gazes, the delegates filed past John Faddle and off the aircraft.

Elmer Pitkin was the last in the queue. He stopped. "Your plane? How'd you pull that one off in that workers', peasants' paradise of yours?"

"From each according to his ability. I buy that part, Elmer. Just like I bought this plane. It's called hard work," Faddle said.

"Hard work? What hard work did you ever do?" Pitkin said.

"Twenty hour days, Elmer. Reading, thinking, pounding the phone."

"You call that hard work?" Pitkin said. He sniffed.

Faster than Buford thought possible, Faddle's hand shot out and latched onto Elmer Pitkin's collar, then jerked him down, pulling his nose against Faddle's own. "That's right. Hard work. I don't know what you call hard work, Elmer. Shootin' rabbits or bustin' broncs or cornholin' jackalopes. But I respect what you boys do out there. From each according to his ability." Faddle squeezed Pitkin's collar closed and Pitkin began to turn purple. "You old son of a bitch," Pitkin squeaked, the corners of his mouth attempting to turn upward in a smile.

Faddle loosened his grip and began to laugh. "Christ. You looked like a fucking eggplant."

"Goddammit, John," Pitkin rasped, rubbing his neck. "Why don't you come home? Good ol' North Dakota boy like you. We need fellas like you in the Republic. Everyone's goin' soft. Or crazy."

"Aaargh," Faddle gurgled, waving Pitkin off.

Roughly, Pitkin placed his hand on Faddle's cheek, then bent over and kissed the other. "I love you, you old son of a bitch."

"Yeah, yeah," Faddle said. "Just do me a favor, will ya, Elmer?"

"Sure. What?"

"Keep those clowns in line. Just a little. You're the right-wing nut. They'll listen to reason, if it's coming from you. Get me? You know what's at stake."

"Yeah, pardner, I guess I do. For the Rocky Mountain Republic and good ol' U S of A, I'll walk the line best as I can."

"That's all I ask," Faddle said.

"All right, Mr. Mayor," Buford said, "what in hell was all that about?" With a self-satisfied smile on his face, John Faddle was reclining against the back of his seat, his hands folded across his stomach.

"Plain as day, wasn't it? Yessir. Plain as day. The bastards mutinied. Gotta give credit where credit's due. Their timing was perfect. Left no time for me to turn 'em around. Which, of course, is what I would've done in Rio. Yep. Give credit where credit's due."

"So, what do we do now, Uncle John? Should we get you over to the hotel?" Carmine said.

"Goddammit, boy! You got shit in your ears? Didn't you hear me say, more than once, in fact, that I'm staying here?" Faddle waved him off. "This crate is top o' the line. Yessir. Top o' the line. It was the prototype for a stealth Air Force One. Well, when we shelved the US of A, we shelved the Presidency, too. So, I bought it."

"You really bought it? So that wasn't bullshit? It is your plane?" Carmine said.

"Nah," Faddle said, waving a hand. "That was bullshit. Remember, I've spent my life selling stocks and selling people. Gotta bullshit a little. White lies. No black ones, though. Don't forget it. No black ones. Say, Buford, would you mind getting me a shot of bourbon?"

"Yessir," Buford said.

"So, you didn't buy the plane?" Carmine said.

"Nope. City did. But I did install a bunch o' fancy upgrades on my own dime. All the latest stealth technology and a few other little surprises," Faddle said.

"Surprises?" Carmine said.

"The kind that could come in handy in case there's *real* trouble. Oh, thanks, Buford," Faddle said, grabbing the tumbler filled with two fat fingers of bourbon. He took a small sip. "You boys run along and save the world and I'll just sit right here and hold down the fort in case there's—" Faddle lifted the glass, rolled the bourbon around then drained it, "*trouble*," he finished. "Jesus, this is good stuff. Single barrel?" Buford nodded. "Hit me again, well ya son?"

"Yessir," Buford said.

"Thanks." Faddle took the second glass, cradling it almost lovingly in his great hands. "I don't know how Jaq and Beele—"

"Nick Beele?" Carmine said.

"That's right, boy. Good to see you're learning your family history. Your extended family history, that is. Yup. I don't know how Jaq and Beele drank that Scotch shit. Tastes like fucking iodine." Faddle drained half of the tumbler.

"Uncle John, you sure you're okay?" Carmine said.

"Hmmm? Oh, yeah. Sure, sure."

"I dunno. You're acting awfully strange. Especially after what those cocksuckers did. Why, I'd've—" Carmine began.

"Almost did, boy. Almost did. Then, the goddamndest thing happened." Faddle sipped the bourbon. "It was as if a voice were speaking to me. Except it wasn't a voice. It was … It was like bells. Little copper bells. Crazy shit, huh? Except the sound was not like anything I'd ever heard before. And they said— not really said, mind you—they said … No, they just seemed to tell me what I had to do. I felt perfectly—released. And yet, completely connected. Almost like a goddamned orgasm. Think I would've had one except I'm so old I'm outta cum. Haven't felt like that since Dana—" Faddle's eyes misted lightly and he drained the bourbon.

Carmine cleared his throat. "Say, Uncle John, you're not too old."

"Beh! Look, you guys run along and I'll hold down the fort. Yep. Hold down the fort," Faddle said, his voice raspy with phlegm.

At the exit door, Carmine turned to face Faddle. "Uncle John?"

"Yeah?"

"About that cum thing. Fuggedaboutit. I'm gonna send over one of those beautiful, bronze, Brazilian octoroons for you. We'll see how old you are."

"Get out o' here," Faddle roared, but without malice, his face beaming like the tropical sun. With great effort he raised his arm and hurled the tumbler at Carmine, barely missing his head. The glass shattered in a half dozen pieces against the bulkhead.

"Time to haul down our flag," Buford said, and led Carmine, at a run, off the plane. As Buford descended the ramp he heard a voice. "Is there a problem, sir?" It was the captain.

"Problem? Yeah! Glass slipped outta my hand. Waste o' good bourbon. Hit me again, will ya, Sky King?" Faddle said.

"Yessir."

"Would you care to join me? I feel like bloviating."

"Thank you, sir. I would like that very much," the captain said.

CHAPTER VI

For the third time, but more insistently now, Buford banged on the door to Carmine's room. "Carmine!" he shouted, losing his patience.

Pressing his ear against it, he failed to detect any movement. "Shit," he swore softly. He reached inside his jacket, withdrawing a long, blunt silver cylinder with a bright blue sapphire tip. "Guess I might as well see if this thing cuts through metal, like they said," he muttered to himself.

Suddenly, there were shuffling sounds and muffled voices within Carmine's room. Unwashed, undressed, unkempt, Carmine poked his head out the door and yawned mightily. "Bu," he said simply.

Someone was tugging at Carmine. Several voices, highly pitched and soft and sweet, were murmuring, pleading, behind the door. Three wide-eyed young women, topless, their skin, brown, black and caramel, glowing softly in the dim light of the room crowded around Carmine. "My, my, Minnie, we do have a sweet tooth, don't we?" Carmine grinned. "Get dressed," Buford said, "we've got twenty minutes before the Plenum Session starts."

"Aw, Bu," Carmine said, chuckling. "You go on. I mean, my head's full of so much bullshit from the last two days I think it's gonna fucking explode."

"Get dressed," Buford said. He was not smiling. Carmine's face fell. Pushing Carmine aside and shoving the door open, Buford burst into the room. The girls stumbled backward and Buford blew past them, into the bedroom and out again with an armful of clothes. "*Favor. Vamoose, queridos,*" Buford growled in Sportuguese, throwing the clothes on the couch in a pile. "Now. *Ora. Prontamente.*"

The three looked at Carmine, who clapped his hands and nodded toward the door. Grumbling, the girls pulled on their pants and blouses and stalked out of the room.

In the cab, Buford hadn't uttered three words. "Look, Bu," Carmine was saying, as they climbed out of the car, "it's like this. It was purely academic."

"Academic?" Buford said as he paid the driver.

"Sure. Take ten books—"

"Ten books? What's ten books got to do with three hookers?"

"Listen. Take ten books, rearrange them one at a time, and how many combinations do you get?"

"I dunno. Fifty, sixty?" Buford said cautiously.

"Three million, six hundred and twenty-eight thousand, eight hundred," Carmine said. "That's ten factorial. Factorial is—"

"I know what factorial is. And bullshit."

"Try it, then," Carmine said.

"Cut the crap, Carmine," Buford growled, waving his hand.

"Bu, for me numbers are intuitive, geometry's intuitive. I could tell you right now the volume of that hemisphere above the Congress. Statistics? I've gotta work at it."

"So what's—"

"I'm telling you. I was just trying to see, empirically, how many combinations—"

"Okay, Carmine." Buford smiled. "But that's only three factorial. That's six. You should've been finished by midnight."

"You forgot me. That makes twenty-four."

Rather roughly, Buford grabbed Carmine by the shoulder. "Ouch! Hey, take it easy. Linen wrinkles."

"Carmine, you've got to grow the fuck up. Learn to prioritize. Your Uncle John gave you an important job to do."

"And I'm doing it! I *am* paying attention. You want me to tell you to three decimal places the value of two standard deviations from the monthly average of kelp production under each of the five scenarios proposed by Q'peesha in yesterday's breakaway on 'Food in the Twenty-Second Century'?"

"Carmine," Buford said.

"Do you want me to extrapolate—"

"Carmine!" Buford repeated, grabbing Carmine's cheek between the thumb and forefinger of his left hand.

"Brr-bu—" Carmine mumbled.

"Minnie, shut up for a minute. Can you do that?" Carmine nodded.

"Look, you're a good kid, but you've got to grow up." Carmine opened his mouth to protest but Buford hushed him. "And do you know what it means to grow up? Do you really?"

Carmine's shoulders slumped and he shook his head. "Ever watch a bunch of kids in a sandbox with toys? They're acquisitive, selfish, and hierarchical. Same as all the coconuts we've been listenin' to in conference rooms, grownup sandboxes, for the past two days. What passes for maturity is the ability to exercise control and manipulate all of those hardwired impulses. And manipulate those same impulses in other people. But do you know what the real clincher is?"

"Hey, Bu. Can ya' le' go o' my fafe. My teef are goin' numb," Carmine mumbled.

"Oh, sure, kid. Sorry. Anyways, as I was saying, the hardest impulse of all to control is impatience. That's what separates the men from the boys. The ability to control immediate gratification. Not eliminate fulfillment, just defer it to a more appropriate time and place. That, young fella, is growin' up."

Carmine pursed his lips. "That's good, Buford." Buford raised his eyebrows, for he had never heard Carmine call him by his full first name. "I never really thought about it like that. I guess I always thought of maturity as a time when you put the toys away for good."

"Some people do, son, but that gets more complicated. Besides, that's something you'll never have to worry about." Buford smiled. "Here comes Limon. Now there's a fella who knows when to take the toys out. My God, that was some night in Ipanema."

"Good morning, gentlemen," Limon called, as he crossed the plaza. He was not smiling.

"What's up?" Buford asked as the three shook hands.

"Today the shit hits the fan," Limon said.

"Well, you don't have to be a rocket scientist to figure out that a Plenum Session would draw flies," Buford drawled.

"That's obvious. But I've been told by my operative that today it will happen," Limon said.

"And what's *it*, Joe?" Carmine asked nervously.

Limon raised his palms upward. "That's my problem. I don't know, my friend. Let's go in and find out."

Carmine stood quite still, staring at the structures.

"What is it, Minnie? Cipherin' again? Calculating some quadratic bullshit or other?" Buford said.

"Nah. It's just that Congress reminds me of the World Trade Center, that's all," Carmine said. Instantly, Limon whipped his phone and began speaking rapidly. "What'd I say?"

Limon hung up. "There hasn't been an attempt on a structure from the air in almost fifty years. The Trade Center was the first and last. Like everybody else, we've dropped our guard. I'd say it's time to put our hands up again, eh? Thanks, Minnie."

"Yeah, yeah, sure," Carmine said. Then, smiling broadly, "Sure. No problem. Fuggedaboutit."

* * * *

Carmine and Buford took their seats, located conspicuously along with those nations that were now referred to facetiously as the Previously Developed Countries, the PDCs, in the rear of the auditorium. At the podium a speaker droned on, while delegates milled about, lobbying and kibitzing.

Carmine let go a long, low whistle. "Boy, I can see why these jungle bunnies are short on cash. They must've blown every last *cruzeiro* on this joint."

Carefully, Buford surveyed the space. Walls paneled with several varieties of tropical wood soared tens of meters upward. Ribbon mahogany and rosewood were inlaid with tan and yellow and lighter toned veneers. Palms and plants burst from the base of the panels and hovered protectively above jaguar and lemur, parrots and piranha. Threading, suggestively, through it all was a ribbon of pure pewter, a silver artery pumping life into the bosky jungle.

As the teak trees drew Buford's eyes upward to the balcony that ringed the auditorium, he also noticed, professionally, an unusually large number of special forces, all in black berets and putty green fatigues, in surveillance. Trouble, indeed? Buford noted the fact, then relaxed and let his gaze wander to the dome enclosing the roof. Delicate inlays of ebony, suggesting the leafy shadows of the forest canopy, ringed the immense saucer protecting the viewer from the terrific beauty of the deep night, a bright pulsing indigo backdrop, inset with a gibbous moon of shaved ivory, yellow-white.

Suddenly, subtly, the room rocked. Buford blinked and turned his head away, but his eyes were seized by a glint of silver. The Amazon no longer ran dully, brushed pewter, but syrupy silver. Pure mercury, elusive, seductive, coursed with its peculiar, cohesive momentum around the great hall.

For a sliver of a moment, Buford could not breathe. Something sparkled, argentine, amethyst and rose, bursting through the bright, metallic surface of quicksilver, then vanished. As if driven by an irresistible impulse to rise and follow the figure, Buford felt the pads of his fingers push against his seat. Yet as he did, the quicksilver stream froze solid into a dull ribbon of pedestrian pewter once again. Buford blinked and pulled out a Lucky, which he began to roll between his fingers, then tapped against his palm.

"Hey, Bu. You can't smoke in here," Carmine said.

Buford smiled a hard, thin smile. "Just fidgeting." Shooting a glance at the wall panels, Buford discovered only a wooden jaguar staring back. "Besides, I've quit smoking," Buford said, jamming the cigarette back into his shirt pocket.

"*Sure*," Carmine said.

"Don Paulo!" Buford hailed across the room.

"Fuck, Bu. What'd you do that for?"

"He's okay, Minnie. He was gonna find us anyway. He's with our delegation."

"I know, but the fuckin' guy's a homo or something. I thought maybe he'd stay lost for the morning. He's always running around bullshitting with everybody," Carmine said sullenly.

"First off, Minnie. Who gives a shit if he's a queer? This is the twenty-first century, for Christ's sake. And, besides, I don't think he is. He just dresses a little funny."

"*Funny*? Acts a little funny, too, if you ask me," Carmine said.

"Those are called manners. Something you ought to learn. Second off, he's doing his job. Politicking. Which is also a skill you ought to be sharpening, seeing as you're the official delegate from New York."

"Temporary official delegate," Carmine corrected.

"Whatever," Buford mumbled. "Ah! Don Paulo. *Buon giorno.*"

Don Paulo La Spada, delegate plenipotentiary of the Republic of Venice and acting chairman of the Delegation of the Republics of New York and Venice, bowed slightly and extended his hand. He was dressed in tight-fitting black slacks and shirt and sported a short, black velvet jacket, decorated on the chest with a single silver medal. Buford wondered if perhaps Carmine hadn't been right.

The boys from the States shook the Don's hand. "Is something wrong, Signor Stemp?"

Buford realized that he had been staring. "Oh, no, sir. I, uh, was just admiring your outfit. I mean, suit," Buford said.

"Ah!" Don Paulo flashed a broad smile and then snapped off an energetic pirouette. "You like it? Give me your measurements, please, and I'll have one made for you. Si?"

"Watch it, Bu, I think he likes you," Carmine muttered under his breath.

"Excuse me, Signor Carmine," Don Paulo said, flashing a smile of small, yellowish teeth. Quite the color of the ivory moon in the dome of the ceiling, Buford thought.

"Um, I, uh—"

"Carmine was just telling me to go ahead and do it. But I don't exactly have the figure for it. But you, La Lama, not only the clothes but the name fits," Buford said.

"La Lama. The blade. Pure coincidence, of course. But I did not know that you were a student of Italian, Signor Stemp," Don Paulo said.

"Buford, please."

"Of course. Buford. Thank you," Don Paulo said.

"I'm not really a student of Italian. I just looked up the name yesterday afternoon online. Although I must admit, I decided recently to brush up on my foreign language skills. It's useful in my business. And I think I may have the aptitude for it." Buford ran his palm over his short, gray hair. "Someone suggested …"

"So, you'll be studying … ?" Don Paulo said, smoothly filling in the uncomfortable silence.

"Latin," Buford said.

"Latin?" Don Paulo said, his eyes widening with true surprise. "But that will only serve you in Hades, where all the dead Romans are, I expect. A brilliant but evil race."

Don Paulo's lips curled up above his tiny, yellowish teeth. Their suggestion caused Buford to glance up at the ivory gibbous. *Hades?* He shuddered.

Don Paulo's eyes narrowed. "But, of course, it is also the great mother tongue. Learn Latin and you'll quickly learn the rest of the Romance languages. Even Portuguese. *Buon Di*, Senhor Limon!"

"Good morning, sir," Limon said.

"I thought we'd lost you," Buford said.

"No. Just observing."

"And?" Buford said.

"Too much security," Limon said.

"You said there'd be trouble. Everyone else must expect it, too," Carmine said.

"Yes. But there hasn't been a terrorist attack at a major international conference for twenty years. People don't prepare like this until after—how do you say it? After the horse is out of the barn you shut the door. Unless …" Limon said.

"Unless something else is up," Buford said. "What in hell are some of those black berets carrying automatic rifles for?" Buford pulled the Lucky back out of his pocket and raked the butt across his cheek. "Seems like there're more police than participants."

"Carmine?" Limon said.

Quickly, Carmine scanned the room. No smart-ass comments, Buford thought. Maybe he is growing up just a little. "Well, there are approximately two hundred and thirty-seven security forces and four hundred and three delegates. Approximately," Carmine said.

"An excessive ratio," Limon said.

Don Paulo turned and scanned the wall behind their table, which was located in the last row. "Security has its place but any ratio greater than zero makes me nervous," he said.

"Fairy," Carmine whispered.

"Excuse me?" Don Paulo said.

"I said, very. Me too. These guys make me *very* nervous," Carmine said.

Don Paulo regarded Carmine with what Buford thought to be an admiring look, like a teacher's for a bright pupil. "Perhaps you are a quicker study than I had thought, Signor Carmine." Carmine flushed. "And I quite agree. Guns make me extremely edgy. What do you say we all move down front where we can, um, see better. There are some empty seats with the Brazilian delegation. I'm sure they would consider it an honor."

"Let's go," Buford said.

As they moved toward the aisle, a young soldier stepped quickly away from the wall and blocked their path. Briefly, Limon and the private exchanged a few curt words. Limon flashed what appeared to be his security badge and the soldier moved back against the wall.

With mind-numbing monotony, the chief speaker for the Club of Rome droned on as Don Paulo La Lama spoke briefly with the Brazilians. Though they tried to protest, it was a short-lived attempt, and soon Don Paulo had succeeded in seating everyone. They were, however, not spared frequent frosty glances.

" ... and so," the Clubber was saying, "it is, ironically, capitalism that will lead to the Socialist paradise that many of you desire. No mind or minds can replicate the efficiency of markets. And no government or agency can minimize the administrative costs of global economic expansion the way that decentralized, atomistic market economies can.

"However, Capital must recognize the enormous potential of world markets and contribute to the creation of basic infrastructure. Clean water, food, transportation and communication.

"Henry Ford said that he would go broke if he could not sell his cars to the people who made them. When the current meteorological crisis has passed, capitalism will flame out, consume itself, if the South cannot buy the goods that it produces.

"And during the transition, those who suffer differentially must be assisted by those who benefit differentially. Thank you."

A smattering of applause was laced with catcalls and booing. On stage the Director General of the Latin American Monetary Fund was introducing the next speaker. "… may I present Senhora Camilla Limon."

When Camilla walked across the stage, there was polite applause and some murmuring. The delegates glanced at their programs. Clearly, they had not expected a housewife from Rio to address them.

Buford sat up straight. "Too bad, Limon, you got your looks from your old man." Limon laughed nervously, his jaw snapped shut. Buford could see that he was anxious, but also proud.

As Camilla Limon began to talk, Buford recognized the speech as the one she had given three days before in her own living room. Glancing behind him, he could see the delegates from the North squirming uncomfortably. Curiously, Elmer Pitkin was nodding, as if in approval.

"You of the North have walked away from our problems for centuries. That time is over. Now, I'm afraid, the problem is about to walk up to you."

The end, Buford thought. But Camilla continued.

"However, we of the South also have a …" Camilla did not finish. A man from what appeared to be the Russian delegation stood up and began shouting. Buford thought it odd that he hadn't seen the fellow before. But Buford didn't have time to finish his thought for the man screamed, "You say we have walked away. Well, you will not!" and pulled out a high-powered pistol with a sighting scope and fired, striking Camilla in the chest.

"No!" Limon screamed as he leapt from his seat. More shots rang out from the back of the auditorium and Buford pulled Limon down with all of his strength. Quickly, Buford looked over his shoulder. The noise of the gunfire was all wrong. It sounded weak. He could see two or three delegates stand and fire at the soldiers. One of them was with the New England, Rhode Island and Providence Plantations. He'd never seen the man before. Then all hell broke loose as the security forces began to fire into the crowd.

Quickly, but nevertheless meticulously, Buford organized what he could out of the mayhem of motion and sound. Curiously, the troops stationed by the exits from the main floor of the auditorium were firing their automatics methodically at knots of delegates from each of the major Northern countries who had remained in their section. Of those who rushed the doors, some were ignored and passed unharmed, while others were shot dead on the spot. The troops exhibited none of the panic that often manifests itself in a police action.

Then, for a moment only, the space was suffocated in silence. *What the fuck now?* A silence, broken by the thunderous report of weapons discharged in synchrony that strained the very walls, followed by the staccato of rifle fire.

"Jesus, fuck," Buford whispered. "A massacre. Carmine, get—" But he saw that Carmine lay huddled up, his face pressed close to the floor, his hands covering his head. "Stay down, kid."

"No fuckin' problem."

"Limon—" A sharp whack caught Buford in the jaw and sent a sickening wave of pain shooting across the side of his head, and as he fell to the floor he heard the unmistakable hiss-pop of a gunshot muffled by a silencer. *I'm dead. The cocksucker ...* He didn't finish his thought. He saw Limon pressed up against his chair, holding his revolver casually in his palm.

Buford glanced over his shoulder and saw one of the Brazilian delegates sprawled awkwardly across a seat, a small, leaking wound in the middle of his forehead, his eyes staring fixedly at Buford.

"Thanks," Buford said.

"No, thank *you*. I lost my head for a moment. It was unprofessional," Limon said.

"It was your mother they hit, for Christ's sake. I'm sorry." Buford saw that Limon was sweating profusely, but the hand that held the revolver was perfectly steady. "But let's cut the bullshit and get up on stage. She may still be alive."

Biting the corner of his lip, Limon nodded. "But how, my friend? Those snipers will pick us off before we reach the steps."

"You guys make a run for it. I'll cover you," Carmine said.

Buford's lips twitched, anticipating the smile that he suppressed. "You watch too many movies, kid. Covering fire won't work. There are too many of them and we have to cover too much distance." Carmine shrugged, his lips pursed in a pout. "But thanks."

"We need a diversion," Limon said. "But ..." His eyes darted about, searching for something he knew could not be found.

Buford snapped his fingers. "I wonder," he said, pulling the small, sapphire-tipped tube out of his jacket pocket.

"What's that?" Limon asked.

"A fucking toy. But maybe ... All right, boys. Pray to your god and cross your fingers. I hope this thing's got the range." Limon lifted an eyebrow and, quite unconsciously, both he and Carmine crossed themselves. "When the shit hits the fan, run for it."

Buford set a small switch to 'on/maximum power' and raised the cylinder, aiming at a corner support beam of the balcony. Gently, he depressed a lever and a thin ray of deep blue light shot from the tip of the tiny cannon, sawing the post in two instantly.

Buford swept his hand in a short arc, slicing two troops in half and taking out the adjacent post. With a thunderous crash, punctuated by shouts and screams, the end of the balcony collapsed, crushing at least a dozen people beneath it.

"Go!" Buford shouted to Limon, as he stuffed the laser back into his pocket. "Go!" he shouted again and shoved Carmine. Taking off at a sprint behind them, Buford paused as he passed the body of the dead Brazilian. "Son of a bitch," Buford whispered, then took off in a crouch and raced up the steps to the stage and over to the podium, which had luckily been positioned near the curtain and wings.

Squatting behind the rostrum, Limon yanked Carmine, who was standing stupidly in plain view, down and behind the curtain.

Briefly, Buford surveyed the section of balcony still standing. Three Asians were fighting their way to the Exit. The security forces' rifles were impractical at close range and one very large man was bashing skulls two at a time while another, more slender figure was doing the best damned impersonation of Bruce Lee he'd ever seen. Both shielded a third man. North Korean observers had been rumored.

He turned to Limon whose fingers lay lightly on Camilla's neck.

"Is she alive?" Buford asked, gasping for breath.

"Barely," Limon said.

"Let's get her over here in the wings," Buford said.

Gently, Buford slipped his hands under Camilla's shoulders and he and Limon slid her behind the curtain. A thin sheaf of papers slipped from her hand when they moved her and Limon scooped them up. Camilla stirred. With what appeared to be enormous effort, her chest heaved as she struggled for a breath. Her eyes slipped open and she stared silently at Buford. "I—" She swallowed. "They didn't allow me to finish." Struggling to move, to rise, Camilla succeeded only in rolling her head to the side. Her eyes caught Limon's.

"*Carinho*," she whispered.

"Mother, please. Don't speak. Don't move," Limon said, his eyes moving to the hole in her chest, seeping bright red blood.

Turning to Buford, his eyes pleaded for any small measure of reassurance, but Buford could only shake his head. Limon nodded.

"*Carinho*—"

"Mother, please. I beg you—"

"No, you listen. I'm no fool." Now her eyes were opened wide, glistening brightly, as if they were lacquered. Buford had seen this before, too many times, with too many friends, and enemies. Enemies, even, who had been friends. Like a small star, the soul often went nova before it slipped away, especially souls of great dimensions.

"What is it, Camilla?" Buford asked.

"Ah! Buford," Camilla said. She searched for his hand with her own and he took it gently.

"Ma'am," he said, simply.

"*Carinhos*. They did not let me finish. I wanted, not just to blame, but to talk, to talk—" Camilla winced and drew a sharp breath.

"To talk about justice, Mother?" Limon said.

"No, *carinho*. Justice is tied to the past. The past can be—Buford?"

Buford took a wild guess. "A catalyst, ma'am?"

"You are my English dictionary, huh? Yes, the past can be a catalyst. It can

teach. But if it stays in the soup, the supper is ruined, no? Please, Jorgezinho—"
Camilla clutched Limon's hand tightly. "Make sure they hear the rest, make—
" Buford felt Camilla's grip weaken and her eyes fluttered. Carefully, Buford
slipped his hand from beneath her head. Once again, Carmine and Limon
crossed themselves.

"Let's get her out of here. *Fast*," Buford said, struggling to
compartmentalize, to amend the mission plan extemporaneously, as he had
always done. *Am I just getting too fucking old?*

"No," Limon said, "stand up. We leave her. She's dead. We've got to make
sure we don't end up that way. People need to know what she was going to say.
What's happened here. C'mon," Limon said, his voice surfing strongly over a
barely detectable tremolo.

"Excuse me, no," a voice said. Stepping around the curtain from the front
of the stage, an officer and a soldier advanced with drawn pistols.

"Ah, I'm glad to see you, Capitan," Limon said, keeping the conversation
in English, clearly for the benefit of Buford. "I am—"

"We know who you are, Senhor Limon. Allow me to express my profound
sorrow," the captain said, regarding Camilla's body. "It seems we have caught the
perpetrators of this heinous crime nearly in the act, no?"

"I'm afraid you don't understand. These men did not shoot my mother,"
Limon said.

"No. I'm afraid *you* don't understand. What is happening here is far bigger
than the truth of the moment." Oh, boy, Buford thought. "Whether they did or
did not shoot her, as far as history is concerned, they *did*. Now, if you will please
step deep into the wings, gentlemen."

"I see," Limon said. "Of course. So, Senhores, please do as the captain has
said." He's improvising well, Buford thought. Hope they buy it.

Limon moved to reach beneath his jacket. "Stop, please, Senhor Limon.
Remove your hand, slowly, please, and step over there with your friends."

"Captain, they are not my friends, they are—"

"Please, please. We all know what is going on here. Let's not be naïve. And
give me those papers, please," the captain said.

Reluctantly, Limon handed Camilla's speech to the officer, who motioned with his pistol barrel for the three men to move upstage. Out in the auditorium, Buford could hear the firing resume once again. But now it was regular, almost methodical. The executions have started, he thought.

"You see," the captain was saying, "we will need more than one martyr to serve as inspiration to the people of Brazil and the peoples of Latin America while Mexico moves on the old States to reclaim what is rightfully theirs. What is happening out there is only the first reprisal against the North for this heinous act perpetrated against the Senhora. I'm sorry, Senhor Limon, but it can't be helped. You can see, of course, that it is for the greater good." The captain shouted an order to the soldier and they both raised their automatics.

To his right and overhead, behind the two Brazilians, Buford noticed the faintest movement, like the shadow of a shadow behind one of the curtains. Almost imperceptibly, one of the curtain ropes vibrated. "So, um, you're a philosopher, huh?" Buford said in an overloud voice, gambling for time.

The captain raised his left hand, signaling to the soldier to wait. He smiled graciously. "A bit. I am a thoroughgoing utilitarian, which I am sure you are as well; otherwise, you would not be in this business."

"Okay," Buford said, stalling, but curious as well. "What's so important about that speech."

The officer shrugged. "No harm I suppose. Her oration was to give a rationale for the South to take what is theirs. But she also admonished the South to look inward and admit their own failings, their rationalizations for their failures. We cannot permit that to become public."

"Guess not. Always easier when you lie to yourself," Buford said. For an instant Buford recalled Jaq telling him about Bildad Proud. "But I suppose that's what a good utilitarian does."

Against the dark folds of the curtain, holding onto the rope with one hand, hung Don Paulo. All of Buford's training locked into place. He did not move a single facial muscle. His eyes saw Paulo La Lama but did not look. "Still seems to me you're more like Machiavelli," Buford said.

As if on signal, Paulo dropped to the stage floor, making no sound that could be heard above the gunfire that continued to pop and burp in the auditorium. Quicker than Buford could have imagined, Don Paulo slid his left arm underneath the soldier's arm and locked his hand behind the man's neck, while his right hand held a dagger pointed at the jugular.

"Machiavelli, you said?" Don Paulo cried. The captain wheeled about, his eyes opened wide, his face a blank mask. "A damned Florentine but one of my heroes, I must admit," he said. "*Capitano*, if you will please drop that gun I would be most appreciative."

"I'm sure you would," the captain said, "but I'm afraid I can't oblige you, Senhor."

"Pity" was all Don Paulo said before he slid his stiletto through the skin of the soldier's neck then deep up into his brain. Jesus, Buford thought, this guy doesn't fuck around.

Turning purple, the captain screamed something at the Don in Portuguese that Buford couldn't quite make out. But he was pretty sure the phrase contained references to "faggot" and "shit." Then the officer fired quite madly at the Don, hitting, of course, only the corpse of the young soldier.

Both Buford and Limon seized the obvious opportunity and pulled their pistols.

But Paulo was too quick for all of them. While they were reaching, he tossed the soldier's body at the captain, knocking the officer slightly off balance, though only slightly. Yet the distraction was enough for Paulo.

He sprang from his spot and rolled across the stage floor. Before the captain could recover, Don Paulo came up from beneath him and slashed at the officer's wrist. Not only did the captain's gun fall to the floor, the hand holding it did as well.

At first, before the pain could register, the captain stood staring at the space his hand had occupied, replaced now by a stump of white bone and a surface of ragged flesh, pumping bright red, arterial blood. Then his eyes turned to the stage floor, searching for the severed hand. Almost comically, Buford thought, it lay there clutching the automatic, expressing intention in exquisite detail.

"Gentlemen, *please*," Don Paulo said, his voice clearly indicating his impatience. Buford and Limon fired, hitting the captain directly in the center of his chest.

Slowly, he dropped to his knees, then fell on top of his dead comrade, his own features expressing neither shock, nor anger but, perhaps, professional admiration, almost wonder, at the magnificence of the surprise.

"That was an extraordinary performance," Limon said.

"Thanks," Buford added.

Nodding curtly, Don Paulo rolled the captain over onto his back. Eyes and mouth remained wide open. Two small holes were paired directly over the heart. "Nice shots," Don Paulo said, smiling. "But now, since we know the why of this massacre, I suggest we find our ways out of here and inform our governments. No?" With that, the Don grabbed onto a curtain rope and shinnied like a large, black lemur up some five meters. He stopped. "You are, of course, welcome to follow me, but I suspect you lack the skills for it and, besides, it is better for us to split up in order to double our chances of getting through. Are my odds correct, Signor Carmine? " Carmine nodded.

Buford smiled. "Good luck."

"And to you, my friends," Don Paulo La Lama replied, then vanished from sight.

"Jesus Christ," Carmine whispered.

"I agree," Buford said. "Now let's move." Quickly, he picked up the captain's hand and pried the automatic loose, scooped up the soldier's small Uzi, still the perfect close-range weapon, and tossed the pistol to Carmine. "All right, Limon, you know this firetrap better than any of us. Let's bust out."

"Right. Follow me," Limon said. At a jog, and without looking back, Limon led them behind a scrim at the rear of the stage.

Guess everybody's gotta do it their own way, Buford thought.

"Here," Limon said, pointing to a ring in the floor. "This leads to a storage area beneath the stage. There's a tunnel out to a loading dock behind the building." Sporadic gunfire continued to erupt in the auditorium.

Once again, the curtains in the wings rustled, but this time more clumsily. Someone was stumbling around. Buford put his fingers to his lips and slipped off to the side, disappearing behind the thick fabric.

Signs of a short scuffle rippled through the velvet. With a few muffled cries, the intruder was led out into the open. "Elmer. Elmer!" Buford shouted in as loud a whisper as he could manage. Elmer Pitkin's eyes went wide and then he closed them for a moment in relief. Buford hushed him as he lifted his hand off Pitkin's mouth.

"Jesus H. Christ, am I glad to see you, old buddy," Pitkin said.

"The others?" Buford asked, abruptly.

"Dead."

"All of 'em?" Buford said.

"All," Pitkin said.

Just in case, Buford laid both of his large hands on Pitkin's biceps and stepped forward, pressing his own chest against Pitkin's. "And you?"

Pitkin glanced down at Buford's hands and smiled. "Nah," he said, "I was just a dumb sombitch like everybody else. Everybody except O'Reilly."

"How do you know O'Reilly was in on it?" Buford asked.

"Buford, I know who he is," Limon said. "He's okay. Let's go."

Briefly, Buford looked at Limon, then without a word, turned back to face Pitkin. "How do you know it was O'Reilly?"

"Well, when the shit hit the fan, the little Mick bastard walked right up to a soldier, calm as you please, and smiled this sick-ass, shit-eating grin. The soldier smiled back and stepped aside to let him pass to the exit." With a snort, Pitkin sucked in a large noseful of snot and swallowed.

"So he got out," Buford said.

"Nope. The solider shot the goddamned Benedict Arnold right through the back of his fucking head. Served him right." Pitkin spat on the floor.

"You sure Q'peesha—"

"Yup. I mean, she was in cahoots on the Faddle thing, but not this. You could tell when the shooting started. She was scared. Scared and surprised. All of 'em were, 'cept O'Reilly. Like I said."

Buford tightened his grip. "And you?"

"Survival skills, old buddy. I'm Militia, remember. I just dove over three fucking aisles and hid out. 'Til you blew the goddamned balcony down. Shit. What—"

"Later," Buford said.

"Anyways, I finally hauled my ass up here when I saw the chance. You found me. That's it. That's my story and I'm stickin' to it," Pitkin said, grinning.

"Okay, Limon, let's go. This is…" Buford said.

"Sounds like the shooting's stopped. They'll do a sweep through," Limon said, then flipped open the trap door and motioned impatiently for everyone to go down. At the bottom of the stairs, Buford looked up to tell Limon to hurry, but stopped. Limon was staring across the stage and crossing himself once again. Softly, he touched two fingers to his lips and, turning the hand toward his mother, stretched his arm as far as he could.

Yup, guess everybody's gotta do it their own way and in their own time, Buford thought. Just like Kate and Jaq said.

The storage room was lit by a few overhead halogens, which had been dimmed, casting a sickly yellow glow across the cavernous space. Concrete walls, covered with slick, gray paint, reflected the light weakly. Only a few objects lay scattered about. A couple of old props, some red light bulbs and an open chest, packed with curtains. The air was laced with the thick, clutching smell of mold.

"All right. That small door on the far wall leads to a hallway that defines the inside perimeter of the building and exits onto the Plaza. The large one on the right leads to a loading dock. I say we make for the loading dock," Limon said.

A heavy thunk echoed down the tunnel that opened onto the dock, and the very tips of a few thin fingers of sunlight slipped beneath the large double doors. Distant voices and shouts were heard.

"Not anymore, old buddy," Elmer Pitkin said.

Limon spat. "*Merda*! Okay, then. I guess we—" Overhead, boots clattered on the stage floor. "Let's move. This way," he said, bolting for another exit door. Again, he waited, motioning everyone through. "Buford," Limon called ahead, "just stick to the main corridor."

Buford took off at a jog, in the lead. Ghastly green fluorescents flickered madly against the ceiling, causing the corridor to swim before Buford's eyes. He was losing concentration. *Dammit!* Light sliced the dense, humid atmosphere into the lumpy shards. Then he heard tiny copper petals rustle. *Of course! How simple and clear.*

"Buford! Come back here," Limon called. Like a single strand of gossamer, the thought snapped and floated away.

Limon was waving. "This way. Quickly."

Numbly, Buford tried to trot, but his ankles felt as if they'd been shackled in lead. Passing a small side corridor, he failed to notice signs of movement in the dim passage.

"Out of shape, old man?" a voice asked.

Buford's mind snapped into focus. *Shit! You're off your game.* Jaguar Black and Cockatoo Blue stepped into the light.

"Bu!" Carmine shouted.

"Run!" Buford yelled.

"No," Limon said to Carmine and Pitkin. "Don't move."

"Limon, goddamn you! What…?" Then Buford saw Carmine and Pitkin backing out of a side passage and back into the main corridor, their weapons raised. Out popped Yellow and Orange.

"Looks like we got ourselves a Mexee-can stand-off, Buford. It's your call," Pitkin said.

"I'm toast in any event," Buford said, falling back on his training, which had snapped into place as soon as Cockatoo Blue had waved his gun. "You're the wild card, Limon. One of the others makes it and you got a chance against these two monkeys." Sharp, hot pain surged through Buford's skull as Black slapped the barrel of his automatic against Buford's cheek.

"Yes, I am the wild card. Gentlemen," Limon said, speaking to Carmine and Pitkin, "I suggest you give me your weapons, and then if everyone would be so kind, let's step into this little room here." He motioned to a door off the main hallway.

"You back-stabbin' son of a bitch," Buford said to Limon as he stepped past him and into the room. "Why the fuck didn't you just shoot us back a ways?"

The question was leading. Buford knew it and he knew Limon knew it. Limon blinked rapidly. *Morse code! Jesus Christ.* 'O-K.' That was the message. Buford grinned. "Next thing you know, somebody'll pull out his Dick Tracy radio watch," he said. Though Limon's lips did not move, his eyes smiled. Buford exhaled quietly.

"What was that?" Yellow asked in English.

"An old American insult," Limon said as he shut the door behind them.

"So, Limon. How come they're not dead already? You told us in Rio that you'd kill them." Cockatoo Blue said. Who's in charge, Buford wondered.

"Shut up," Black said, sharply. Cockatoo's head snapped around and the wrinkles on his forehead smoothed out, sending blue ripples snaking across the top of his skull, like a dangerous animal laying its ears back, flat against its head. But he said nothing. Guess that settles that, Buford thought.

"So, Limon, how come they're still alive?" Black said. "You have your mother's speech, don't you?"

"Yes," Limon said.

"I am sorry," Black said, the words seeming completely incongruous coming from such a savage figure, NOHMS Die scrawled across his chest. A look passed between Black and Limon. Buford couldn't be sure. Black crossed himself, as did Cockatoo and Yellow. Orange stood apart, sucking at the large gap where his front teeth should have been and preening the brilliant orange spikes of hair that shot from his skull in a thin line. Yellow nudged him. Orange looked up and Yellow touched his own forehead. Orange made a sloppy cross.

"Limon?" Black said. "The speech, please." Pulling the speech from his pocket, Limon stared at the folded yellow papers for a moment with what appeared to Buford to be a mixture of great sorrow and great pride, then handed them to Black. "Thank you." Black seemed far too polite and intelligent. Protocol? Maybe. Cockatoo was smart and dangerous. Pumpkin Eater was just plain dangerous. Buford couldn't quite figure Yellow.

"Hey, what the fuck're you doing?" Carmine was shouting.

"Nice *assento*, motherfucker," Orange cooed, circling Carmine while dragging the barrel of his pistol across Carmine's buttocks.

"Stay cool, Candy," Buford said, softly.

Though Carmine was trembling, he made no move to stop Orange.

"Cool?" Orange said. "Seems to me our little man is hot, no?" Rivulets of sweat began to pour off of Carmine's forehead, running down his cheeks and dripping off the end of his nose. Stooping slightly, Orange, standing now in front of Carmine, reached out and grabbed Carmine's crotch. Hold on, buddy, Buford thought. Carmine held on. *Good boy.*

"Enough!" Black snapped. "We're wasting time."

"Yeah," Cockatoo said. "Let's kill the motherfuckers and get out of here."

"Fine with me," Orange said, straightening up and shrugging. "I'll fuck him after. A bunghole's a bunghole."

That was it. Carmine snapped. Feinting with his left to distract Orange for a fraction of a second, he planted his feet and hit Orange smack in the face, sending him reeling backward and splattering blood and a couple more teeth on the ground.

"Looks like we'll have to shoot him," Cockatoo said, laughing. "I don't think you could handle him unless he was dead." Unclipping the garroting wire from his ears, Orange sneered at Cockatoo, then lunged at Carmine, lashing him across the face and cutting him deeply across his left ear and jaw.

"Stop!" Black said, in a tone that permitted no objections. "We're wasting time. I asked you a question, Limon. Why are they still alive?"

"I believe they may be valuable assets," Limon said.

"I don't," Black said.

"That's not your decision to make. I am senior, remember," Limon said.

"Yes. But this is my mission—"

"Which I've completed by hand-delivering the speech," Limon said. For a moment, there was silence. Black made no reply. *Maybe Limon is going to pull this off*, Buford thought.

"*Merda*," Cockatoo snarled. "You told us in Rio that you'd kill them. Maybe you've become too involved. Or maybe you're a traitor?"

Limon glanced at Cockatoo, then faced Buford. "All right. Up against the wall," Limon said, motioning toward the flat white space behind them, gleaming, almost antiseptic beneath the overheads. Like a dissection table in the morgue, Buford thought. *So this is it. One of the risks of the job. No tears.*

Limon was okay, Buford was sure of that. But he couldn't take out the four street creeps, or whatever they were, by himself.

Buford, Carmine and Pitkin lined up. Looking over at Carmine, Buford could see that he was shaking all over, but trying very hard to control it. He winked. Carmine took a deep breath and grinned. "You're all right, Carmine," Buford said.

"Thanks, Bu," Carmine said.

"Any last requests?" Limon said.

"Cut the crap, Limon," Cockatoo said. "What do you think this is, some fucking movie?"

Black held up his hand. "The request is reasonable. These men are in our profession, no?" Black gave Carmine a hard stare.

Carmine cleared his throat and looked Black in the eye. "Don't let Pumpkin Eater here fuck me when I'm dead, okay?"

Black nodded. "He won't." Orange glared at Black.

"You?" Black said to Pitkin.

Pitkin spat a wad of dip on the floor. "Through the heart." Black smiled and nodded.

"And you, old man?" Black said to Buford.

"Well," Buford said, as he began to reach for his shirt pocket.

"Hold it!" Cockatoo said.

"They're just cigarettes," Buford said.

"You want a smoke, eh? This *is* like a movie!" Cockatoo said, chuckling.

Buford pulled out a Lucky and rubbed it across his cheek. "Nah, gave 'em up. What I'd like is for Limon here to kill you three instead of us." Buford grinned.

Limon laughed and so did Cockatoo and Orange and Yellow. Limon shrugged. "Okay," he said simply, then smoothly fanned the hammer of his pistol, sweeping the barrel across a small arc, striking Yellow and Cockatoo both in the middle of the chest and Orange square in the stomach, just a fraction of a second before he could squeeze off a shot.

Black was standing very quietly. "I thought maybe," Buford said to him.

"You guessed right, then," Black said.

"I was wondering about that fucking peashooter," Buford said.

"Much more efficient than a clip in a tight spot, when the odds are poor," Limon said.

Behind him, Buford heard an ugly groan. Carmine was leaning against the wall. He was bent over at the waist, grabbing his knees and retching violently.

"Minnie?" Buford walked quickly over to his friend and put his arm around the boy's shoulder. "Shoot, there's hardly any blood, boy. Jorge missed the heart on Blue and Yellow, though you can't blame him, and ol' Pumpkin Eater's gut shot."

"It's not that *they're* dead, Bu. It's that *I* almost was. Brother!" Carmine straightened up and Buford tousled his hair. "I'm all right," Carmine said, wiping his mouth with his sleeve.

Buford dabbed the blood on Carmine's cheek almost lovingly, with his sleeve. "You are that, boy."

"But we won't be if we don't get out of here fast," Black said. "They're doing a very thorough sweep. They want no survivors."

"Okay. Let's disappoint 'em," Buford said.

"I'll go into the corridor and see if it's clean. If it's not, I'll lead them away and you're on your own," Black said.

Elmer and Buford nodded and Limon returned their guns to them and to Carmine.

Conspicuously, Black walked out into the corridor. Clearly, he was regarded as an asset. '*Merda*," Buford heard him say under his breath. Black reached back into the room, flicked off the lights and closed the door.

"Nothing here," Buford thought he heard him say. There was the sound of perhaps a dozen jack boots hitting the floor, which grew fainter as Black led them down the hall and away.

When the sounds had faded, Limon opened the door a crack and peered out into the hall. He held up his hand. "There're ten or so heading down a side corridor. Must have split off from the bunch that Indio decoyed," Limon whispered. "Okay. It's clear. Let's move across the hall and out. Fast. And quietly."

Pitkin bolted. As Buford prepared to exit, he heard what he thought was a low grunt behind him. Turning, he saw Orange with his automatic raised and pointed directly at him. His own gun was in his belt. *Too late.* To his left, a loud boom startled him. Where Orange's right eye had been, a gaping hole gushed blood as his head dropped to the floor, hitting the concrete with a sickening crack.

"We're fucked!" Limon shouted. "Move." Buford and Carmine bolted out the door and across the hall, followed by Limon. Shouts, a couple of distant shots, then a loud boom were heard as Pitkin fired off a couple of rounds as cover.

"Minnie? Where'd you learn to shoot like that?" Buford said as he sprinted down the hall.

"Video games. But I saw that shot in an old movie. Remember the Jew guy in Vegas in the Godfather?" Carmine said.

"Yeah, yeah. And thanks," Buford said.

Limon was in the lead. "We've got maybe forty meters between us and them, but I think it's enough. There! That door and we're out!" Off to the side a door opened and a pair of troops stepped into the corridor. Behind, the sounds of their pursuers were growing louder.

"Trapped like rats," Pitkin snarled.

Surprised, the soldiers froze for a couple of seconds. Their hesitation gave Limon just enough time to orient himself. "In here!" Limon shouted, grabbing the handle of the door to the stairwell. The soldiers hadn't seen him. "And let's have some cover!"

Carmine and Pitkin squeezed off several rounds at their pursuers, who were just rounding the corner, and Buford's fire forced them back.

"Okay," Limon said once they were all inside. "Two flights up to the Plaza, then you're on your own." They all raced, two steps at a time, past the next landing to the Plaza level. "I have to go back for Indio. He still has the speech on him. It has to survive this. I have to get it back before they find it."

As they reached the platform fronting a metal catwalk, perhaps twenty meters from the exit, Buford realized that Pitkin was gone. Looking down, he saw Elmer squatting on the landing below.

"Elmer!" Buford cried. "Get your skinny ass up here."

"Now if I did that, my cover wouldn't be worth much of a shit, would it?" Pitkin said. "Besides, they can see me through the window. Once I move, they're in."

"Mr. Pitkin, please. I'll provide the cover. Quickly, please," Limon said.

"Yeah. And if—" Pitkin began. Below him, the door blew open and, mixed with shouts and oaths, the firing began as the first wave of troops entered the stairwell. Pitkin squeezed off three or four rounds and the soldiers retreated quickly. Buford could see that at least two had been hit.

"Mr. Pitkin, please, I can—" Limon began.

"Yeah. Yeah. I'm sure you can. But then *your* cover's blown. I figured out who you are. Oh, and sorry about your momma." Limon nodded. "Anyways, in a pinch, you can use me as an alibi, for bein' where you ain't supposed to be, like this stairwell. Might even help you get to Indio quicker."

"Elmer, listen—" Buford began.

"Buford Stemp. This is what I trained myself to do. This is what I like to do. I'm Militia, old buddy.

"That speech is pretty important, I'm thinkin'. Wouldn't let her finish it. Far as I can figure, it must be a humdinger. And—" The door below blew open and a half dozen soldiers stumbled in. It looked to Buford as if they'd been shoved in. Fear was pasted all over their features. Pitkin shot the first two. As the rest turned, shots rang out from the corridor and they fell. Buford shot Limon a hard, questioning look.

"*Los Ossos*," Limon said. "The Death Squads are here. The regular troops are fodder."

"That's pretty fucked up," Buford said. Limon nodded.

"One, maybe two more waves and you won't be able to hold them, Mr. Pitkin," Limon said.

"I already told you—or you told me—there's nothin' more important than getting that speech into the right hands.

"I've been listening real carefully the last three days, Buford. And while we've had it bad up North, seems to me like they've had it worse," Pitkin said. "Maybe I can help. Just a little."

"Why, Mr. Pitkin," Limon said, "I thought your republic was known for its prejudice."

"There's some that's incorrigible. And prejudice can have a foundation in truth, Mr. Limon. But no one is all good or all bad. And I figure you boys down South aren't half bad which means you're more'n half good and that's enough for me." The door below swung open and shots rang out, a few bullets ricocheting off the wall with a menacing whine.

"Buford," Elmer shouted. "Let's cut the bullshit and, please, get your asses outta here!"

"He's right," Limon said. "You and Carmine must get to safety."

"Why us?" Buford asked, grasping Limon's meaning and eyeing him suspiciously.

"Because *La Cobre* told me, that's why."

"*La Cobre*?" Buford said.

"Ur, the copper-haired girl. She said your safety was important. No, imperative," Limon said.

"And you believed her?" Buford said.

"Explicitly and implicitly," Limon said, then raised his eyebrows in a very serious, questioning manner.

"Yeah, so do I," Buford said, reaching into his pocket for a Lucky and dragging the butt end across his cheek, scattering a few flakes of tobacco across the front of his shirt. He pulled a matchstick out of his pants pocket and scraped the top against the wall, igniting a burst of bright orange flame that hissed menacingly. *Give 'em up tomorrow.* Buford lit the cigarette and took a deep draw. "All right. Let's go, Minnie. Elmer, good luck, old buddy."

"See ya in I-dee-ho! Mebbe," Pitkin said, turning around and grinning at Buford.

"Go," Limon said.

But just as Buford and Carmine stepped onto the catwalk, the entrance to the open stairwell from the floor below, but above Pitkin, opened and the lead troops of a squadron stepped through. Seeing Buford and Carmine, they opened fire, sending them back into a recess on the landing.

"Shit fuck," Buford said. He could hear the soldiers coming slowly up the staircase. Dashing out, he squeezed off a few rounds, inviting scattered return fire and pressing them up against the wall. He could hear them gathering on the landing above Elmer.

Buford took another long drag. He could hear sounds from below. It sounded as if *Los Ossos* were preparing for a final assault. "Suck it up, pardner," Buford said to Pitkin.

"I hear 'em," Pitkin said. A long grinding moment of complete quiet passed.

"Say, Buford!" Pitkin cried suddenly. "You still got that Flash Gordon ray-gun?"

"Yeah," Buford said. "Yeah!" He pulled the small instrument from his jacket pocket. Buford hesitated.

"Goddammit, Buford Stemp, will you quit arguin'?"

Buford flipped the little silver tube to Pitkin. "This looks simple enough," Pitkin said. "They put the directions right on the side here. Now, boys, when the rest of 'em come in below, I'm gonna blow that fucking landing right down on their goddamned heads."

"And yours," Buford said.

"Hope not." Elmer pulled a cigarette from his pocket and lit it hurriedly. "Limon, I'm gonna scrinch sideways-like under these iron railings and pray. You dig me out, if you can. Deal?" Pitkin said.

"Deal, my friend. And don't drop that toy, Elmer," Limon said, smiling. "I'll need it for my alibi. It's the only way I can dispose of all the witnesses."

"Deal," Pitkin said.

With a loud bang and a gust of furious cries, the stairwell door below them was shoved open and a small horde of berserkers streamed in.

Pitkin pointed the little silver tube at the landing above and a blue ray shot out. With a crack, the concrete gave way, and amidst screams and the odd, hollow knock of rubble tumbling off walls, the landing and the soldiers fell five meters down and on top of their own in a cloud of dust.

"Run," Limon said quietly.

"Get him out if you can," Buford said to Limon, who leapt then began to scramble over hummocks of cement and steel toward the spot where Pitkin had been.

Buford and Carmine ran like hell, reaching the exit at the opposite end of the catwalk in seconds. Tossing his cigarette aside and raising his pistol, Buford opened the door and peered cautiously outside.

CHAPTER VII

On the Plaza Grande, scattered troops were racing around, rifles raised. Cars and trucks zoomed about aimlessly like mindless bugs.

Smack in front of the exit not two meters away sat Donna's electric pink Volkswagen, shimmering strangely. But Donna was nowhere to be seen. Behind the wheel sat *La Cobre.*

With an expression that was more serious than usual and an impatient wave, Ur gestured quite clearly to the two men to get their asses into the car.

Ten meters away a jeep screeched to a halt and at the same moment, two soldiers, obviously elite guard from the black uniforms they wore, appeared from around a corner and immediately froze in their tracks.

Carmine must have been as astonished as the soldiers by the pink VW, rippling mirage-like before him. He stood slack-jawed, simply staring.

"Minnie! Get your Guinea glutes in the car," Buford screamed.

From the jeep, the driver shouted something to the two troops facing the car. Carmine blinked. The soldiers shook themselves out of their stupor, as if they'd stuck their tongues into a light socket.

"Oh, shit," Carmine said, and dove into the back seat.

The blacks raised their rifles and an officer sprang from the jeep, yanking his automatic pistol from its holster.

Ur floored the pink Beetle and once again the soldiers stood motionless, their faces unfolding into featureless masks, undone by disbelief.

Abruptly, Ur decelerated and calmly turned the car around, coming within a foot of the two soldiers who were now talking excitedly to one another. The officer raced toward them. Ur missed him by millimeters. Or did she drive right through him, Buford wondered.

No one spoke. Ur downshifted and the pink Beetle buzzed toward one of the exit ramps off of the Plaza. Several times Ur slithered between trucks and jeeps and through knots of soldiers heading for the Congress Hall.

As Ur hit the ramp, which led to the boulevard, Buford saw a troop truck heading, against the grain, directly for them. "Lookout!" he cried. Ur jammed the gearshift forward and with no room at all to spare, slid past the truck and out onto the main thoroughfare.

Buford leaned back against his seat and squeezed the pack of Luckys in his shirt pocket. Slowly, purposefully, he stretched his neck and shoulders. Delicate, sharp shocks radiated down his back and out through his hips. *It's been one hell of a day so far, Buford Stemp.*

All around them Brasilia was a pot at full boil; kinetic, chaotic, but contained. All of Buford's instincts and training were telling him that he needed to survive, to get out of Brasilia as fast as he could, so that he might provide the strategic intelligence he possessed.

Staring straight ahead through the Bug's tiny windshield, Buford instinctively began to count the number and type of military vehicles in the battle zone and their vectors. There were jeeps of ancient twentieth century design, and black and green troop carriers, oddly half empty. Maybe not so odd, since no ground force opposed the indigenous army, Buford thought. Suddenly, several new Chinese Dragon Mobile Artillery Platforms flew over them at low altitude, wheels down, clearly close to their targets.

Everything was headed away from them and toward the airport. *The airport! Of course.* The massacre must be complete. Buford began to speak, then checked himself. He felt that there was a purpose to this joyride Ur was taking them on that transcended normal behavior. *Ur?* Deep inside his brain, Buford raised a mental eyebrow.

They had to turn around and get to the airport and rendezvous with Faddle. But Ur must know that as well. And there were a few things that Buford wanted desperately to find out, like the fact that they seemed to be slipping unobserved through the general mayhem, just as Ur had walked across the Avenida Atlantica that night in Rio. Gnawing at him even more was the deep conviction that he was connected to Ur, in a way unrelated to the great events unfolding around them.

Carmine was curled up on the backseat in a ball. "It's all right, Candy, we're clear. Sit up and enjoy the ride."

Gripping the back of Buford's seat, his hands shaking, he eyed Ur. "Thanks."

"You're welcome," Ur said.

Buford cleared his throat. "Miss? Where'd you learn to drive like that?"

"My name is Ur. I believe we've passed the point in our relationship, Buford Stemp, of being overly formal."

"It's just an expression. I wasn't being—" Eyes fixed straight ahead, Ur said nothing. "Shoot." Buford hung his head and rubbed his forehead.

"You see, I'm trying very hard to learn some of the protocols of human interaction. While I've learned a great deal from Uncle Nick and Frankie—"

"Frances Howard?"

"Yes," Ur said.

"Jesus," Buford whispered. "She disappeared from Ketchum about the same time as Nick."

"That's correct. They are--a couple. We all live at New Spall, but it's a very small community, and there is little diversity in social conventions. It is much more complicated here. There are so many variables." Ur flashed her perfect, clenched-teeth smile.

Buford blinked. "I've heard of Old Spall, but where's New Spall?"

"Elsewhere," Ur said. "But we're straying from your question. While I learned to handle Rock Cats on Spall, these machines require different skills. Donna let me drive a good deal of the way here, and since driving is part of my essential nature, I learned quickly. That is my primary purpose here, to be a driver."

"A driver." Buford ran his hand through the gray stubble on his head. "I'll say you've learned a lot." All around them vehicles continued to scream past. Brasilia had become thoroughly unglued. Ur downshifted.

"Fangool!" Carmine croaked as Ur cut through two lanes of traffic.

They slipped around vehicles, and as they did Buford noticed an odd iridescence, a slithering at the margins.

Buford slipped a Lucky out of the pack in his pocket and rubbed it against his cheek. "I meant, how'd you learn to drive like *that*?"

"I see now. Your original question was imprecise," Ur said. "The referent of the demonstrative pronoun 'that' was unclear."

"Right. I think," Buford said.

"Buford Stemp, we are traveling through space-time. Or, more precisely, along a world-line of less probable existential reality," Ur said. Buford swallowed hard. "It's simple, really." Ur made a sharp turn at a broad intersection, dropping behind a fire engine, siren blaring, of the type that carried pressurized CO_2 cannons. "Ah, this is better."

A smile played at the corners of Buford's mouth. "The referent of the demonstrative pronoun 'this' is unclear," he said.

Ur shot him a glance, then her face burst into the more supple smile coaxed out by her laughter, which showered the cab of the car in copper.

"Pennies from heaven," Buford said softly.

"I'm sorry?" Ur said.

"Your laugh," Buford said.

"And a song," Carmine said. "Buford used a 'double entendre.'"

"Double—yes, of course. French. A double meaning. Frankie likes to sing that song. And you think that my voice is metallic?" Ur asked.

"No. I mean, yes, but—" Buford began.

"You must understand that subtleties, like double entendres, elude me still. It is part of my nature; or, rather, *not* a part of it. It is a vestigial deficiency, like Uncle John's stutter. You've noticed how he repeats himself," Ur said matter-of-factly. But Buford was no longer paying attention. Instead, he had become focused on the truck they were following. "Buford?"

"Excuse me. I was going back to work. Habit," he said.

"A good one. So?" Ur said.

"I was wondering about that fire truck we're following," Buford said.

"That's what I meant when I said *this* is better. Donna taught me that if you follow fire engines, police cars, any official vehicle, you can minimize traveling time."

"You mean you can speed," Carmine said.

"Yes!" Ur said. "And it is exciting, especially all of the noise."

"I didn't mean that," Buford said. "I was wondering why they deployed a truck with CO_2 cannons. I don't see any fires at all, let alone fuel-based fires. I hope it's not something at the airport. It'd be a bitch if they've blown up our ride home. But they're headed in the wrong direction."

"I don't think they can destroy Uncle John's jet, in any event," Ur said.

"But all it's armed with are a couple of pop guns. Isn't it?" Buford said.

"Hardly," Ur said. She accelerated the bubble-gum Bug and for a moment Buford thought they were going to drive right over the rear bumper and straight into the back of the fire engine. He gripped the dash tightly and could feel Carmine's hand slip behind his back as he latched onto Buford's seat.

"That is where they are going with the cannons," Ur said, pointing at the two towers that soared above the Congress Hall. A small black shape was diving at a steep angle toward the south tower. It was one of the old American F-series fighter jets with RMR on side. The roar of its engines could be heard above the din in the streets. A loud boom reverberated through the thick, humid atmosphere as the aircraft breached the sound barrier. Almost immediately a second loud roar followed, as the plane smashed into the tower and exploded in a ball of black breath and orange fire.

"This will happen in approximately ten minutes in this reality," Ur said.

"Jesus, they thought of everything," Buford said. "They dispatched that engine before the blast. They planned it. The North strikes with a Rocky Mountain plane, or that's the way they've made it look, and the South gets to take the moral high ground. We've got to stop it!" Buford said.

"You can't, Bu," Carmine said. "You heard her. You'd be changing the future. It's not allowed."

"That is an interesting theory, Carmine, but it is only partially correct," Ur said.

"So what are we waiting for?" Buford shouted. "Let's drop out of warp and see if we can contact somebody who'll shoot the thing down. You said Faddle's plane's got artillery."

"Actually, that attack will not happen in your world, Buford," Ur said.

"What in hell are you talking about now?" Buford said.

"We're seeing just one of many futures, many universes," Carmine said, his voice quiet and calm. "Is it really true, Ur?"

"Yes," Ur said. "That is a very good deduction, Carmine. You both needed to see the possibility of a different worldline, since you may need to deal with it before all of this is over."

"I knew we brought him along for something," Buford said grumpily. Gazing up through the windshield, Buford watched as black plumes of smoke belched from the crippled building as if it were coughing out its own guts. *Madness. Human beings are utterly and incorrigibly mad.*

Buford's mouth had gone sour, the taste of the cigarette he'd smoked turning his stomach. He shoved the unlit Lucky back into his shirt pocket. He blinked. The fire engine was gone. He looked up at the towers. They stood pristine, erect, windows blazing hot white, defiantly hurling the sun's own light back into its face.

"All right, Einstein. Which goddamned universe are we in now?" Buford growled.

"Beats me. You gotta figure there are infinitely many permutations of possible states given initial conditions. Infinite but countable. So, ay, who knows?" Carmine said.

Despite the maelstrom of motion and sound all around them, Buford became acutely aware of context. Yellow lines, like markings down the back of a deadly viper, snaked along the black asphalt of the boulevard. Gleaming white marble buildings sat pasted against the light blue jungle sky of morning, like cardboard cutouts.

Buford cleared his throat. "Ur, you still haven't answered my question. Not really. Why don't I, this *I* sitting here, just shuffle back in time a step, stop that jet, and to hell with screwing with some other, what's it called, world-line?"

"Because this *you*, sitting here, exists in a physical universe without a kamikaze jet. Another you in a universe where no massacre occurred in the Congress Hall. Or perhaps *that* you perished in the suicide attack. Besides you have work to do here."

A smile played at the corners of Ur's rich, supple lips. He hadn't observed that degree of subtlety of emotion in Ur before. Of course, he hadn't spent all that much time with her, had he? Buford felt his insides flow like thick, warm honey. He stirred. *Dirty old fucking man.* Buford frowned.

"Don't look so glum. While you exist in only one physical universe, there are many moral universes that will unfold as well, because of the choices you will make." The subtle smile faded from Ur's face and she turned her eyes back to the road. "Besides, I am the driver, Buford Stemp, and when I am driving I can claim certain prerogatives, such as the choice of route, that are otherwise not allowed."

"Krishna," Carmine whispered, but Ur ignored him.

"So, you've both seen the possibility of many worlds and I assume you're both accustomed to this mode of travel by now. I think we'll take, in both a Euclidean and a relativistic sense, a shortcut to the airport," Ur said.

"Which is?" Buford asked, somewhat nervously.

Accelerating directly into the oncoming traffic, Ur slipped and zipped the pink Bug around, between, over and under—had it actually been *under*? Buford wondered—the dense, fast, moving mass of cars and trucks. Yes, under a police car, around a half-track rocket launcher, over a hook and ladder. Buford's heart pounded furiously against his ribs.

"Candy, you okay?" Buford said.

"Fuck no. But yeah," Carmine said.

In the distance, the airport loomed, bristling with antennae and dishes and brightly colored, old-fashioned wind socks. As they got closer, Buford could see jets taking off, or trying to, only to explode in balls of flame from ground fire. *Shit.*

"When we stop near Faddle's jet, we'll be back on your original world-line. We'll be visible and exposed. Get out and run like hell," Ur said.

"We'll need cover," Buford said. "I'll—"

"We're expected. I gave Donna the precise temporal coordinates, so Faddle will be able to provide cover. But, as you know, Buford Stemp, cover is only that. There will still be risk," Ur said.

The pink VW stopped abruptly. Buford felt sick for an instant. "Go!" Ur shouted, and all three bolted from the car and toward the steps sitting against the fuselage of the jet.

Racing toward them, not a hundred meters away, were two jeeps and a mobile launcher. The mobile launcher braked hard, apparently stunned by the sudden appearance of the bright pink car. Buford heard gunfire and the whistle of a few random bullets buzzing by his ear. *This is going to be close.*

Suddenly, behind them Buford heard a blast, followed by a whoosing sound over his right shoulder. *RPG.* The grenade hit the first jeep, and the blast caused the other two vehicles to veer and brake.

Shooting a quick glance behind him, Buford saw the three North Korean 'observers' he had noticed fighting their way out of the balcony at Congress Hall. The big man, and the two others, along with a half dozen troops.

"Go, go!" the thin uniformed man from the Hall shouted, and they were off. Their escort made short work of the Brazilian troops in the other two vehicles.

Quiet, Buford thought; but not for long I expect.

Faddle's jet had turned into the wind and the big man was at the head of the ramp shouting, "C'mon, c'mon," and waving them all in.

As they hit the steps, Ur scrambled up after Carmine, but the North Korans pulled up.

"Thanks," the man in civvies said. "But our ride's on the way."

Behind them Buford heard the 'thwak, thwak, thwak' of rotary blades. "That's one big helicopter gunship," Buford said. "But I suppose big makes sense if they're pickin' up Go Jumong."

"Pleased to meet you too Mr. Stemp," Jumong said. Buford raised an eyebrow.

The big man signed furiously to Jumong. "Okay", Jumong said. "Perhaps another time, Mr. Stemp?" Buford nodded.

"Get your asses moving," Faddle shouted. Then he signed to Fuong Ba. A look of surprise crossed Fuong Ba's face, and then he smiled and signed something back.

"Go!" Faddle shouted again. "We'll give you cover." And as the copter touched down on the runway, they were off. But just before Jumong started to run, Buford saw him glance, for just a second, up into the cockpit of Faddle's plane. His eyes locked onto the pilot's, but so briefly Buford wasn't sure there was anything to it.

Around the corner of the hangar careened an armored vehicle with a rocket launcher, nearly on two wheels. Shit, Buford thought, no RPG'll take out that tank. Buford stopped and saw the launcher's rocket carriage leveling for a shot. "Fuck!" A small burst of flame erupted around the vehicle as the missiles roared toward their target, Jumong's ride home. But before they were halfway to the copter they exploded as they hit a broad, blue wall of light. "I'll be double goddamned," Buford whispered.

"Buford Stemp! Get your ugly ass up here. Time's wastin'. Yessir. Time's wastin'," John Faddle was shouting. Buford scrambled halfway up the steps only to be grabbed by the shoulders and hauled in by Faddle himself. The old man's strength surprised him.

Donna sealed the door; and the jet wheeled about and screamed down the runway, throwing Buford backward. "Hang on, Buford. No time to buckle up," Faddle said as he deposited himself with an enormous, authoritative thud into his seat.

Buford and Carmine each held onto an armrest for their lives. Unexpectedly, the aircraft cornered sharply, throwing both men across the aisle. Buford heard a nasty thunk behind him.

"If the goddamned wind hadn't shifted, we'd be long gone," Faddle roared. "Ur, can't you help?"

"Yes, Uncle John. But no."

"Aaargh," was all Faddle could manage.

Ur was perched on a seatback, in the crisp white capris and a tight short sleeved shirt she had worn at the bowling alley in Ipanema, staring out of the window. Buford started to shout a warning to her but stopped himself. *Who're you kidding, old buddy?* "Faddle? We goin' vertical?" Buford shouted, breathing heavily.

"What do you think?" Faddle said.

"Shit, Minnie, c'mon," Buford said, grabbing Carmine by the arm and with enormous effort hauling him up and into the seat beside him. A nasty gash lay open across Carmine's forehead. Blood was running down his nose. "Between Pumpkin Eater's garrote and that armrest you look like you were in a car wreck. You all right?"

"No. But yeah."

"Good kid." Hurriedly, Buford secured Carmine's seat buckle.

The pilot was speaking to Faddle over the intercom. "There's another hostile, sir, and I've got to pull up in four seconds. We don't have circumferential shielding."

"Just get us out o' here in one piece," Faddle growled.

"Yes, sir," the pilot replied.

Carmine was secured. On an impulse, Buford turned back toward Ur again. She was watching him intently. *A test?* Mentally, he shrugged.

Leaning over as far as he could and pressing his cheek against the window, Buford caught an obstructed view, dead ahead. He could just make out the side of the rocket launcher. A blue beam shot from beneath their wing and the launcher exploded as the pilot pulled up.

Almost immediately the angle of ascent shifted to 90 degrees. Thrown backwards against his seat, Buford gripped the armrests for all he was worth. As the G forces increased and the trajectory stabilized, Buford struggled to strap himself in. He was pretty sure the ride would get rougher. He was right.

A few random explosions were heard behind the plane. So it has fore and aft shielding and laser cannons, Buford thought.

"Everyone, please, hang on," the pilot said. "I'm going to exercise a few evasive maneuvers as a precaution. We've experienced some random fire but it appears to be uncoordinated. The situation on the ground is chaotic. I'll have to say, Mr. Faddle, I believe we scared the shit out of them,".

"You scared the shit out o' me, that's for sure," Faddle rumbled into his mike.

"Sorry, sir," the pilot said, and Buford heard the intercom snap off.

Gently, the jet decelerated, rolled, and then with a roar dove straight down from fifteen thousand feet. Buford heard Carmine gag and watched him grab an airsick bag and shove it over his mouth.

The pilot pulled up, rolled again, and began to zig back and forth and zag up and down as he climbed discontinuously higher. Carmine retched violently. Buford patted him on the shoulder.

Suddenly, two explosions were heard behind the jet. A little too close, Buford thought.

"They must've put some fighters in the air to prevent any escape," the pilot's voice crackled over the intercom. "Our aft shields will hold them, but I've got two on radar closing fast in front of us. I can't shoot and shield at the same time."

"Whadda ya mean?" Faddle roared.

"Well, sir, it's like the old Klingon Warbirds. You can cloak or you can shoot but you can't do both. Excuse my language, sir, but I don't believe we should fuck around. I'd like permission to take out the two bandits behind us and go where they can't."

"Do it," Faddle said.

Pure, focused blue light flared from beneath the wings and blazed aft. Two massive explosions rocked the jet slightly, and Buford caught a tinge of orange afterglow. "Done, sir," the pilot replied.

"Poor, goddamned, dumb-ass jungle bunnies," Faddle said. "Say, Sky, nice shootin' but what about the fighters up ahead?"

"I'll be goddamned, sir."

"Huh?"

"Two friendlies, North Korean, by the looks of the big red stars on their tails, just took out the hostiles," the pilot said.

"Hah!!" Faddle shouted, smiling and rubbing his hands together. "I'm sure glad I convinced the rest of our 'confederacy' to give the Koreans that old beat-up carrier, like they asked, as a thank you for helping us take out Necros and shutting down their nuclear program in the bargain."

"We're heading to sixty thousand feet," the pilot was saying. Oxygen masks dropped from overhead.

Gently, Buford placed his palm on the back of Carmine's neck. "You okay? We've got to put on oxygen," Buford said.

Carmine opened his eyes and lowered the bag from his mouth. The smell made Buford's own stomach turn for a moment. Buford tried to take the bag from Carmine but Carmine pulled it away and closed it tightly, then placed it beneath his seat. "Sorry, Bu," he said in a weak voice. "I've been waiting to finish that job all morning, ever since I almost got my brains blown out."

"Fuggedaboutit," Buford said, with a grin.

Carmine attempted a weak smile. Buford handed him a yellow mask. "Put this on." Carmine wiped his mouth with his sleeve and secured it.

In minutes they were level and flying Mach 3 at sixty thousand feet. The silence, Buford thought, was exquisite. All he could hear was the sound of his own breathing, calm and steady, inside his mask. Looking out of the window and down through a cloudless sky, he gazed on the dark green jungle awash in the glare of noon light, and off in the distance, the gray-blue of the South Atlantic. No one would follow them there. Not yet, anyway. But Buford knew that soon, hordes would be heading north.

CHAPTER VIII

"Thing is," *Faddle was* saying, "it's a goddamned shame about Q'peesha. I mean, I'm sorry about the rest of the bunch, 'sfar as loss of human life is concerned, but she was special. Had guts and brains." Faddle slurped his bourbon deeply.

"But I am truly sorry for all of 'em, except that goddamned, no good son-of-a-bitch O'Reilly. Almost wish I'd been there. I'd of—"

"No, no *favorito*. Then you'd have been killed too, and I'd have died of a broken heart. Or had to kill myself. No, no," Donna said. She was sitting on Faddle's lap, her hand placed lightly on the back of his neck. The jet carried fewer than half the seats of a normal aircraft, and they could be swiveled so that the passengers could face one another during the flight.

"Kill yourself? Honey, you didn't even know me two days ago!" Faddle said, raising his big, bushy eyebrows.

"So? Maybe you don't love me the way I love you," Donna said, slipping her hand off Faddle's neck and pushing her full, red lips into a pout; but her eyes were twinkling.

So were Faddle's. Letting go an enormous whoop, he slapped her on the thigh. "*That's* why I love you," Faddle said softly.

"Why's why you love me, *favorito*? I don't understand," Donna said.

"Because you remind me of Dana. Hope that doesn't bother you, honey. I just have to be honest." Faddle slurped his bourbon noisily. "It's a compliment."

"I like that you're honest. Most men aren't," Donna said.

Faddle grinned. "Buford? Carmine? Doesn't she remind you of Dana?"

Shifting nervously in his chair, Buford cleared his throat. "Well …"

"Ay, Uncle John. Aunt Dana was tall, and blonde and blue-eyed and, and quiet," Carmine said. Dana, Faddle's wife and Ur's nurse, dead some five years, had looked like a Valkyrie, or so Jaq had described her. And she had been a deaf-mute. "Donna's. Donna's …" Carmine gestured with his hands. Donna was tall, but much like her mother, darkly beautiful.

"Aaargh!" Faddle growled. "Here, honey—" Faddle patted the seat beside him. "My leg's going numb." Gracefully, Donna slid off Faddle's lap. "Carmine, you're missing the point. Missing the point entirely. She's only the second person … Well, third, including your daddy, Ur." Ur was sitting very quietly on the floor, lotus position. "Anyway, she's only the second *woman* who's focused me. That night, back in ninety-three, at your mom and daddy's house, Ur, at the Winter Solstice party, Dana whipped my ass in ten seconds flat in a wrestling match. Lifted me up and over her shoulder and, bam! Thought she'd killed me."

"I thought it was five seconds, Uncle John," Carmine said.

"Shut up, son," Faddle grumbled. "Anyway, that incident focused me. Or started the process anyway. I began to see how goddamned narrow and insulated my life was, selling stocks. Living alone, selling stocks. I was a real one-dimensional dickhead.

"And Donna here has focused me, too. I'm ninety but I'm no goddamned invalid. I'm a man still. Yessir," Faddle said.

"I've got to admit I was surprised when you hauled me into the plane," Buford said.

"Lot of things might surprise you, Buford. Right, honey?" Faddle flashed Donna a little smile. Donna laid her head on Faddle's thigh. Playfully, he took it off. "Cut that out, Donna. Not now.

"Carmine, when we get back to New York I want you to throw that goddamned wheelchair away, or give it to Goodwill or something. 'Course—" Faddle patted his stomach. "I'm gonna have to lose a few pounds. My knees aren't what they were. That's my problem! Goddamned knees. I think I'm going to need all of my strength for what's coming."

"You will, Uncle John," Ur said. Everyone turned toward her. "All of your strength, physical and mental. "But Carmine's not going to New York."

"No? Where're you sending me?" Carmine asked with an edge on his voice.

"I'm sorry. I phrased that badly. I hope you won't be going to New York. It's your choice," Ur said.

"Sure. Okay, so where?" Carmine said.

"Chicago," Ur said.

"Chicago!" Carmine shuddered involuntarily. "Chicago's a twenty-square-mile friggin' ice cube."

"I know. But I'd like you and Buford to go there. And then I'd like you to go to Ketchum," Ur said.

"What's in Chicago?" Buford asked.

"Who," Ur said. "I want you both to go and see Professor Irwin."

"Irwin! He's a kook. Fuggedaboutit," Carmine said.

"A kook and a genius," Ur said.

"Genius? He perfected a titanium-graphene coating for glass spacecraft. There is no space program anymore. I don't get it," Carmine said.

"He also invented the technology that packed all of that power into my pen, and this plane. Xasers. A practical x-ray laser," Buford said.

"And the North will need them both," Ur said.

"For war?" Buford said.

"Yes. And so there'll be a possible future when it's over," Ur said.

Buford pulled a cigarette out of his pocket and raked the tip across his cheek. He knew that was about all they were going to get out of *La Cobre* on that subject. "Why Ketchum?" he said.

"To fetch my father."

"Jaq? Why? He's damned near ninety!" Buford said.

"So what in hell's wrong with ninety?" Faddle barked.

"My father's perspective may be useful," Ur said. "And he possesses an equally valuable technology."

Buford exhaled loudly. "Okay. Then?"

"We'll see," Ur said.

Buford pulled out the pack of Luckys and shoved the cigarette back inside. "I'm game. Of course, I'll have to check with the Agency," he said.

"And they'll have to check with me," Faddle said. "And I say yes."

"That's very nice, Buford. And thank you, Uncle John. But my suggestions are directed at Carmine. He possesses the intellectual skills to realize the potential of the technology," Ur said.

Buford slumped in his chair. That's right, he thought, I'm just a dumb spook. He started to verbalize his hurt, then checked himself.

Staring at Buford for a moment, Ur pursed her lips, then turned to Carmine and waited patiently for his reply.

Carmine shrugged. "Well, I guess I sort of got my sea legs today. And if Buford's with me ..."

"Buford's with you," Stemp said quietly.

"Thank you, Carmine," Ur said.

"So, what's the plan?" Carmine asked.

"I've told you," Ur said.

"But—" Carmine began.

"The details will unfold," Ur said.

"I suppose you'd like us to drop them off in Chicago," Faddle said.

"That would be helpful," Ur said. "And lend them your plane."

"Sure, sure," Faddle said. "And we____"

"Will go back to New York. You are the only one that has any chance now of pulling together the Americans," Donna said. "And Ur said you'll need all of your powers. I think I may be of some help." Donna ran her finger across Faddle's knee.

Faddle grinned. "I bet you will. You coming with us, Ur?"

"I'm going to Venice," Ur said.

"Venice. Jesus!" Faddle slammed his fist on the arm of his seat. "I have to contact Maria. I 'd almost forgotten."

"That would be prudent. But you'd better do it quickly, for soon she'll be difficult to contact," Ur said.

"Why?" Faddle asked, squinting slightly.

"The primary threat in this conflict will launch their attack against Venice," Ur said.

"Primary threat?" Faddle said.

"Of course," Buford said. "The Islamic Axis. Venice is the closest major target and Venice and New York are the only Western states possessing atomics.

The Latins' attack on America will be a secondary diversion to keep our resources tied up."

"That is insightful, Buford Stemp," Ur said.

"Well, thank you. I'm glad I have some skills besides being a bodyguard." With his molars, Buford clamped on the inside of his cheek. *Shit. Well, I'm only human.* Again, Ur regarded Buford for a long moment, but did not say a word.

Faddle harumphed. "After we drop the boys off in Chicago, should we catch a flight to Venice? Or do we do it the other way around?"

"You don't have to do it at all. But thank you anyway," Ur said as she walked up to Faddle, then planted a kiss on his cheek. "Good luck."

Faddle smiled, then wiped the expression off his face, replacing it with as curmudgeonly a mug as he could manage. "What's luck got to do with it? Seems to me as if you've got a crystal ball."

Shaking her head, Ur said simply, "No." She picked at a finger, then gazed at John Faddle. "I can see possibilities. Sometimes, even, I may—" she paused. "Suggest," she finished, caressing the soft sibilant. "But God's the one who plays dice."

"I thought he bet football," Faddle said.

Ur grinned a toothy grin, turned a slow cartwheel and rotated right out through the fuselage.

"Holy Mother of God," Carmine said.

Donna crossed herself.

"I'll be a son-of-a-bitch. Yessir. A son-of-a-bitch," Faddle whispered.

Buford simply sat in silence. As he had watched Ur slide through the light aluminum skin of the aircraft, he had felt as if she were holding onto fine threads that were attached to a spot deep in the middle of his chest, and that they had unraveled and then slipped slowly from his body. Now he was empty.

A moment later Ur appeared again, spinning gracefully in shimmering luminescence, into the cabin.

Neither Buford, nor Carmine, nor Donna moved. Faddle flinched. "Forget something?" he said, gruffly, as if she were catching the last train to New York.

"Actually, yes. May I speak with you?" she said, addressing Buford.

Woodenly, Buford rose. Ur took his hand. Buford's own felt as if it had folded around a swarm of warm mayflies. She walked him toward the back of the plane, then looked up into his eyes, her own flashing cobalt, framed by fiery copper.

"I just want to tell you—" then she picked at a finger. "I just didn't want you to feel hurt. Unimportant," she said.

Buford shook his head. "No worries. I've been around long enough to be able to look in the mirror. Doesn't mean I always like what I see, but I'm old enough, I think, to take some of the disappointment."

"But mirrors are only useful in this present. They can't show us what we'll become," Ur said.

Buford scratched the side of his nose and smiled. "I got myself a Latin grammar book."

"That's good. But that's only partly what I mean. I can see futures, except my own. And I can't see yours."

"What—?" Buford began; but Ur placed a finger on his lips.'

"I don't know," Ur whispered, then traced the tips of her fingers across his lips and kissed him lightly on the cheek. "I really must get to Venice now," she announced.

"You gonna—?" Faddle made a circular motion with his arms.

"Sure am, pardner." Buford began to laugh. "I'll have to admit that I wasn't sure I could do it the first time when I was a child at New Spall. The probabilities are, well, very tiny. This will be my third attempt and I'm not following a different world-line. But Carmine can explain to you. Can't you, Carmine?"

Carmine jumped up and with a very serious expression, gave Ur a big hug. "Good luck," he said hoarsely.

"Thank you. Anyway, thank goodness space and time are elastic. It is great fun." And this time Ur smiled her odd smile, broadly. Taking a great running start, she did a handspring and disappeared through the tail of the plane.

For a few minutes, no one moved. At last Faddle smacked his palms against his thighs. "I need a bourbon. Anybody join me?" A babel of yeses swelled until it felt as if the thin skin of the plane would burst.

"I'll get the drinks," Donna said.

"I'll help," Carmine said.

A few minutes later the sound of ice cubes rattling against glass had replaced the general hubbub. Faddle grabbed the intercom. "Sky King?"

"Yes, sir."

"We're going to Chicago first," Faddle said.

"Yes, sir. I'll alert our escort," the pilot said.

Surrounding their jet were six fighters from the New Confederate States.

"Do you think they'll get involved? I mean *really* involved?" Buford asked.

"The CSA? I dunno." Faddle slurped on his bourbon. "Probably not. They have the most to lose. But I think they'll help in a pinch." Faddle clenched and unclenched his hand. "Buford, what you told me about Elmer, do you think he'll be all right?" Buford shrugged.

"If anyone can save his ass, it's Jorgezinho," Donna said defiantly.

"I agree. If anyone can," Buford said.

The cabin was quiet. Everyone had drained their drinks and the ice cubes had melted. "Time to get to work," Faddle said. "This is some goddamned mess we've got here. Donna? Hand me that cell phone, will you? I've got to call Maria Valesqua. I hope I'm not too late."

Buford smiled to himself. *Too late? What in hell does that mean, really? Space and time are elastic.*

THE END

ACKNOWLEDGEMENTS

I would like to thank a few people without whom this book, and the Ur Legend series, would not have been written. First, John Barnes, my editor and 'book doctor' in Denver, who is a brilliant novelist in his own right. Also, Gene Harris, for his imaginative and striking cover designs.

A special thanks is due to Joyce Krieg, another terrific writer, who not only performed the almost impossible work of typing my manuscript from freehand composition books, but gave me invaluable editorial advice, both in detail and in overview. William Neish also offered incisive guidance and comments.

Once again thanks to Lynn Pigott for her photo of me and my wife, Linda, above my bio.

None of this would have been possible without the counsel and guidance of my publisher, Patricia Hamilton, who has 'held my hand' as I have learned the functioning of an industry that had been foreign to me.

Lastly, I have to thank my wife and Katherine's mother, Linda, who has supported me in the realization of a life in print for our daughter.

○ ○ ○

ABOUT THE AUTHOR

AJAX MINOR was born in Danbury, CT on September 11, 1950. He 'prepped' at Danbury High School and received an A.B. from Princeton in 1972. After graduation he moved to New York City and began a career as a bond trader. He and his wife, Linda, lived in Manhattan and Brooklyn for twenty years, and spent another twenty in Denver, CO where their daughter, Katherine, was born, and died. Presently, they reside in Monterey, CA.

Minor began writing after the death of Katherine. Her passing, and her life, served as the inspiration for the 'Ur Legend' series of fantasies, of which The Girl from Ipanema is the second of three books. Book 1, Sun Valley Moon Mountains, was published in 2016. Though the novel is his preferred medium of expression, he has also written a few short stories and some poetry which are available on his website, ajaxminor.com.

www.ingramcontent.com/pod-product-compliance
Lightning Source LLC
Chambersburg PA
CBHW070924190726
48292CB00004B/1093